Dirk van den Boom

Uprising

DIRK VAN DEN BOOM

THE EMPEROR'S MEN

UPRISING

ISBN 978-3-86402-610-2

Cover © Timo Kümmel
Editor: Rob Bignell

www.atlantis-verlag.de

1

"That is your proposal, Mr. Engineer?"

While it was quite unusual for Rheinberg to emphasize formality in his closest circle, the slightly disbelieving undertone, accompanied by an amused headshake immediately took the severity out of the salutation. Dahms grinned at Rheinberg. They sat in the narrow messroom on board the *Saarbrücken*. The cruiser was moored at the pier of the "German City" specially built for the ship, a settlement that had now developed into a veritable city district of Ravenna.

Dahms with his finger painted a circle in the small wine pool that clumsy Langenhagen had caused. The first officer of the *Saarbrücken* looked at the engineer somewhat irritated, but, like all of the others, noticed the twinkle in the man's eyes. Was the proposal not meant to be serious? "Oh yes, Captain, Sir," Dahms paid back with the same coin, and his grin broadened. "That's the suggestion."

"I wish Köhler was here," Langenhagen muttered. The boatswain would have expressed his displeasure about the idea of the engineer with most well-chosen words.

"I want to repeat as I understand it," Rheinberg said now, slowly, raising a pointing finger. "You have the intention of setting up a strategic collection of shit!"

Dahm's face grew serious. "It's exactly like that. Actually, I'm less concerned about the shit, if you allow me. I am concerned with saltpeter."

"Which do you want to get from shit?"

Dahms raised his shoulders. "We haven't found a natural saltpeter source yet. I'm sure there is such a thing in the realm – perhaps somewhere in Asia, at any rate there were some existing in our time. But we can't wait so long, especially not in the current situation. We have to get away from the steam catapults and build proper cannons, and we need black powder. What we have gathered so far is sufficient for the experimental part of our work. But if we want to go into a real mass-production, this won't be enough. We need saltpeter, and much of it. The best source is cow shit. Properly deposited, saltpeter crystals form on the underside of the dung. We need that. I don't want the crap itself. What I want is an organization of people who are trained by us roaming all latifundia and courtyards, and with a suitable tool ..."

"... rip through the shit," Langenhagen completed the sentence. "Imperial shit."

Dahms nodded. "Exactly. In the short term this is the best source for a substantial saltpeter reserve – at least until we have found a natural one. I hope this will soon be the case. But until then ..."

Rheinberg looked for a moment doubtfully at Dahms, but then lowered his head and resigned to the inevitable. "All right," he said softly. "I will confer your request to the Emperor. He'll be irritated."

"We've been doing a lot of things that have been irritating since our arrival," Langenhagen said dryly.

"I can't contradict you," Rheinberg replied, reaching for his wine glass, without lifting it to his mouth. "Gratian is used to us. This will certainly not bother him too long, even if it is very peculiar."

"I'm responsible for the peculiar," Dahms reminded his superiors. "I stamp an industrial revolution out of the ground here. And this is based, at least in the field of weapon technology, on a nice heap of shit."

Rheinberg frowned, smiling. "I'm sure I'll chose a different wording for my conversation with Gratian."

"It will be better," Dahms confirmed. "But to return to the seriousness of the situation, I'm now in a dead end with the development of weapons. We are so far as to produce smaller pieces with drilled barrels and also successfully fired one as a test. But if all this is to be of military sense, it will be time to set up a proper artillery company. It has to be trained, very carefully. And I need a good measure of black powder. Before I have a reliable source for saltpeter, we are really stuck. I have now advanced to the refinement of the steam catapults, but we must clarify this question soon." Dahms leaned back. "I expect large saltpeter deposits in the Nile mud. I also know that there have been sources in Hungary in our time. However, we still need time to develop the appropriate course of action. We should certainly involve Gratian. But for the immediate needs, the solution proposed by me is certainly the best and fastest."

"As I said, I'll bring it to the Emperor," Rheinberg said. "He arrived in Ravenna the previous day, although only for a short visit. Since he is here, he is easier to reach. I'll meet him at court tomorrow, and then I will discuss it before he leaves for Trier again."

Rheinberg looked for a moment out of a porthole. The *Saarbrücken* was not alone in this newly established navy facility – even if the latter was at present not much more than a long pier and the dry dock still under construction. Visible in the waters was the *Valentinian*, the first steam-war ship of the Roman fleet, recently returned from northern Egypt, without Köhler and Neumann on board, who were both painfully missed by Rheinberg.

But with an unexpected guest.

It was an officer, a young man, the closest follower of the traitorous former First Officer von Klasewitz, about whom they hadn't heard anything since that disastrous night. Until now.

Rheinberg took a deep breath. His injury was still noticeable, a pain that had accompanied him since the failed assassination attempt on his life in the summer palace of the Emperor near Saravica. He wondered how he had managed to recover so quickly. It must have been a combination of a good bodily constitution, a competent doctor, and the unconditional will to be cured. Although the wound had now healed completely, he felt its existence; sometimes surprising, but sometimes when he expected it. The pain also reminded him that his enemies were everywhere and were not afraid of anything. Up until then, the failed assassins had not been linked to a specific source. The men had all died on the scene and hadn't carried any traitorous hints.

Ever since the incident, Rheinberg suddenly would awake at night, his hands clenched around the pistol, which he always carried with him. Small movements, sudden noises, all that was enough to tear him from sleep. He didn't want to raise the issue with anyone, but the mental wound that the assassination attempt had torn was obviously deeper and more lasting than the physical one.

Rheinberg had to deal with a lot of anxiety lately.

He closed his eyes. Where had he begun to digress? Ah, yes, von Klasewitz and his supporter, the young ensign ...

"What do we do with Tennberg?" Langenhagen asked, as if he had guessed the Captain's thoughts.

Dahms made a contemptuous grunt. Rheinberg knew what the engineer had in mind as to the fate of Tennberg. It had something to do with a fixed rope dangling from high. "We will proceed with caution," Rheinberg replied. "I've made up my mind to conduct the interrogation myself, now that he has been knocked around for a while by his comrades. I'll see him this afternoon."

"I want to be there," Dahms growled. "And if he doesn't bend, I'll beat his soul out of his body."

Rheinberg smiled and shook his head at the same time. "No beating, at least not yet." Before the engineer could reply, Rheinberg raised his hand and signaled him to keep quiet. "I once made a mistake with another ensign. I haven't properly understood what it means for some of us to enter this new world. I'm very sorry now."

Dahms wasn't entirely convinced. His regret for Thomas Volkert seemed to be within narrow limits.

"We cannot compare Volkert's case with that of Tennberg," Langenhagen said.

"Both are deserters," Dahms murmured.

"Both are deserters," the First Officer confirmed. "But Volkert we have driven more or less toward it, and he is a young fellow who acted out of love. Tennberg was not compelled to do so, and he became a deserter because he was a failed mutineer. And that we have forked him up under certain circumstances in Egypt at least shows to me that he continued his betrayal without any remorse."

Rheinberg smiled. He was delighted that his new deputy had the degree of human compassion that he himself had lacked in the past.

Dahms growled again but didn't contradict. Rheinberg knew that the engineer missed Volkert and that he was basically willing to forgive him. But far and wide there was no trace of the ensign, and it was to suspect that he went underground somewhere in the Empire. And, last but not least, there were political reasons that didn't allow an all too hasty amnesty.

"I'll handle Tennberg carefully," Rheinberg said. "He should get his chance."

"He deserves nothing," Dahms replied emphatically. "Volkert, yes, all right. But Tennberg? No way!"

"I won't accept him back into the crew," Rheinberg conceded. "But I'll give him the prospect of an honorable exile. If I give him no perspective, the success of von Klasewitz is his only chance of a normal life, and he will not voluntarily pull out of the conspiracy."

"Oh no. Let me spend a few hours with him alone. Or let our Roman friends do the 'talking.' I have heard that they are not too squeamish."

This was indeed correct, as Rheinberg knew. Torture was a common and hardly questioned interrogation method. But the young Captain didn't think anything of it. For him, such an approach was indisputable.

This attitude must have reflected in his facial expression, for Dahms let it rest.

Again his gaze wandered out to the *Valentinian*. Two other ships of the same type were already under construction, and Dahms was busy day and night building the two bronze steam engines needed for the new crafts. Rheinberg should be optimistic and proud. They had reached a remarkably great amount in a very short time. But since Tennberg had reappeared, something nagged at him, a dark premonition.

He finally rose and looked at his comrades.

"See you tomorrow evening," he said. "Then we'll know more about Tennberg's intentions and the chances of collecting shit from the whole Empire."

Dahms grinned. "I only need the saltpeter crystals. Raise the shit, scrap off crystals, leave the shit behind."

Rheinberg raised his hands.

"Spare me the details, Mr. Engineer!"

2

Tribune Sedacius sat in front of the crackling camp fire. Everyone was grateful for the dancing flames, as it had cooled down in the evening. Erminius, the leader of the Quadians, squatted close to the Roman officer and was silent. The mood between Rome and the Quadians was not good. Only a few years earlier, Rome, largely unprovoked, had killed the king of the neighboring tribe and thus created a military conflict finally won by the Empire. Erminius, the successor of the murdered king, knew that his people were full of a deep and truly justified hatred against the traitors. But he also knew that there was a much greater danger approaching from the East – and that this threat had come very close, even closer than the Romans had assumed.

Thomas Volkert, although no one knew him under this name, rested at the fire as well. Sedacius had insisted, though Volkert's rank was little more than that of a simple legionary. But the young man's watchful intelligence had not escaped the Tribune's attention, nor the story that had led to the sudden promotion of the soldier, who had once been involuntarily pressed into the service. At that time, he had led a column of green recruits in a surprise attack by the Sarmatians to an unexpected victory, after the actual officers had fallen. Volkert didn't think of it as a feat. His friend Simodes had died in that battle. And it was hard to make friends here.

Erminius was silent because he had talked for a long time. In every detail, he had listed the previous encounters of his people with the Huns. Their attacks, quick, from the small, fast-paced horses, who had little work with the Quadians. Their courage, their unreservedness, their determination, the abilities of their leaders, who knew exactly how and where the tactical advantages of a mobile cavalry army could be put to proper use. The fact that the Quadians still existed depended on the fact that the main body of the Huns was relatively far away, and so far only smaller rutting group had been involved in fighting – as well as those groups of apostate Huns who refused to be subservient to the current leaders of their people and had sought their luck on their own.

But still. When the Quadians had succeeded in making some prisoners, it was clear that something was wrong, at least for Thomas Volkert, who knew a version of the story in which the great mass of the Huns appeared close to the Roman borders some decades later. This led to the Battle of the Catalaunian Fields and the legend of Flavius Aetius, the last great Roman general, who had been able to turn fate away from the possible ruin of Rome, only to be subsequently murdered by his own emperor.

Erminius had credibly told them that the main force of the Huns was now moving steadily toward the West and would be reaching the borders of the Empire much earlier than had been thought. It was highly probable that in a few years the Empire would suffer serious attacks. The Quadians didn't have a proper idea of the extent of Eastern Europe, and Volkert felt that the speed with which the Huns knew how to travel was still underestimated, despite all their experiences.

The young German felt hot and cold listening to the descriptions.

Rheinberg's elaborate plan to prevent the attack of the Huns against Rome by a counterattack threatened to collapse like a house of cards. If what the King gave up in bitter open-mindedness corresponded to the truth, the great exploratory mission, to which Volkert belonged, was only of limited use. The advance warning had rapidly diminished. The enemy was nearer than everyone thought and instead of continuing into the depths of the East, it was necessary to put the Empire in a state of readiness.

Volkert had to smile involuntarily at the thought. He hid the potential cause for misunderstanding behind a wooden mug of beer from which he had already drunken too much.

The Empire has been in that state for decades. But that wouldn't be sufficient, as history had proved. But perhaps the Germans could make the difference, the difference between the tragic overthrow of Western Rome and its survival as a state. In Volkert, everything was urging Sedacius to send a message back to the authorities as soon as possible. But he was only a decurion. So he remained silent, waiting for his opportunity.

The Tribune said nothing. He, too, held a wooden beaker with beer in his hand, turned it slowly between his fingers, and looked at the reflection of the crackling fire in the murky liquid. He had proved himself as a good diplomat, and he drank the beer, although everyone knew he preferred wine. But insulting Erminius and questioning his hospitality, even to a certain extent, didn't even occur to the Tribune.

It was an ability for which Volkert was quite grateful. The Quadians were in their heartland, deep in their territory, and the Roman column was very vulnerable, despite the presence of German infantry.

Volkert always had to shake off the feeling of being watched from the darkness. He felt uncomfortable since they had entered the great camp of Erminius, but he didn't notice anything out of the ordinary, despite all his attention. Nor were the Quadians of a threatening demeanor, against which his intuitive mistrust could have been directed. They were reserved, defiant, grumpy, but just because of this they were honest, and the motivation for their willingness to cooperate was credible.

There was something different.

Volkert hid his face again in the cup. After all, the drink was quite enjoyable.

"So what are you Romans doing?" the King finally asked.

Sedacius hesitated visibly. He was only a tribune, and could scarcely anticipate the Emperor's decisions. Nevertheless, he had to find an answer, because the good will of Erminius needed an adequate reaction if one didn't want to recall the horrors of the past. The predecessor of Erminius had paid his trust with his life. Sedacius surely cursed those responsible. Volkert was certain that the Tribune wouldn't repeat that same mistake.

"I can't say what my lord will decide. Nevertheless, we were sent out to explore the danger posed by the Huns and to find out their exact distribution. Your help is very important to us. Rome will fight against the onslaught of the enemy as soon as possible."

"What about us?" Erminius replied. Volkert knew at once what the Quadian wanted. Rome might be arming itself – and where in this game was place for his own people?

"I'm sure there is a solution. Perhaps the status of *foederatii* and a joint defense here at the border? I doubt less about the possibility of such an offer from our side than your willingness to accept it."

Erminius grimaced.

"As if we had a great choice, Tribune."

"Be assured of our good will."

"This time for real?"

Sedacius raised his arms. "I can only say what I think and feel. I am a small tribune."

Erminius nodded and sank for a few moments back into a pensive silence. Then he nodded a second time, more violently, and took the floor. "Prove your good will, Tribune, and find a way to learn more about our common enemies."

"And how?"

Erminius gesticulated into the darkness. "Not far from here, no more than 50 Roman miles, there is a larger host of the enemy. We've been watching it for a while. It seems like they're waiting for reinforcements. We don't want to find out what happens when those arrive."

"Not more than 50 miles?"

"Toward the sunrise."

"How many?"

Erminius pursed his lips. "Two-thousand, rather 2,500. All on horseback."

"I have scarcely a thousand men at my disposal," the Tribune said.

"I offer 4,000 or 5,000 of my men, all that remains after the Empire was finished with us." The bitterness in the King's voice was unmistakable.

Sedacius didn't pretend as if he didn't notice it, and nodded expressively.

Volkert observed the Tribune carefully. He learned.

"So 6,000 men, if all comes together," Sedacius said. It was left unspoken that the Roman soldiers had a very special reinforcement, which could be quite beneficial to the success of any attack.

"The chief of the Huns is a man named Octar. It is said that he is very close to the current leader, one of his closest advisors and commanders. Even if we can't get hold of him, a few prisoners could help us." Erminius had been waiting with this piece of information until the end.

Volkert realized that Sedacius was more and more inclined to seriously consider the proposal of his counterpart. "How did you learn name and position of that fellow Octar?" Volkert slipped.

Sedacius turned aside, giving the Decurion a half-blaming, half-appreciative look.

Erminius did not seem to mind the fact that someone else than the Tribune had asked the question. They all sat by the same fire. "Our friend spoke of it," he said lightly, pointing to the mutilated head of the Hun, now lying decoratively on a wooden plank behind him, the flames reflecting on his empty face.

"I'd like to talk to your military leaders, your clan-chiefs," Sedacius said.

"No problem. So you are interested, Tribune? Such an attack must take place soon. Who knows when the reinforcement appears? Then it could be too late even for our joint effort."

The Tribune narrowed his eyes. Volkert sensed what was going on in his head. And when he made his demand, the young German knew that he had anticipated correctly.

Sedacius wanted to know how desperate Erminius really was. "I am commanding the attack," the Tribune said.

Volkert watched the King closely. There was a resistance felt by the man, which was easy to discern. Pride as well, despair, but also fear and insecurity ... and then, even before he opened his mouth, Volkert saw that Erminius had made a decision.

"I myself have other tasks to fulfill," the leader of Quadians answered slowly. "My older son will take command of our warriors.

He is well-acquainted with Roman customs; he served five years in the border troops until ..."

"Until we betrayed you and murdered your King," Sedacius completed in a quiet voice. "Then your son left the service and fought against our troops."

Erminius smiled at the Roman. "You're taking command. Luvico, my son, will not be enthusiastic about it, but he will understand your orders." The King waved toward the darkness. "Bring Luvico and the scouts." He looked at Sedacius searchingly. "We'll begin at once?"

The Tribune lifted his cup. "Not if you have anything else to discuss."

Erminius grinned.

3

Adulis, according to Chief Köhler, was worth a trip. Although their latest experiences had been a bit uncomfortable, the long voyage had proved to be largely uneventful. Köhler wasn't sad about it. Alexandria had shown them very urgently what powers were secretly directed against them. Still, no one knew how well their opponents were actually organized – or who actually belonged to them exactly. The fact that von Klasewitz, the apostate, had become a bitter enemy after his failed mutiny, wasn't one of the great surprises. But the extent to which the resistance to the influence of the time-travelers was actually rooted in the imperial hierarchy was ultimately guesswork.

Here, outside the immediate Roman area of control, the situation was somewhat different – possibly simpler, but perhaps even more complicated. Adulis was the economic center of the Empire of Aksum, the predecessor of what Köhler had known from his time as the Empire of Ethiopia, to which the German Reich maintained friendly diplomatic relations. In addition to the capital Aksum itself, Adulis was the second major urban center of the North African empire, which, if Köhler was right in remembering the historical lessons of Rheinberg, was close to reach its zenith. Its special position as a Christian empire of its own kind wasn't of importance so far. At that time, Roman North Africa was largely christianized as well. Islam as a great, competing world religion did not exist yet.

The port of Adulis was, of course, by no means as great as that of Alexandria. But the coastal sailor, which they had ascended in Alexandria, had to look for his jetty with an effort. From here, almost the entire trade of Aksum, in and out, was settled. The long quay walls were hardly recognizable because of the numerous ships. There was lively activity in the harbor basin and the noise of a heavily frequented transshipment area was already clearly perceptible during their approach. Their captain, a gray-haired sailor with many years of experience, was well-informed about the navigational hazards of their trip, so that Köhler was content to leave the nautical details entirely to him.

"Impressive, is it not?" Behrens and Africanus looked up, as the infantryman came nearer. "There is a whole new world to discover. What does it look like in the east? Or in the south? At this time, we are not making any real sense of our world."

"There is still much to explore," Köhler agreed. "And we're obviously just right in the middle. Africanus, what does our next step look like?"

The Trierarch held a parchment roll in his hands. "This is the letter written for us by the Prefect of Egypt. We shall report to Josephus Diderius Latius. He is something like the resident ambassador of Rome to Adulis. His main task is trade rather than politics, but he knows his way around and will be able to establish the connection with the Aksumite government for us. He can also help us find the quickest way to Aksum."

"Where does Latius reside?"

"Our Captain says he knows it, and we will be led there by one of his men. The ambassador is supposed to occupy a town-house near the port."

"Our own accommodation?"

"I hope Latius will accommodate us. Otherwise, the Captain will be able to provide us with lodging that is not too dangerous."

"We'll manage, I'm sure."

Africanus looked a little astonished at Köhler but didn't reply. The Trierarch felt that the Germans had prepared themselves with a good mood, and above all, Köhler seemed to be so much at ease that nothing could make him nervous. The Roman officer even suspected that the Germans, in any case, saw this as an exciting adventure, which they wanted to enjoy to the fullest. Probably a better way to deal with fate than to think day by day of lost family members or friends who had vanished in the stream of time forever. Since, however, with all his enthusiasm Köhler didn't lack the necessary precaution and care, Africanus couldn't find any evil in this attitude. In fact, he himself was very anxious about Aksum, for this too was his first visit to this kingdom. So far, despite all his experience at sea, he had been staying only on the Mare Nostrum. Therefore, he entered new territory, and that in the truest sense of the word.

It took another hour for the coastal sailor to be moored properly. The Captain kept his promise and sent one of his men to show them the way. In addition, he promised to have the goods the expedition brought along well-guarded. His ship would remain here for four days; until then, the expedition had to find another safe place for their valuables.

They had spent a lot of gold in Clysma to buy valuable Roman products, which they could transport easily as well. Among these were, first and foremost, fine fabrics, but also exquisite wines as well as some of the artistic craftsmanship known to be in high demand among the elite of rich cities, eager to place anything exotic in their villas and mansions. All in all, the goods were less intended to cover their livelihood in Aksum – the Roman coin was gladly exchanged against the local currency or could even be used directly – but rather to present suitable gifts to the king in Aksum, and probably for important people in his court.

After all, they wanted something from him.

Köhler, Behrens and Africanus formed the delegation, which, under the leadership of a bullish sailor, finally entered the quay and dived into the streets of Adulis. The weather was hot, and the sun was burning from an almost completely cloudless sky. The swirling crowd, the noise, and the rapid movements of their guide, who obviously knew perfectly how to navigate in the city, quickly generated sweat not only on their foreheads, but the light cloths with which they were adorned were completely drenched as well.

Although the estate of the Roman envoy was "near the port," they were on the road for a good half an hour. The early afternoon had begun, and as the three men, in their quest to visit Latius as soon as possible, had departed without taking a snack, they felt a throbbing hunger as well as thirst. But they were full of confidence to be able to enjoy the hospitality of the envoy, and the prospect of chilled wine and a meal bolstered the agility of their progress.

Soon they had entered a side street. Here, too, the expedition moved quickly and the tall, white walls gave a relaxing shade. They had arrived in a quarter of the city where obviously more prosperous citizens lived. In some of the courtyards the travelers saw a few of the gigantic stelae, like the Aksumites used to erect them, marked with inscriptions. It seemed that they shared the same passion for impressive monuments as the Romans did. Like the Germans as well, Köhler thought to himself. Some things just lasted forever.

Then their guide stopped so abruptly that the three men almost bumped into him. They were standing in front of a white wall. A big wooden door stood open. In one of the two door wings, a sturdy "SPQR" was artfully carved into the wood. That this was the house of Latius there could be no doubt.

"The door is open. This isn't normal, is it?" Africanus said. He looked at her guide. "Is this customary?"

The sailor shrugged, pointed to the door.

"I should only bring you here," the guide said. "Everything else is none of my business. I have done my duty." He raised his hand to greet them, turned away without comment, and disappeared, relieved of his obligation. Whatever was going on here, he obviously didn't want to have anything to do with it.

Africanus, Köhler and Behrens looked at each other. There was mistrust in her eyes.

The time-travelers drew the pistols they carried with them. They were not recognizable as a weapon for the random observer, so they wouldn't immediately be considered as a threat, should the open door only prove to be irrelevant.

Köhler nodded to Behrens. That was his area of expertise.

The Sergeant touched the door carefully with his toe. It swung wider, without any squeaking from the hinges, opening to a view of a courtyard in Roman style. Latius had built a small piece of home in Adulis.

Behrens stepped forward, his scrutinizing look wandering vigilantly. Nothing moved. Africanus and Köhler followed him. A gentle breeze blew from the coast to the yard and gave them some needed cooling.

Slowly, observant, they pushed forward, entered the pillared main building with the painted walls and the mosaic floors, artistic architecture that bore witness to wealth and taste.

No servant stood up to them and asked for their request. The house was silent. The only sounds came from the street.

They entered the atrium, and there they saw Latius, as he smiled amiably at them. A handsome man, the toga swung around the body like a senator, with a large, bulging nose, wrinkles around his eyes, and short, Roman-style hair. He had raised his hand to the salute, the symbolic gesture best known to any Roman, greeting as the master of the house.

A life-size statue of himself had been placed in the atrium, carefully marked with name and rank, a modesty that helped them to unambiguously identify the beheaded corpse that lay directly in front of the statue in its blood. The head had rolled a little further, had been coming to rest under a bed-chair, the facial expression rather unfriendly, showing traces of the agony and horror Latius must have felt at the moment of his death.

Africanus looked at the corpse with a professional look.

"A clean, well-executed blow. This man here wasn't a warrior. He was at the mercy of his opponent."

"Where are the servants?" Köhler asked. "Latius must have had slaves."

Africanus looked around, paused for a moment, lowered his gaze in attention. "I hear something."

In fact, footsteps approached, hurriedly. Several men.

Heavy steps.

Then a half-dozen Aksumite soldiers, armed with shield and spear, plunged into the atrium, led by two men, who could be identified as slaves. The two seemed to be quite excited.

For a moment, both groups glared at each other.

Then everyone's eyes fell upon the beheaded body of the Roman envoy.

One of the slaves, trembling, lifted his right arm, his mouth

20

desperately trying to form the words that Köhler already anticipated. When the finger pointed toward the three visitors, the trembling man said something in a foreign language, but there could be no doubt about the content of the message.

The soldiers lifted their spears. They'd found the culprits.

4

Petronius entered the empty church and paused for a moment. An uninvolved observer might have thought the priest just remained silent, but instead the man looked around imperceptibly. The big room was empty, oil lamps flickered on the walls. It was already evening in Ravenna, and the high, narrow wall windows didn't allow a lot of light inside. Finally, the man's gaze fixed itself on the collapsed figure, who, apparently inoblivious of anyone, crouched before the altar. Petronius knew that this person was waiting for him, but he had been informed by a messenger only that morning of the imminent arrival of this important personality.

He hurried forward. He didn't even think about why he had been requested to come and not his master, the bishop. He knew who was calling for him, and it was only logical that the old and unreliable bishop was not involved in this conversation.

When he had reached the figure, the person rose silently and slammed back the hood of his garment. Petronius was not astonished when he recognized the man's face at once; indeed, a feeling of joyful expectation filled him.

He lowered his head respectfully. It was always a good thing to show Ambrosius, the Bishop of Milan, the necessary reverence. After all, a good relationship could only help him to become Bishop of Ravenna, as soon as the elderly man currently occupying that position has finally withered away.

"My brother," the Bishop said softly, and a gentle smile greeted Petronius. He bowed his head and let himself be blessed. Then he crouched next to Ambrosius and looked at the flickering tallow candle, which stood before them. He didn't say anything. The Bishop had called him, and he'd speak at the appropriate time.

"How is Liberius?" the visitor finally asked for his brother from

Ravenna. Petronius listened carefully. The question was not totally of a harmless nature.

"My master is doing well, as much as he can expect in his old age," he replied. "I talked to him this morning and held a prayer. He looked tired."

"Time makes you tired," Ambrosius replied, his crooked eyes facing the priest again. "And for an old man like Liberius, all of this is certainly very hard to grasp."

"He carries his burden bravely."

"You're helping to carry it. Without your help, Liberius couldn't fulfill his duties, everyone says that."

"I serve where God has commanded me to. If I serve well, I'm pleased."

"You're doing very well," Ambrosius said. "In fact, I suspect that your services will one day enable you to claim the highest office in Ravenna."

"I don't expect so," Petronius replied modestly. Both men knew it was a lie, and both of them didn't bother.

"I have friends in Ravenna," Ambrosius said.

"You have friends everywhere," the priest flattered.

"Not everywhere. At the moment I am less popular at the imperial court."

"A very regrettable circumstance."

"I couldn't phrase it more adequately."

"It is necessary to change this."

"That's why we meet."

For a moment, Ambrosius said nothing, looking only at the sluggishly flickering candlelight. "Say, Petronius, what have we learned from the failed attempt to attack the metal ship of the demon worshipers?"

Petronius had a spontaneous answer on his tongue, feeling somewhat out of balance by the sudden question, which still put a finger on the painful wound of his recent failure. But then he swallowed the answer and thought about it more. The Bishop wouldn't ask him in order to blame him. The meaning behind this question went further. It was necessary to answer it the right way.

"We mustn't underestimate them," Petronius began cautiously.

Ambrosius bowed his head. He didn't comment.

"Violence against them is meaningful only if we have created a situation in which they are clearly in an inferior position," Petronius warmed to the topic. His next sentences came quicker, more eagerly, without waiting for a possible reaction from his opposite. "They must be far from their weapons, or the advantages of their weapons can't be put to use properly. A clear superiority of our numbers and greater determination would also help."

Ambrosius allowed the hint of a smile. "You think like a soldier, my brother." Before the latter could reply, the Bishop raised his hand. "That was no criticism. We live in times when you, as a man of the church, must think like a soldier. We are disciples of Jesus, Petronius. We are leading a great crusade, and the enemies are many. These are not only the time-wanderers themselves, but also those who support or at least tolerate them."

Petronius whispered, "But this also includes the Emperor ..."

"Yes, the Emperor. What do you learn from that conclusion, my friend?"

Petronius thought for a moment. Although the Bishop had said that nothing was wrong with his argumentation, he suspected that something more was expected. "We should find ways other than direct confrontation. We must first find allies, influence moods, spread rumors. We must tear or at least shake the foundation on which the strangers are standing. They must be on their own once we attack again. No one should help them. And if they are beaten, no one shall think of revenge or retribution."

Petronius looked into the Bishop's eye and recognized respect and affirmation. He felt the man's hand on his shoulder, the gentle pressure of his fingers. He saw his smile.

"Petronius, you will get far."

"I serve the Lord and his church."

"Very far, my brother, very far. But before we talk about gratification and recognition, we have to talk about what you have just made clear. Let's talk about this village, the settlement with all the demonic things that are built there. Let us talk about the people who work there and who are helplessly exposed to the evil influence of the demon worshipers. Let us talk about what is to be done to free them from the claws of their spell, cleanse their souls and lead them to the light – and let us speculate about what the population of beautiful Ravenna can do to help us with our plans."

Petronius' eyes were shining. Whatever the Bishop of Milan thought, it was entirely according to the taste of the priest. "I'm anxious to hear your suggestions," he replied eagerly.

Then they put their heads together.

Whoever happened to enter the chapel by chance, would see two priests who were quietly and passionately praying, a constant, eternal litany in honor of the Lord.

And the plan slowly took shape.

5

Markus Tennberg was tortured.

No one was poking him with glowing irons. The Ensign in the Imperial German navy, even if he didn't believe that he would continue to occupy this position any longer, was fully aware of the fact that the Roman state had the most capable and experienced torturers in his service and little scruple to employ their talents against anyone from whom one hoped for information. At the present time, however, the young man wasn't exposed to such physical torture. This didn't mean that this couldn't change, and this thought made him as uncomfortable as any kind of real torture he might be subjected to.

Tennberg sat on the straw bag, which served him as a bed. He looked out of the narrow hole, barely a brick's size, in the wall, through which daylight penetrated his dungeon cell. There wasn't much to see. He stared directly at an opposite wall. The cold winter air reached his nose, mixed with the warmth of the fire, which pushed through the grilles from the other side. The cell had no door but a wall of iron bars, as did the six other cells of the small prison. All the metal walls were aligned to a wide corridor, which ended on a heavy wooden door. In the middle of the corridor, a fire burned in a half-open fireplace, and the three legionaries who guarded the prisoners were sitting in front of it.

Tennberg was currently the only inmate. The Romans largely ignored him, talking quietly, chewing on something, playing a game. Scarcely ever a glance struck him. Twice a day, morning and night, a meal was given to him, nothing special, but enough to keep him properly fed. He received water all day. Nobody wanted him to go hungry or thirsty.

This wasn't the torture either.

The real torture consisted of the visits of his shipmates.

No, he always corrected himself – his former shipmates. In most cases, they were men of the infantry, not even his old navy friends. Hard men, and in their faces a lot of determination as much as contempt. It was this contempt that made him feel sleepless at night. The coldness in the eyes, without compassion. Each of these men would kill him, without hesitation, if the order would be given. Tennberg knew why the interrogations were not carried out by the men of the *Saarbrücken*. Tennberg had followed von Klasewitz because he had been promised a rapid career in the Roman Empire. But he had never been the angry grinder and arrogant asshole like the nobleman, not more than a little ensign who had wanted to take an abbreviated climb on the way up. This abbreviation had, after a few detours, brought him directly into a dungeon cell in the small settlement close to Ravenna, which had been created around the cruiser, and where Dahms was concerned with initiating an industrial revolution.

Tennberg tried to guess what would happen to him. He had retained his knowledge on the whereabouts of von Klasewitz and his plans to that day, awaiting to be beaten or worse.

No one had struck him. Every day the same questions were asked. Where is the nobleman? Who has he allied with? Who helps him? What is he doing? What kind of knowledge does he give his friends? What resources are available to him? What was he doing in Alexandria?

No word had passed his lips. He had reaped glances of contempt and disgust, but no one had raised his hand against him. They gave him food and a warm bedroom. Every three days, hot water was brought, and he had to wash his whole body. He was supposed to live and to do well – according to the circumstances. Everyone waited for Rheinberg's return in order to bring affairs to an end.

What would Rheinberg's order be? Tennberg didn't remember him as a particularly cruel officer. But he must have changed now that he was among the leaders of the Empire. Politics, as Tennberg has already learned despite his young age, was often more important than individual preferences and desires. "Reason of state" was the overriding concern. And sometimes people like him fell victim to it.

And there were good reasons why he could become one of these victims.

Tennberg felt a shiver run through his body. He didn't tremble because of the cold air.

He turned around as someone opened the door. It was a familiar face, expressionless, with cold eyes. The high grown man wore the uniform of the infantry, as all his conversation partners so far. His badges identified him as a lieutenant, perhaps a platoon leader. Tennberg couldn't remember his name. The man had probably never mentioned it.

It was like a ritual. Tennberg was to sit on the only piece of furniture in his cell, a coarse-tiled stool. Then two men entered, the lieutenant and an infantryman with a raised weapon whose barrel was directed directly at Tennberg's skull. The lieutenant went behind the prisoner and tied his hands together with a shackle. When Tennberg was secured, the infantryman lowered the weapon and stood watchful in a corner.

The lieutenant began his encirclement.

He walked around the sitting Tennberg. No word came over his lips. He made his rounds. Tennberg had begun to count them. The interrogation usually didn't begin until the lieutenant had finished his fourth round. He was predictable, and so the menacing posture of this ritual faded. It got boring.

Tennberg would be careful not to show that. He made sure that he seemed intimidated, even frightened. His boredom was his treasure, his tiny advantage, and he clung to it fervently.

"Well, Ensign?"

The cold voice intersected his thoughts. Tennberg twitched involuntarily. He had to accept that his nerves were not in good condition.

"What does your future look like?"

Tennberg was confused for a moment. Was this a new question? No one had ever wanted to talk to him about this topic. He also didn't believe that this question was asked out of genuine concern. "I do not know," the prisoner replied truthfully.

"No wishes, ideas?"

"They're no longer important."

"Why?"

"I am trapped, a mutineer, and a deserter. My punishment is inevitable."

"So you know your future?"

"As far as the end of this process is concerned, yes. Execution awaits me."

"Aaah, yes. Execution. A simple and obvious solution."

Tennberg said nothing.

The lieutenant made a round and spoke. "It's not that easy, Ensign. We are no longer in our time and our country. Things have changed."

"I was told that the laws of the German Reich continue to be valid. And even the laws of Rome clearly state what has to be done with mutineers. I do not see what has changed."

"You've been dealing intensively with these things, have you?"

"I'm informed."

"Then why did you mutiny?"

"It seemed to me to be the right thing, and a superior officer had strengthened me in this view."

Tennberg had expected a burst of hatred comments for his reply, but nothing of the sort happened. The Lieutenant seemed rather thoughtful. "Yet something has changed, Tennberg. We are fighting for our survival. We are by no means as superior to the Romans, as we would have liked. We must convince and impress them."

Tennberg said nothing. He didn't even feel that these observations were addressed to him.

"I see your future somewhat different from you," the Lieutenant finally said. He went to squat before Tennberg, looked into his face. "You count on your death, Ensign?"

The prisoner nodded.

"What if I offer you your life?"

Tennberg made a comprehensive hand movement. "And this is my life? It would be like a death, but much slower and more agonizing."

The lieutenant looked at him searchingly. "Many people in your situation would seize the opportunity and hope for future pardon."

Tennberg shook his head. "Not me."

"You underestimate Captain Rheinberg."

"Maybe."

"The offer could be better than you'd expect."

"Like what?"

"Your life and more."

"More?"

"Exile. The Empire is great. A Greek island perhaps, a life as a farmer or fisherman. Retired, yes, but as a free man on his own soil. A woman and children, why not? With your knowledge, you would be of value; you might even be very popular with the local population and could be of help. No one needs to know why you have settled there."

Tennberg looked at the Lieutenant and could hardly suppress the hope that had suddenly arisen in him. What the man offered him, seemed to be a probable way as punishment for his deed. And it was better, much better than execution or a life in a cell. But was it also meant to be serious?

The Lieutenant must have considered his concerns. He smiled a thin, cheerless smile. "Doubts, Tennberg?"

"For sure."

"Good. I will not take you on that road now. Perhaps the Captain, if he accepts your cooperation, will, and he arrives shortly. Maybe he doesn't like my idea. You are so far away from any trust, comradeship, or any security in dealing with us, that I can well imagine that your way back is long and difficult and perhaps not open at all."

Tennberg nodded. What else could he have said? The man was absolutely right. He felt the fetters loose. He rubbed the wrists, looked at the Lieutenant questioningly.

"That's it. Think about it. Consider whether Captain Rheinberg is a traitor or an honorable man. Do not close yourselves to others. Consider your opportunities."

So the man turned away, and the two soldiers left the cell. The door closed.

Markus Tennberg was alone with his thoughts.

6

Von Klasewitz looked pleased at the destruction. At first sight, it didn't seem to be particularly impressive – a simple wall of stones, connected with loose mortar, which was still moistened by the weather, stood before him. There was a big hole in it, caused by a round ball of solid granite fired by his cannon. Probably the wall would have been damaged if the two legionaries, who stood beside the German, would've thrown the bullet with muscular force. Nevertheless, everyone was satisfied. Among the observers, Roman officers, some craftsmen, and other legionaries guarding the site, there was a good mood. Klasewitz allowed himself a smile.

It was done.

Almost lovingly, the time-traveler looked at the marvel of technology to which he owed this success. The cannon was made of bronze, the simplest alloy to be produced, and a second one, made of cast iron, stood directly beside it. This one had not yet passed its test.

The bronze cannon had been cast from one piece, a belly of about three meters in length, erected on a wooden stand, tied with ropes. The setback had caused the buck to tremble, and the craftsmen were still working on a more stable version, but the cannon had been static enough to be able to target and deliver its volley. The powder had ignited as expected, the ball had left the pipe, the pipe didn't break – this weapon would be able to fire again.

The first Roman cannon. Von Klasewitz was certain of it. If he was sure of anything at all, then of the fact that he was the best expert on artillery on board the *Saarbrücken*.

Had been, he corrected himself immediately.

This, and the support of the Comes Maximus, Rome's governor in Britain and usurper-to-be, had led to the ability of von Klasewitz, despite all setbacks and problems, to equip his army with field artillery. He had carefully observed that the production process of each piece was accurately recorded. A detailed production manual was also written for this bronze gun, with steps described and provided with drawings from skilled hands. The nobleman himself had contributed extensively, and the hard work had finally paid off.

While he glanced at the new cannon, the foremen had given orders in the background, in the large manufactory hall. The workers immediately began to produce further pieces on the basis of the records of the successfully tested cannon. They would work day and night, and according to von Klasewitz's estimates, he would be able to hand over forty cannons of this type to the Comes in four weeks' time. And they had enough black powder, because unlike what he knew about Dahms' progress, they had found a source of saltpeter and used it wisely.

Forty cannons on a battlefield against the usual Roman formation, closely patterned, shield on shield – and then, that was the hope of the German, no longer with simple balls made of stone but with thin-skinned iron balls with a primitive impactor or even with sacks filled with shrapnel – the effect would be devastating, not least the psychological one. Von Klasewitz didn't have any illusions about the fact that Rheinberg and his men would do all they could to even this advantage again, but this one, the first battle, would certainly be a joy for the enthusiastic observer.

The preparations for the downfall of Gratian also proceeded according to plan. The escaped ex-Emperor Valens was dead, his attempt to betray their plans luckily failed. General Malobaudes continued to hold the Emperor's trust and knew what needed to be done at the appropriate moment. The fact that the young Goth who had helped Valens had escaped, remained to be the only regrettable aspect. But who would believe this man if he reported, torn and wounded, to any Roman authorities that he had escaped from Gaul with the dead Emperor Valens?

Nobody thought this a serious problem.

General Andragathius, the closest confidant of Magnus Maximus, finally stepped forward, throwing a short, well-studied look at the shattered wall, and then turning to von Klasewitz before the eyes of all. "Today is a great day for the Roman Empire," he said loudly. None escaped the fact that he laid his right hand on the shoulder of the time-traveler. "This man has given us the instrument with which we can lead Rome to a new prosperity, to new strength, and above all to new justice."

There was loud applause. Legionaries hit their shields with their swords. Shouting ensued. There was great enthusiasm everywhere, as they were now convinced of the destructive power, as well as the functionality, of the new weapon. Von Klasewitz was careful not to dampen the euphoria. It was clear to him that any improved onager would have achieved the exact same effect with this hastily erected, brittle wall – or even more so. But it was not about the comparison of the punch-through force, it was about completely different effects, ultimately about questions such as range, fire speed, and the type of ammunition to be used. The use of artillery was by no means foreign to the Roman army, and the expert builders were masters of constructing mighty catapults and onagers, miracles of mechanics with considerable power. However, these were generally designed as siege machines and played a very subordinate role in the classic field battle, if at all. This was what von Klasewitz wanted to change, or even revolutionize. The artillery as an integral part of a battle, with the clear task of exerting as much destruction as possible before the beginning of the actual fighting, with the demoralizing effect of "invisible" death, the noise, the cruel mutilations that a hit necessarily brought with it. And if he had a whole company, or even two or three, who bombed the battlefield in regular staccato, one after the other, so that the first had already loaded again, while the last ones were still firing ...

The nobleman could not resist a joyful grin. The effect would be overwhelming. Yes, the Roman troops had discipline and fighting spirit, there was no doubt about that. But the legionaries could not be compared with the mercenaries of a *terzio*, who, in the Thirty Years' War, marched through the rain of cannonballs and bullets with stoic serenity to finally to put an end to the enemy with their pikes. Of course the legionaries, who survived the first of these battles, would at some time get accustomed to this new mode of warfare, but Magnus Maximus would have already achieved a lot during his advance. The German enthusiasm and the ability of the time-travelers around Rheinberg to prepare and equip the Emperor's troops in their own way were no longer limiting the confidence of the nobleman.

It would in any case become to be a very bloody war.

Andragathius leaned forward. Von Klasewitz alone could understand his words. "Production has now begun and is being continued. Whatever you need, it is to be procured for you."

"Good."

"You suggested that a training schedule has to be started."

"Our own legionaries must be accustomed to the guns. They must not be frightened once they are fired, they must become familiar with the injuries that can be caused by them, and they must be prepared for the thought that they can be shot at some time. As soon as we have some pieces ready, we must begin with appropriate maneuvers and marches."

"Shot?" Andragathius frowned. "You mean, if Rheinberg equips Gratian's troops?"

"That too. But we're talking about a battle with ultimately mobile troops. Has it never happened that the occasional catapult was also aimed accidentally in the direction of your own soldiers in a battle?"

The General nodded thoughtfully. "This is true. It happens."

"It will happen again. Only this time the consequences, especially for the troop's morale, could be even more negative."

The old general stroked his impressive and well-groomed beard. "I concur. Maneuvers and plenty of them. And what kind of marches?"

Klasewitz suppressed a sigh. It was difficult for him to communicate the necessity of testing the artillery in combat, before going on a trip to Gaul and challenging the Emperor.

"We have enemies on which we can try these weapons. Is there not a tribe in the north of the Hadrian's wall, to whom Rome is not well-disposed?"

"More than enough. With most, however, we have valid agreements. We should not provoke them unnecessarily. That would be a bad signal to the others."

"Most of them?"

Andragathius' facial expression got thoughtful. Then he grinned. "I think something could be arranged ..."

Klasewitz grinned back.

7

Godegisel could only guess the impression he gave.

For a moment he stopped, looking down at his dirty legs. The constant rain ran down his neck, but he almost didn't notice it. His clothes were completely soaked and filthy after several days outdoors without any protection from the weather and driven by the fear of being pursued.

He had to admit that he had not seen any pursuers. Nevertheless, he continued to march steadily. He avoided the large streets that connected the cities and mostly had military posts. Who knew what kind of news the traitors, the murderers of Valens, had spread. A transient gothic rebel, a violent barbarian to be seized and killed instantly? It was possible. It was actually very likely.

Godegisel was sure that not even his mother would have recognized him in his present condition. His beard was overgrown and unkept. His hair stuck greasily to his head and shimmered. His skin looked pale and his cheeks fell. He hadn't been able to eat much the few last days. Here and there he had fed on what nature offered him. Armed only with a sword, it wasn't easy to hunt, and his abilities as a trapper were limited, and he didn't have time to wait for a rabbit to meet him and to present himself as a meal. Berries and fruits, he had sought in vain at this time of the year. From a farmstead, he had stolen fresh bread that someone had put into the open window for cooling. It had been the best meal for a long time, but now already two days ago.

There was plenty of water – God blessed Gaul with a constant rain, not very intense, but permanent, which went through everything –, and the paths the young Goth used were transformed into almost impassable mud courses. Thirst was the only thing Godegisel didn't suffer from. But the drifting hunger, which had started to become painful and established itself as his permanent companion, weakened him with every step. He felt reminded of the arrival of his people on the Roman frontier, a time which seemed to him to be an eternity and yet not two years ago. Even then they were all very hungry, exhausted by the flight from the Huns. Hunger was well known to Godegisel, and he had learned to hate that feeling fervently. He would have to eat something soon. If not, he couldn't continue his way.

His way.

The young Goth wasn't sure where he was going. Maximus and his supporters had great influence and would certainly have placed their men at important positions. Godegisel didn't know whom to trust. In the end, he had no choice but to speak directly with the Emperor, which he thought was unlikely, or he returned to Fritigern, his people, and let things take their course. But Godegisel was no fool. All Rome would suffer under the civil war, which would inevitably break out as soon as Maximus put his plan into action.

The course of events could then turn out to be very unpleasant for his people, especially if it became public knowledge that Valens had survived the Battle of Adrianople and had been surrendered by the Goths to the enemies of Gratian. Godegisel wanted to curse Fritigern's plan, but told himself that he had allowed the opportunity for serious opposition to pass him when he had had it.

Of course, he might be able to get in touch with the time-wanderers.

Godegisel didn't feel too well at the thought.

It had been his sword that had killed one of their leaders. He hadn't been punished for it, and had been allowed to return to his family after the conclusion of the peace treaty, but it would be silly to assume that his role had been forgotten.

On the other hand, if the Goth who had killed a leader of the Germans, came and warned of great danger, wouldn't that increase the chance to be heard by a clever and intelligent man, such as the new Magister Militium?

Godegisel wasn't sure, but there was only one method to find out. He would have to go as far as Italy to make direct contact with his former enemies.

But until then there was still a long way to master.

Godegisel raised his head, glanced at the cloud-covered sky. The weather wasn't so cold, and he guessed that he had moved fairly steadily toward the southeast since his escape. He might have traveled between 150 and 200 Roman miles. As he avoided entering large settlements and had no particular knowledge of how these towns and villages were scattered in Gaul, the only way left to him was to maintain a roughly southerly route. He hoped to be able to make his point but was aware of the fact that his current condition was not adequate to arouse great confidence in other people. He'd noticed the peasant's eyes on the fields, as he had walked past them. No one had stopped or called on him, but his ragged appearance made every Gallic peasant appear as a nobleman in comparison.

Godegisel now avoided the fields. The time of sowing had come, and the land's population was busy. Nevertheless, it was clear that he wasn't doing very well. Clean and tidy clothes, some cash, a bath and a shave, all this would help him considerably.

Night fell. The Goth looked at the edge of the nearby forest before him. In there, he might find shelter, set up on a tree for protection from bears or wolves. He hadn't eaten anything all day, just drank, and felt the weakness of his limbs. He wouldn't be able to walk much further without a rest. Perhaps there was something to eat in the forest. In any case, a mighty tree crown could hold back the rain. Luckily he could sleep for a few hours.

He needed about half an hour until he reached the forest. It wasn't as dense as seen from afar. Carefully, the man entered the edge. When he had advanced a few yards into the undergrowth, the stumps of two trees, which had just been felled, became visible. Were there any forest workers at work who had brought building material or firewood for one of the nearby villages? Perhaps a careless man had left some food. The probability was low, but Godegisel clung to this thought, as he followed a barely recognizable forest path, on which traces of sand could be seen. Every now and then he passed another tree stump. Whoever was responsible had been careful not to cut the wood randomly, and not to take a group of trees completely. In addition, the impact could not be seen from the outside, the signs began only a few meters inside the woods.

After a few minutes, Godegisel came to a small clearing. The light of the setting sun was becoming more sparse, but that wasn't a problem, because the building, which he observed from hiding in the scrub, gave off both light and warmth. It was a large cone-shaped structure, glowing from the inside. Little holes were drilled into the structure, behind which the glow of a slow-going fire could be discovered. Godegisel didn't have to think long in order to recognize what he was looking at: In this carefully constructed device wood was processed into charcoal. Once such a pile had become active, it would slowly burn for several days, and would need constant supervision in order not to consume itself. The charcoal burner working here wanted to produce coal, not ashes, and was therefore compelled to guard the embers day and night, to supply air, or to block holes again until he could open the pit and remove the finished charcoal.

That meant two things. On the one hand, a worker was present in the immediate vicinity, perhaps on the other side of the kiln. And on the other hand, this man was either unattentive or simply not proficient in his line of work. Godegisel wasn't an expert in charcoal, but he knew that the greatest danger was that the pile caught fire and consumed himself and his valuable contents. And the smoldering of the openings, as well as the smoke coming out of them, suggested that this time came closer.

He circled the construction with great caution. He enjoyed the warmth it exhaled. It gave the promise of dryness – dry skin and dry clothes.

Godegisel concentrated on his surroundings. One thing after the other.

As he circled about halfway around the miller, he saw a small wooden shed that wasn't even worth being called a hut. It was merely an oblique roof of branches, resting on two wooden beams, fully open at the front. In front of it was a small, now extinct campfire. Godegisel saw a bundle with something that looked promising like food. Two feet protruded from the shed. The Goth guessed that the man was asleep, one of the greatest dangers that this occupation entailed.

For a moment, he hesitated. People like them were not rich. And this one would be in big problems when his work flared up in flames. To steal one of his possessions ...

The Goth pushed the thought aside. He was hungry. That was all he could think of now.

He went on carefully, peered into the opening of the cagelike structure. Then he relaxed.

There was no reason for special caution.

The man was dead.

The man was already somewhat old, at least he looked so. Life here caused people to age early so that from their appearance it was difficult to judge their real age. He had, however, long since crossed the zenith of his time. There was no sign of violence. The old man, he thought, had been engaged in his work and then died in his sleep. It couldn't have been so long since the pile had not yet destroyed itself.

The young Goth knelt. He shied away a bit from squatting right next to the corpse, although it looked remarkably dry in the hatch – the roof seemed to be tight. Godegisel's hands went through the belongings of the deceased. In the bundle he found a dry shirt, freshly washed, but also a hard piece of cheese, an edge of bread, and some grains which could be made into a mash with warm water. Next to the extinct fireplace stood a metal bowl, in which water could be boiled. Finally, Godegisel found a small amphora, closed with a stopper made of wax. He opened it and sniffed. Diluted wine that smelled slightly sour. Godegisel took a cautious sip. After all the hardships of the last few days, he felt like the most noble drop he had ever tasted. He closed his eyes and took another sip.

"Who are ... Father?"

A bright voice, a woman, full of terror and fear.

Godegisel stood slowly, turned around, his right hand visibly on his sword-grip. Before him stood a young woman, not yet twenty years old, in a filthy, simple dress. In one hand, she held a kind of pot with a wooden lid, from whose steam evaporated. It smelled auspicious. Soup.

Soup for the dead father.

Godegisel looked into the woman's face and was looking for tears. He saw into the weary eyes, looked at the folds that had already dug into her skin, saw the dirty, black-gray hands. No daughter of a Roman noble or even a wealthy craftsman or trader. A woman like one he often met among his own people. He had lost his father to the Huns, his mother died on the flight, the little brother on the border to the Roman Empire, starved to death, and his sister sold herself to a Roman officer for a slaughtered dog. Her gaze was that of someone who had so much suffering and deprivation in her short life that even another death was nothing that would tear her from emotional dullness after the initial shock had subsided.

As if to confirm that, her gaze caught him filled hopelessness as well as silent grief. "And? What will happen to me?"

A simple question, made without any emphasis, almost businesslike. Godegisel wondered at his own emotional reaction, felt sudden shame. "Nothing. It wasn't me. I roamed the forest in search of food. I found your father lying here, he was already dead. See for yourself. I didn't touch him. He isn't hurt."

She looked at the corpse again, now seemed to be consciously aware of it for the first time. She took a step forward, remembered the pot in her hand, put it down awkwardly. Another step, then she bent over the lifeless body, looked at him closely. Then again the look in Godegisel's face. Sadness still but somewhat less hopelessness. That was at least what the Goth himself hoped to see.

"You may be right," she muttered. "He was sick, my father. The constant cough. However the pit had to be supervised, and he was supposed to sell coal on the market. Since mother is dead ..."

Godegisel just nodded. Then he pointed to the pile. "It's about to burn up. We should ..."

He didn't have to say anything. The young woman turned around at once, took a tool, looked at the heat with a professional look, and began to close some of the openings in the pile, reducing the air supply, and thus the risk of an all consuming flare. Godegisel watched her for a few minutes, looking at the slender, almost droughty body, as it tensed, the muscles flexing, and focused on work. Then he joined her without a word, likewise a bronze shovel in his hands, and did as she told him. Twenty minutes, thirty, perhaps, they were struggling for the survival of the charcoal, the value of which the young daughter, now on her own, would surely be able to feed herself from for a few weeks.

Then the young woman paused, wiped soot-sweat from her forehead, and looked at the Goth. Was there a certain degree of respect, indeed appreciation, in her gaze?

Godegisel might be fooled.

Then they stood again before the body of the father. When the daughter took the corpse by the shoulders and looked at Godegisel, he took his feet and dragged the body away. The young woman had a remarkable strength and knew her way around. With occasional glances behind her, she led the Goth, both connected by the corpse, along a narrow path to a coarse-framed hut, which stood on another clearing. Then she let the body slip to the ground. Godegisel's eyes followed her. A little distant from the hut, he recognized a simple gravestone, hammered from sandstone, with a carving of a crude image of a charcoal pit. No writing. Godegisel guessed that the father had made it for the deceased wife – and that he could neither read nor write, and therefore had left only a simple picture. "We bury him here."

It hadn't been a question, more a statement. Whether the young woman was still assuming that the Goth was responsible for the death of her father, and now trying to exploit his guilty conscience as long as she could or whether she was simply expecting, hoping, and doing things, Godegisel didn't know and maybe it wasn't so important anyway.

He just did as she did.

It was a formless, but not unworthy, funeral. Godegisel said nothing, remained silent beside the now freshly dug tomb. The family of the man had been Christians, as he now ascertained, for the daughter fetched a wooden cross from the hut and placed it on the grave, and said a prayer as far as he could interpret the murmur. She didn't expect Godegisel to join her in this.

Godegisel suspected that the next graveyard was quite distant, and the daughter wanted to save herself a proper burial ceremony for monetary reasons. The Goth said a silent prayer, out of respect for the daughter.

"The pit!" she finally said. "We must look after it." Resistance stirred in Godegisel. He had not come here in order to do the work of a charcoal producer. For him, bigger things were at stake.

"There's soup," the woman added, looking at his hungry face. "Bread and cheese. Cervisia. I'll share it with you."

This was an argument that felt very convincing to the young man. And though he could have done it, he didn't want to steal anything from this thin, almost frail, yet powerful woman. In a sense, Godegisel thanked God for preserving this degree of humanity in him despite all the confusion.

It took another half an hour – now it had turned dark –, but then the pit seemed to glow to the satisfaction of the young woman. Without pausing for a moment, she put the pot, which had stood all the time in the grass as if forgotten, to the fire-place, ignited a bonfire, took bread and cheese from the bundle, handed Godegisel the amphora with the wine, and went to fetch beer from the hut. The Goth declined the beer with thanks, which the woman silently accepted. Minutes later, a warming fire burned, and finally the Goth received what he had dreamed for days: a warm meal. The bread was hard, but the hot soup made it edible, and the cheese tasted surprisingly spicy.

On the other hand, in his condition, almost everything that was offered to him would have been excellent.

The woman shared with him, as she had promised. That meant she left him the bulk of the food, stared silently into the fire, and probably thought about her deceased father and her own future. Would she be allowed to continue the father's business? Godegisel was not yet well-versed with the Roman customs and laws, but he doubted it. His eyes fell on the comforting glow. It was the legacy of the dead man, and it would probably be the last one that had been put up in his family.

When he looked back at the fire, his eyes fell into the young woman's eyes. It seemed as if she had had similar thoughts and had come to a comparable conclusion.

"What's your name?" she finally asked.

"Godegisel."

She grimaced. She had a small snub nose, which she could curl nicely. It contrasted with the hard look of her gray eyes. "What is that for a name?"

"Gothic."

"Goth, yes?"

She glanced at the fire, set down some twigs. "We don't have many Goths here. Franks, yes, but Goths … You are Romans?"

"Yes, very recently."

"Freed?"

"No, I never have been a slave."

She nodded, obviously satisfied with the answer. "My parents were freed. They have since lived worse than in times of their slavery, but they were glad about it."

The Goth didn't answer.

"I'm Pina."

"I'm sorry about your father," Godegisel said. She nodded again. "What are you going to do now?" He made a gesture toward the pile.

"Right now? Finish work, sell charcoal. And then I have to look for a man. My father said that I should have done that long ago – at least in his view. But out here …"

A shrug. A glancing, weighing, quite calculating, in Godegisel's direction. No, he corrected himself. The look of a fox, taxing a hare. He took another sip of wine.

"What is your craft?" Pina asked casually.

"I am … a warrior."

"Legionary? You are too young to have completed the service."

"No, not with the legions. I fought until recently against the Romans. Then there was peace, and now I am a Roman. I have not fought since then." This wasn't quite true, but Godegisel saw no point in spreading the whole story.

"What kind of work are you planning to do?"

Godegisel looked down at himself. He was now quite dry under the protective barrier and in front of the flickering fire. He felt better, with a warm meal in the stomach and wine to it. But he had no illusions about his outward appearance.

Pina glanced at his eyes, unconsciously tweaking her hair. Then she smiled. "Where are you going? Are you looking for a job?"

"I want to go south, to Ravenna."

If Pina was disappointed with this answer, she didn't show. "You have work in Ravenna?"

"I don't know that yet. But I have to meet someone. It's very important."

The woman seemingly accepted this explanation, however weak it sounded. She threw a meaningful glance at the charcoal. "The coal is ready in two days," she said abruptly. She turned her head and looked at Godegisel meaningfully.

He didn't reply.

Pina pushed the bundle with her right foot in his direction. "My father's dry things. I cannot wear them."

The Goth took the bundle, held it for a moment, then pulled out the fresh tunic. "I …"

"There is hot water and soap in the hut."

For some reason, Pina always seemed to guess what he was going to say. Godegisel was in dire need of both. He rose quietly and followed the path to the hut. Visibility was better than imagined, because the moon was nearly full and the clouds had vanished. He reached the building and entered it. A single, simple living room that reminded him of the fisherman's family in Britain who had helped him and Valens cross the Channel. A fire spot in the middle, still generating some heat. Godegisel rekindled the fire. Above the fire, a heavy, cast-iron kettle full of water hung, which was still lukewarm, but soon began to heat again. On a small table on the wall, soap and a wooden bowl lay, as well as some cloth rags, which were probably used for scrubbing.

46

Godegisel got rid of his clothes, poured hot water into the wooden bowl, and began to clean himself thoroughly. It was a wonderful feeling to be able to rub the encrusted muck of a battered march from his skin, and he didn't ration the water. When he had finished and even eliminated the dirt under his fingernails, he looked for a beard scraper or a knife. He found some small blades and examined them, attacking his wild beard with the sharpest one. He hoped to look a little manly afterwards and not like an animal anymore. He threw his filthy clothes in a wooden wash-tub, pouring the rest of the hot water and brushed them with some soap. He would soak the clothes overnight, and maybe he could then persuade Pina to wash them thoroughly if he guarded the charcoal.

At this point, Godegisel noticed that he had decided to stay for some days.

He paused for a moment, thinking about it, a little surprised by his own resolve. Meanwhile, he dressed in the dry clothes of the deceased father, who had had roughly the same stature. The fabric was coarse, and the pants and shirt were of a very simple cut, but it was a nice feeling to wear clean clothes on clean skin. Godegisel closed his eyes and enjoyed it for a moment. After all the hardships, he felt like newborn. He took a deep breath, then took some of the things he thought useful – especially food – and set off on his way back to the pit.

As he entered the clearing again, he stopped involuntarily. Beside the shed, Pina squatted, to be seen clearly in the pale moonlight and the fire. She had exposed the upper body, washed herself with the water from a leather tube and a rag. She hadn't noticed his return. The young Goth couldn't help but notice her small, pointed breasts, whose warts had hardened in the cold. Her belly was slender, thin, and he could see her ribs as they peaked under the white skin. She washed herself with precise movements, as if she had memorized every step of the process, and once a slight shiver ran through her body, as the wind rustled through the forest and hit her wet upper body. Then, after a minute, she pulled the dress over her head and squatted close to the fire.

Godegisel consciously stepped on some branches in front of him and pretended he had just arrived. Pina looked up and directly at him. Her face was also free of dirt and soot, and when she smiled, as she did now, her snub nose was even more charming than usual.

The young Goth smiled back. Yes, he would definitely stay for a few days.

8

The Quadians knew the area and what to look for. Luvico, the son of the King, proved to be less bitter and distrustful than they had all assumed or that his father had so clearly expressed his order to cooperate fully that the son had buried every reservation in his mind, in order not to spoil the mission. He was almost thirty years old, a giant of a man who had grown at least one head above his own father, with muscles that made Volkert appear as slim and almost thin. He had served five years in the Roman frontier legion, the *limitanei*, and had left service once treason had been committed to his father's predecessor. He spoke good Greek and broken Latin, but above all, he understood how a Roman force was functioning; he had a definite idea of what questions Sedacius would ask to prepare the attack on the advance division of the Huns.

It didn't take two days until the Quadian-Roman armed force was ready. The approximately thousand men under Tribun Sedacius were strengthened by more than 4,000 fighters. Normally. the barbarians would be used as auxiliary units. They were relatively lightly armed with spears and arches. Only nobility carried swords, which were usually longer than the rather short arms of the Roman legionaries. Even fewer were properly protected; it was only the handful of tribal leaders who carried metal armor on their bodies. The average warrior had only what he would wear as everyday clothes, maybe supplemented by a helmet or cap, rarely made of metal, much more often from leather. Some wore leather straps around particularly vulnerable places, such as joints or the crotch, knowing that a well-executed stab with the sword would destroy this protection fast. The Quadians were not used to the strict organization of the battle and the discipline of the Roman soldiers, but they were obviously willing to defend their native country, and, if necessary, side by side with the truly hated, treacherous Romans.

Volkert had begun to like the tribal warriors, to whom some of his comrades were quite contemptuous. They were simple men, hardly anyone could read or write. If they were not warriors, they earned their livelihood as peasants or craftsmen. Professional soldiers in the sense of a standing army they were not, their military threat to Rome had been, as with all barbarian peoples, in their great numbers and the wildness of their attacks. The men who most closely corresponded to the ideal of the Roman professional soldier were those who had once served in the legions – which, as Volkert had to discover, were not too few – and the small group of warriors acting as the King's bodyguards, maintained by his purse. It wasn't surprising to either Volkert or Sedacius that Luvico had appointed the deserters from the legions, many of whom had served with him, and who left together, to be his officers, not quite unlike the status which Volkert had as a decurion. This didn't mean that the tribal men would fight with the same organization and discipline as the Romans, but their leaders would understand the tactical instructions, immediately grasp their meaning, and try to implement them as best they could. That was all they could expect at the time.

In addition, almost all of the Quadians were mounted. Together with the mounted Romans, this constituted a considerable cavalry unit, even though Volkert harbored no illusions. The Huns, who were able to fire from the backs of their horses with their almost magical arches, were superior to their own riders.

For this, the Romans had the infantry.

Volkert had been able to keep himself away from the troop. But he had not escaped the demonstration by which the barbarians had been made familiar with the special abilities of German weapons. As was to be expected, the presentation, especially of the machine gun, didn't miss its purpose: Luvico and his followers were impressed by the fact that they were far more secure than before. Probably they would have assumed that the weapons were magical and their bearers wizards, if Sedacius hadn't introduced them with quiet and clear unambiguousness as Roman soldiers with special equipment.

Volkert was aware of the fact that the demonstration had a further side effect: If their new allies turned out the be treacherous, or if they were secretly planning a campaign against Rome, the demonstration of this power would surely teach them to reconsider.

At least this, quite obviously, was the hope of Sedacius.

It was an early morning, the mist still deep in the trees and the meadows when the mixed troop finally departed. The barbarian riders took front as they knew the surroundings better than the Roman ones, and an advance party had already started the night before to explore the way to the camp of the Huns. It was now expected, during their progress, to receive timely warning of any impending danger from them.

Volkert rode next to the Tribune. He wondered why. There had been so much work to do, that he hadn't really noticed when Sedacius had asked to join him in his work, sometimes even with the centurions and other officers. Was Volkert, in the eyes of the Tribune, such an extraordinary, even promising man that he wanted to keep him close, to train and to promote him for higher tasks? Or was it an expression of mistrust? It belonged to the paranoia of a deserter who felt like a fugitive that he saw the negative and the menacing in everything. Volkert was well aware of this. Again and again he told himself that there was no point in judging the now, the moment, just from the experience of the past, instead of seeing it as what it was. This rather impassionate distance, which he believed to be a prerequisite for many successful leaders, helped to avoid misjudgment. By considering a situation as it was, and not disguised by the fears and bad experiences of the past, which would lead to false assessments and wrong decisions, a clearer view could be obtained. Volkert wanted to be so calculating. But the thought that execution by rifle or the sword was waiting for him, should his true identity be revealed, forced him to look at everything through a spectacle of fear. This distorted reality, he realized. But he couldn't help it.

He had an easy way out – to execute the orders given him by the Tribune. In doing so, he only postponed the discussion of his anxiety, but at the same time it remained to him to do the things that were to be done and to think about the consequences another time.

But the privileges given him by the Tribune had not escaped others. As always, Decurion Septimus Secundus, his old comrade, emerged as a valuable source of information. On the evening before the departure, sitting at the camp fire, when they had both gazed silently into the half-empty wine cups, Secundus, abruptly or not, had shared some information, and Volkert couldn't quite discern why his comrade offered them.

And even without any consideration for compensation.

The young German became quite suspicious.

"You are often with the Tribune."

"He's calling me and giving me orders."

"Sure, but I think you should know who you're dealing with."

"Sedacius? What is there to know about him?"

Responding to such a question, Secundus typically showed a particular facial expression of "know-it-all" that had become his trademark. The immediate reaction was usually that everyone around the fire collapsed and urged the Decurion to share his freshly acquired news.

"Sedacius is related to the Emperor."

Volkert nodded. He had expected a bit more. So many Roman nobles and officers were in some way related to the current and probably over the centuries to a whole bunch of emperors. As marriage policy was an important means of establishing personal networks of power and influence, such a network of relationships seemed almost inevitable.

"There are many," was his only comment.

"But Sedacius is one of the few who didn't take advantage of it. That is why he is a tribune."

"I don't understand."

"He is a tribune, because he has chosen a military career made on his own strengths, and has come as far as he could have done without the protection of the Emperor. And he is a tribune, because everyone thinks that the Emperor somehow supports him, though this is not true – which his superiors, however, don't know or don't believe."

"Secundus, you're talking rubbish."

The Decurion sighed and took a sip of wine before answering.

"Sedacius is under pressure to prove that he is his own man and able to make the career he wants without wiping anyone's butt."

"Good, but he isn't alone in this. Any officer who wants to be something has to show what he can do if he wants a successful military career."

This was a subject Volkert knew better than he wanted to confess. However, he knew that the same problems – namely, protection from higher positions for officers who simply had the right background – hadn't been uncommon in the Imperial Navy of his time.

"No, he's not alone in this," Secundus admitted. "But it forces him to gather people around him who, in his opinion, make it possible to quickly achieve the necessary successes – and from whom he expects to continue to participate in his successes. So, in short, he builds his own group of clients, loyalists he promotes and who promote him, irrespective of everything that his proximity to the imperial house could add to it or not."

Volkert narrowed his eyes. "Secundus."

Just the one word after a long break. The Decurion had meanwhile drunk off his wine and stared at the empty cup with an expression of regret. He looked up and grinned. "Thomasius, my friend."

"I guess I know why you're telling me that."

"Is that so?"

"You have two reasons."

"Two at once? You overestimate me."

Volkert knew that Secundus wasn't an outstanding soldier, and had too many illegal businesses running to bother too much about climbing the hierarchy of the armed forces. This was less connected with the nature of these transactions than with his unwillingness to share the profits with his superiors. He preferred to try to multiply his earnings or lose them in gambling. But dumb he was not.

"The first reason is that if Tribune Sedacius adds Thomasius to his retinue, and with the desire that said Thomasius will distinguish himself, the good friend of Thomasius, who until now has been largely undisturbed by promotions, may profit from it."

The face of Secundus lit up. "Ah, how beautiful. You call me a friend."

Volkert grinned. "I just tell you your own thoughts."

Secundus waved his hand. "That is to complicated for me. And the second reason? It doesn't seem to be quite as obvious to me as you have just assumed."

Secundus was definitely not stupid. Volkert became serious. "The second reason is that you can tell yourself that Sedacius, before long might try what many have tried before him, and many have also succeeded, in attaining the purple and proclaiming themselves as emperor." Volkert had whispered these sentences. It was not advisable to express such speculations too loudly.

Secundus looked at him in astonishment. It was obvious that the content of what had been said wasn't surprising for him, but the fact that Volkert himself had come to this conclusion. "Thomasius, I can see that I am right."

"Do not expect too much. Sedacius would fail."

"You are too sure."

Volkert couldn't tell him where his confidence came from. At the same time, however, he wondered whether this categorical assessment was still justified. Had not already changed too much in the history he knew? But no one had ever heard of an emperor or even of a usurper named Sedacius!

"I ... have it in my mind," he said weakly.

"Levantus is more confident."

"The centurion?"

"He is one of those who voluntarily or involuntarily serve the plans of Sedacius."

Volkert shook his head, took a sip of wine, and made a mouth because of its sour taste. Then he put the cup on the floor with a determined gesture and stretched. "The conversation leads to nothing."

"These are speculations, but they are not unfounded."

"We'll see what's happening. Now we have to fight the Huns. Who knows who of us still lives in a few days?"

Secundus shrugged. "I have your back, Thomasius. This might help me as well."

He rose and left Volkert alone by the fire.

The young German stretched his hands toward the flames, so near that they almost touched them.

Nevertheless, he was very cold.

9

Berhan cherished three things in his position: wealth, power and slaves.

Especially the slaves.

He rose from his bed, and stretched himself. He merely wore a cloth wrapped around his loins. The heavy wooden doors of his bedroom were locked. He knew that hardly a sound could get out of the room.

And there has been a lot going on. Berhan regarded himself as a very strong man, a man who had to prove this strength, even if only for himself. That he expressed contempt for his wife, he was quite aware of, but didn't care. The marriage had in any case been subordinated exclusively to political ends. Thus, he had tied himself more closely to the house of the Emperor, and in this way he had finally attained the position he had so cherished a good half a year ago, that of the Governor of Adulis, the representative of the Emperor, residing in far away Aksum, the second-largest city of the Empire.

He turned and looked at the body of the young woman who was still lying on the sheets. Whoever looked closely realized that the chest was neither raised nor lowered. She was dead.

With the expression of slight regret, the Governor sighed. The bloody wounds that he had inflicted on her everywhere had certainly not led to death, he knew, for this was not the first time he had amused himself in such a way. But when, in wild ecstasy, he had laid his hands around the neck of the barely 20-year-old, he must have pressed a bit too long.

Berhan was a strong man. He admired his muscular arms. Women who didn't know his preferences considered him an attractive man. Even his own wife had once considered him a good-looking spouse and consented to marry, instead of leading the miserable life of a distant relative at the imperial court. She had stopped rejoicing quite fast.

Berhan didn't beat her, of course. He didn't want to jeopardize the favor of the Negusa Nagast, King of Kings, the Emperor of Aksum.

It was bad enough that the Emperor was so different in his attitudes. Mehadeyis was a good ruler, they all said, perhaps somewhat feebly and too much prone to the suggestions of his advisors. Berhan belonged to this illustrious circle, so he could do more or less what he liked. If not only ...

He grimaced. The good humor he had felt had vanished. This always happened when he thought of the young Ouazebas. This man was not even eighteen years old, and he, too, had the ear of the Emperor. Moreover, there was the rumor that he was chosen by the old Mehadeyis, himself without a son, as his successor. Not only did Berhan despise this. Ouazebas was honest in an almost absurd way. He was diligent, able to read the Holy Scriptures in Greek and Latin, and he had already several times focused the imperial mind on the needs of simple subjects and the poor. His great role-model, it was said, was Ezana, the predecessor of the Mehadeyis, who had brought Christianity into the country.

A wise and honest ruler, gracious and righteous. That's what Ouazebas strived for, there was no doubt about it.

Berhan spat on the floor.

He and his allies wouldn't allow that to pass.

Ouazebas was one who would get rid of someone like him, especially if he were to learn of the little jollies of the Governor.

Gebre Berhan cherished his newly acquired position too much to take this risk.

He sighed again and dressed himself. The day was before him. His servants, discreet as always, would dispose of the dead body, as they had already done one time or another when Berhan's strength had led to similar results. Not a topic he'd waste too much thought on.

As he dressed, he began to focus on the biggest problem that lay ahead of him today. It was the delegation of Roman travelers, who had been found in the ambassador's house alongside the apparently murdered body of this most important representative of their neighbors. There were no ordinary Roman travelers; they carried the seal of the Emperor with them, had a letter of escort from the Egyptian governor, and rumors said that some of them belonged to the time-wanderers of whom strange stories had been heard in Adulis.

The suspects had spent the night in a dungeon, and now the Governor, Gebre Berhan, was expected to make a decision.

Berhan sighed a third time.

This was the problem with power, wealth and influence. They resulted in a certain commitment to do certain things.

If he didn't like one thing, then it was obligations.

Once he left his house, he had already forgotten about the dead slave in his bed.

The path took him from his villa to the residence of the Governor, a splendid white stone building, not far from the port. The port was Adulis' life-line, from here almost the entire foreign trade of Aksum was carried out – and also any military expedition that couldn't be done over the mainland. Aksum was an expanding empire and thus one that gained great riches. Only 30 years ago had the kingdom of Kush been conquered. Further conquests in the East followed. And this phase had not yet been completed. Aksum was one of the four greatest empires in the world and was named in a breath with Rome, Persia and distant China. The palace of the Governor, in which Berhan resided, testified to the self-esteem of an aspiring magnificence.

When the Governor was led by his guards to the auditorium and had taken his place on the elevated chair, which was worthy of his position, the officials poured into the room. Berhan felt only contempt for this class of the Aksumite administrators, even though he was fully aware of the necessity of their existence. The imperial bureaucracy, as his impression was, developed a disastrous life on its own with the expansion of the Empire. It was as if there was another power next to the Emperor and his deputies, a power that couldn't be grasped with hands, which seemed to be submissive and attentive, but one even a Negus had to show respect for. Berhan, too, found himself, already from a natural tendency, to rely more and more on the services of the officials and not only to delegate tasks to them, but to give more and more freedom in the manner of execution. He had already begun to lose sight of all affairs attached to his office.

The Governor shook his head slightly.

There were things he could not leave to the officials for political reasons. One of these matters was now imminent.

He focused his mind.

The doors were opened and some tired and slightly filthy figures were led into the room. Like everywhere, the stay in an Aksumite dungeon was by no means agreeable, and that was clearly visible in the prisoners. Some of the men, who were now standing before the Governor, were remarkably tall for Romans. Berhan remembered the rumors about the time-wanderers and wondered if he was in the presence of some of them.

An interpreter stood next to the prisoners. Berhan waved his hand. He spoke Greek fluently and expected from a delegation from Rome that they all mastered this language. He didn't trust translators.

"Bow down to the Governor of Adulis," the Master of Ceremonies proclaimed, also in Greek. The men understood the order and produced a bow Berhan almost rated as appropriate. He was usually used to a bit more respect.

He turned to the commander of the town guard, who had also entered the room with the prisoners. The soldier, a veteran of the war against the Kushite empire, once served as the Nagast of a Sarawit, the leader of a regiment, and he had been given this prominent position in return for his merits. The gray-haired Nagast stepped forward. His bow was even less impressive than that of the prisoners. Berhan had to live with it. The old man had good political connections and was close to the generals at the court of the King of Kings. His son served in the guard in Aksum. He was imperturbably loyal and completely unimaginative. It wasn't worthwhile to begin any shady business with him.

"Speak!" was all Berhan had to say.

"Lord, these men were arrested in the house of the Roman merchant and ambassador Diderius Latius. They had obtained illegitimate access, and beside them lay the murdered figure of the ambassador. We took the men into custody."

"Have they resisted?"

"No, sir."

"Have they been questioned?"

"Yes, sir. They have legitimization from the Roman governor in Egypt. They are on an official mission, not ordinary thieves or assassins."

"What did they want in the house of Diderius?"

"He had been mentioned to them as a contact person for accommodation and further organization of the trip. They claim that the outer gate was open when they arrived, and Diderius was found dead."

"You have not seen anyone else?"

"No."

"What did the slaves see?"

"Most of the slaves were out for work today. The major-domo found Diderius murdered in the morning, and at once ran for a guard for support. When he came back with the soldiers, the prisoners were present. The slave has blamed them for the murder."

"Ah, has he?"

Berhan looked at the prisoners for a moment. They didn't seem to be particularly intimidated, and they obviously trusted in their official status as ambassadors of Rome. The Governor had to admit that this trust was not completely unjustified: In fact, one wouldn't be able to deal with them as with ordinary murder suspects. Besides, the likelihood that these men had just arrived in Adulis was very likely to have had something to do with the death of Diderius.

Berhan knew this quite well, he had himself paid the assassin and dispatched the man in time to let it look like the Romans had assassinated him.

He allowed himself a fine smile. In this elegant way, he had at least learned that the attempt had been successful. "The slave was interrogated?"

"Under torture, sir."

"And what proof does he have for his accusation? Were these men seen killing Diderius?"

"No."

The Governor frowned. Again, he looked pensively at the prisoners. Listening to the whole conversation with the soldier in Greek, they must have understood most of it. "Who speaks for you, Romans?"

A man whose ancestors apparently came from Africa stepped forward. "Aurelius Africanus, Trierarch of the Roman Fleet."

"Africanus, yes?" Berhan allowed himself another smile. The arrogance of the Romans was sometimes a bit too much, he thought.

"Yes, sir."

"What is the goal of your mission, Trierarch? I heard you wanted to go to Aksum."

"That's true, Governor. We seek an audience with the King of the Kings."

"What does Rome want?"

"We ask permission to look for commercial goods in the highlands."

"A trade mission, then? The rumor is that Rome is in search of allies in the struggle against the Persians."

Everyone knew the archemnity between Rome and the Persians. The rule of the Sassanids was a thorn in the eyes of the Romans. They argued about Armenia and always waged war with each other. Finally, however, it was heard that Shapur III was interested in a peace settlement with Rome. Nevertheless, Berhan's assumption had not been unrealistic, not least because Aksum had far-reaching interests in the East and therefore could have the intention of forming an alliance that excluded the Persians.

"I don't know about these rumors," Africanus replied. "But the Emperor has other problems, I think."

"The Goths," Berhan said musing. "In Adulis, we've heard of Adrianople. Valens is dead, they say. I regret the loss of your ruler."

"We're sorry, too. The Goths are now pacified."

"The news of the Battle of Thessaloniki has also come to our attention." Berhan glanced at the tall figures who had not spoken to each other so far. "There are also rumors about so-called time-wanderers and a mighty, steely ship with gods as crew."

"There have indeed been many remarkable things happening in Rome," Africanus replied evasively. It was clear that if he wasn't forced to do so, he just wasn't interested talking about these things.

"You were found in a compromising situation."

"The death of the ambassador surprises us as much as it does anyone. We have counted on his help to get to Aksum."

"Did he have trouble in Rome? Has his family fallen into disgrace?"

"I'm not aware of anything related to him. He was named to us as the most important contact in Adulis. The Governor of Egypt spoke with respect about him."

"In fact, your envoy was very much respected and popular here. A successful trader, too." *Too successful for his own business interests,* the Governor added in his thoughts. But the problem was solved now. At this hour, his men were already active in taking over all those parts of the small Roman trade center that Berhan had long been concerned about.

"That's how we heard."

"A very regrettable occurrence," Berhan said. He turned back to the commander. "Was the house of the murdered man searched?"

"The major-domus had it checked, sir."

"And?"

Berhan knew the answer, at least he had given appropriate orders.

"Gold is missing, Roman and Aksumite coins. As much as two men can easily and unobtrusively carry through the streets."

"Ah," the administrator said. "And this gold was found among the prisoners?"

The officer looked to the ground. "No, sir. Maybe they hid it in time."

"Nothing in the house."

"No."

"I understand."

The gold Berhan knew in the pockets of the assassins. By this, the victim had paid for the balance due for his own assassination. The Governor thought this a very practical solution. He smiled at

Africanus. "It seems to me as if you your arrest can be called a bit premature."

The Trierarch bowed his head. "It is only proper to investigate events from all angles."

"Excessive caution can cause damage. We want good relations with Rome. If a shadow falls on our relationship with the Emperor, this wouldn't please the Negusa Nagast."

"We agree. We want everything to be clarified in regard to this case. The death of Diderius is a loss for the Empire."

"Your cooperation is welcome," Berhan said. He leaned back. "Bring chairs for my guests."

This made it clear to all parties that the man had made a decision. Berhan watched under half-closed eyelids as the former prisoners visibly relaxed. He suppressed a smile. And then he remembered another idea he kept in mind, to which he immediately congratulated himself. Fate was in his favor and put everything together.

When the former prisoners had made themselves comfortable, he rose again. "Please be so kind and don't tell the Negusa Nagast too much about this little misunderstanding," he asked Africanus, but turned to all of them.

The Trierarch bowed his head. "We do not want to make anyone uncomfortable. But perhaps we don't even get an audience with the Emperor. Diderius had wanted to help us in this regard."

Perfect, Berhan thought. *Life is perfect.*

"You will surely get an audience. I myself will give you a letter of recommendation to the Negusa Nagast. And you will have a guard that will lead you to Aksum. Unfortunately, the trade route to the capital is also infested by robbers. I don't want you to be harmed."

"Thank you very much, Governor. Above all, a letter of recommendation should help us a lot."

"I'll personally seal it. And you need gifts for the Negusa. The old man has a sentimental soul, and we all respect him very much. If your wish is to gain certain trade concessions, it will be necessary to influence his mood positively. He has his preferences."

"We would be very grateful for any advice in this regard."

Berhan waved to an older man who had been waiting in the background. He stepped forward and bowed. "Haleb is here to support you wherever he can. He knows the esteemed Negusa almost better than I do. He'll advise you. He will immediately provide you with suitable accommodation in my palace. You have spent the night in the dungeon, and you are tired, hungry and filthy. You certainly want a bath and a good meal."

The mention of both sparked an expectant glow in the eyes of his guests, and Berhan knew he had chosen the right words. "Haleb! Bring these men into the palace. They are to receive everything necessary for their well-being. Prepare the trip to Aksum. I wish our Roman friends to be equipped with everything. Help them wherever you can!"

"Yes, sir!" Haleb bowed again. Berhan rose.

"Trierarch, let us continue this conversation once you have been taken care of. Recuperate and feed yourself. Haleb here will show you the way."

"We thank you, Governor!"

The Romans also rose and left the hall under bows. When Haleb wanted to join them, Berhan waved toward him. They put their heads together for a few moments. No one could hear the soft murmur, but Haleb nodded several times, then hurriedly left the audience hall.

Berhan looked satisfied. One could rely on Haleb. He had held him in his service for over ten years and had never regretted it. Haleb was discreet and inventive. He had already removed the remnants of the previous night without anyone noticing it, he had taken care of the two assassins who had killed the Romans, and he would provide the gifts for the Negusa Nagast, for him and for his successor, the young Ouazebas. Dignified, precious gifts, as expected from a foreign delegation. Haleb would have to spend a lot of money on it.

But it would be worth it.

Berhan was quite sure of that.

10

"I don't understand you. I actually don't want to understand you."

Rheinberg looked at the tabletop in the Captain's cabin of the *Saarbrücken*. From outside, he could hear the gentle rippling of the sea, the waves breaking on the steel body of the cruiser. He had felt a strange emotion of peace when, after so many weeks, he had returned to the ship. He had villas and palaces opened for him, wealth and luxury for the highest military dignitary of the Roman Empire, but it was here, in the small steel chamber of the Captain's cabin, in which Rheinberg really felt at home.

His well-being had been severely impaired once the two infantry-men presented Markus Tennberg. The Ensign had been tied up, and Rheinberg had ordered to untie the cords. Tennberg had sat down and said nothing. Although Rheinberg had expressly given instructions not to cause him any physical damage, the man looked wary, a little sluggish. The dungeon was not a summer holiday for anyone.

When he looked at Tennberg, the thought of Thomas Volkert had involuntarily creeped upon Rheinberg. Another a young man, of Tennberg's age, and with the same legal status, a deserter. And yet Volkert's decision had a different background, leaving behind other feelings in the Captain, more regret and compassion, and some understanding for his youthful impetuosity.

For Tennberg, he didn't feel much more than contempt. Rheinberg sighed barely audibly. It was not his intention to kill anyone else of his crew. Each of the time-travelers was indeed invaluable. They were, whether they wanted it or not, a community of a very special kind, assembled by destiny. It was by no means that Rheinberg had developed an understanding of Tennberg's and Klase-witz's motives, or pretended to accept their wrongdoing without punishment. But for the moment, he had the impression that the young Tennberg had been the victim of a seduction of quite different kind, though not half as innocent and romantic as that of Thomas Volkert.

No matter what you read in novels, Jan Rheinberg could not find anything romantic about mutiny. He looked in the eyes of Tennberg and found what he had hoped for.

Resignation and a tiny pinch of hope.

He could probably work with that. "Tennberg, where is von Klasewitz?"

The young man said nothing, stared at the wall.

"You know in what kind of situation you are in, do you?"

Tennberg shrugged. "Do what you think is right."

"What do you think is 'right,' Ensign?"

His opposite looked into his eyes. "There are laws that answer this question."

Rheinberg made a comprehensive gesture. "I am the law on a cruiser of His Majesty."

"Then you decide."

"You don't make it easy for me to make that decision."

Again the shrug but with hardly measurable delay.

Rheinberg couldn't help smiling. "We can, of course, proceed according to the letter of the law," he mused. "German and Roman law. In both cases, I can only tackle you hard; I don't want to threaten you unnecessarily, you know what is possible. Ever seen a Roman torture room? I must say that in these procedures our new friends are quite proficient."

Tennberg lowered his eyes. Was there fine sweat on his forehead?

"I'll make you an offer. I believe that during the interrogations you were already made aware of the fact that I'm ready to save you from your death."

"Yes," Tennberg replied hoarsely.

"You can stay alive, Tennberg. I will take you out of the navy, and you'll get rid of your rank. But you should live. And not in a dungeon, but in exile, at least initially. A Greek island. There is a choice. You stay there and have a simple, peaceful life, and I'll leave you alone. For this, tell me all about the plans of von Klasewitz. If you lie to me, and I find that out, our deal is dead. If you tell the truth, you still have a very sunny future. Now, what's it gonna be?"

Tennberg pressed his lips on each other. "How can I be sure that ..."

"I keep my word! I'm not a traitor like von Klasewitz. My word is that of a German officer whose honor is still intact. Isn't that sufficient for you? Have you gone so far from your old ideals that you have lost all confidence in honor and an officer's commitment to truth?"

Tennberg seemed to think for a moment, then breathed heavily.

"Well. I agree with the deal."

"Very well. Where is von Klasewitz?"

"In Britain."

In Rheinberg's head, his machinery of thought started to move. Britain, the province of Maximus, who would rise up against Gratian in the other, the original timeline, and kill him. The Maximus, against whom, despite all the demands, no action had yet been taken. "What does von Klasewitz plan?"

"I don't know about his exact plans. He immediately sent me to Alexandria, once he set out for Britain."

"Who helps him?"

Tennberg made a vague movement with one hand. "Influential Romans. Clergymen among them."

"Ambrosius?"

The Ensign shrugged. "I don't know. No one has been introduced to me. All talks have been conducted by von Klasewitz himself. But a high-ranking official named Maximus was there. He has also been mentioned several times."

"What was your mission in Alexandria?"

"Contact potential allies of Maximus and prepare them."

"Prepare for what?"

"Well. Insurrection. Revolt. Uprising."

Tennberg now looked directly at Rheinberg, all the tension and premonition had disappeared from his attitude. He had made his decision and wouldn't be afraid to put the cards on the table.

"An uprising," he said. "Against Gratian and against the time-wanderers. Especially against your influence. Maximus is to become the new emperor – as in our past. Only this time he gets help, which he didn't have before."

Rheinberg nodded thoughtfully. It all made too much sense for the young man, and he had thought of it before.

"When will it start?" he asked the important question.

"I don't know. I was sent to Egypt quite early. Klasewitz obviously wanted to get rid of me."

The first reflex of Rheinberg was to dismiss this answer as a lie. But Tennberg didn't look away, glanced openly into the eyes of his former superior.

"Didn't you talk about it with von Klasewitz?" Rheinberg continued to ask.

"I don't think he makes the decisions. And if I don't think I enjoy his trust so much that he would have told me everything."

"Who decides? Maximus?"

"Yes. And others who support him."

"What role does von Klasewitz play then?"

Tennberg shrugged. "That is hard to say. I'm not sure if he knows it himself. As I see it, the insurgents use him only to learn the use of modern weapon technology as best they can. I'm pretty sure that he considers himself more important than he is."

Rheinberg couldn't suppress a grin. That sounded like von Klasewitz very much.

"What kind of promises were made to you?" Tennberg hesitated as if the answer was embarrassing.

"I should get the rank of a *dux*," he said. "A province for me, as a governor of the Empire." Again the shrug. "I never really believed in it. I've been part of it because there was no way back for me."

"What was promised to von Klasewitz?"

Tennberg looked directly at Rheinberg, as if to see exactly how the latter responded to his reply.

"Your post was promised to him, Captain."

"As a Magister Militium?"

"As captain of the *Saarbrücken* in the rank of a Navarch. Don't know whether there has been more promised to him than that. I guess so."

Rheinberg nodded, more to himself than to Tennberg. He didn't believe for a moment in new modesty in the nature of that man. Whatever had been promised to him – and Tennberg's version was as plausible as anything else –, he would be looking for more. If only to compensate for his vanity, and the disgrace of his initial defeat.

But in order to achieve this ...

"What plans does he have with me?" Rheinberg asked.

"Death," Tennberg answered briskly. "This was a condition of von Klasewitz for his cooperation. He wants to see you dead. Very simple."

"I'm sure, everyone will be glad about this condition," Rheinberg said dryly. Tennberg allowed himself a weak smile, ran his hand over the tangled, unwashed hair. He didn't add anything.

Rheinberg thought for a moment. Whether trustworthy or not, he felt that Tennberg had told him the truth. Of course, he would be questioned even more thoroughly, because there might be important details, about whose significance he wasn't all aware, but that was not a task that Rheinberg would take over. Tennberg would talk, and then the Captain would keep his promise.

The Captain rose and called for the guards in front of his cabin-door. They stepped in, waiting for a moment. Tennberg also left his chair.

"You will be interrogated. You won't be tortured, I promise you," Rheinberg said, saying goodbye. "Stay with the truth and say everything you know, and I will make sure that a beautiful Mediterranean island is waiting for you."

Tennberg bowed his head gratefully before he was led out.

When the door closed behind the men, Rheinberg dropped back into his chair. He put his head in his hands.

Well, so was to fear, something was about to happen that he had wanted to prevent from the beginning. A civil war.

And he would have to fight it.

Jan Rheinberg had a peculiar taste in his mouth.

11

"No, Martinus, remember the consequences."

Martinus Caius, whose puffy hand still massaged Julius's left breast, paused. His face so close to hers, she smelled his stink as the coarse pores of her husband exhaled the odor of too much wine. He had hardly drank for a day and a night, but the consequences of his last drinking bout still enveloped him. Since, unlike most other Romans, he was not quite as enthusiastic about the principle of physical cleanliness, the smell was strengthened. His tunic had old, dried red wine patches.

"Consequences?" Caius echoed, withdrawing his hand back completely.

Julia suppressed a sigh of relief. "Yes, consequences! You are a learned man, my husband, and have enjoyed the highest education by the best teachers!"

In fact, his father, Julia's father-in-law, had spared no expense and effort to give the young Caius knowledge and scholarship. Caius, on the other hand, had spared no expense and effort to escape the teachers, and instead tried to investigate how far drink and easy girls could be of his benefit. This was a research area he had achieved true expertise – and he still seemed to discover new aspects in it. "Uh …" Caius said.

"I like to remind you of some facts, my dear," Julia whispered, and moved a little from her husband to escape his stench. "It is well known that there is a great danger when you penetrate a pregnant woman like me!"

"Danger?"

"Yes, my darling! You are a man full of strength and endowed like a bull! When you gave me my child at that time, I felt as if a hot-forged sword had impaled me and pierced to the back.

You don't even know in the slightest what your little Martinus is capable of!"

A flattered smile flitted around her husband's mouth. He involuntarily pushed out his chest, an effect that lost its effect because of the unequally voluminous belly. Of course, that night of passion had never happened, for Caius had been totally drunk. But Julia had told the story so often that he believed in it by now. And since then, she had managed to escape his desires by means of colorful and creative excuses. "But ..."

But she interrupted him at once. "Now imagine, if you pound me again with all this male power! Yes, my screams of pleasure would be too widely heard, the whole of Noricum would talk about it! But the danger to our child!" She lowered her voice. "It could be hurt! Your son! The pride of the family! The pride of your father!"

Caius Martinus looked at her with widened eyes. "For real?"

"But yes," she whispered almost conspiratorially. "Isn't that known to you? The fruit of your loins injured by your loins! You can not seriously want that, my husband!"

"But no, no," he said.

As his unsteady gaze wandered around, Julia had already prepared the chalice filled with wine. "Here, my dear Caius," she sneered, as he grabbed it eagerly. "Just relax. Soon, soon, our son is born. And then, after half a year or so ..."

Caius almost swallowed the wrong way. Wine splashed on the tunic and renewed the stains. "Half a year?"

"Well," Julia said, with raised eyebrows. "It takes so long for a woman to be ready again. You know we bleed very much and smell like fish. This will be even worse right after birth. Men can get sick by that." She patted the soft shoulders. "And we won't trouble the little Martinus, wouldn't we?"

"No," the great Martinus confirmed. "We don't want that."

He looked into his cup, which had been replenished, as if by magic. He drank.

There was no greater fool in this world than her husband, and Julia was quite happy about it.

Otherwise she was just bored.

The long stay in Noricum approached the end, which was the good news. Julia had never had much time for the province, but she had been persevering in the hope of hearing something from Thomas Volkert, the man who was the real father of her child. She had used the contacts of her father-in-law in the region as discreetly as she could have. She had to be careful not to arouse any suspicion; on the other hand, she also didn't have many possibilities for obtaining information. There was no clear indication of what might have happened to the troops sent eastwards. However, she didn't want to exaggerate her worries; such campaigns, even those to explore the situation, could ultimately take months or even years, and the troops had only been on the road for some weeks.

Julia couldn't win much from any fatalistic view. She hoped that her Thomas would find a way to leave the troop, and she would be free her from the prison of her marriage with an unloved, tumultuous drunkard. She wanted her child to grow up with her biological father and not with someone who was not really interested in it.

But the hope that this perspective would become reality was dwindling with every additional day. Her pregnancy was now clearly visible and advanced. The midwife, whom she regularly sought for advice, attested to her that everything was developed without any problems. Julia was at times sick in the morning, and she made a loud and, if possible, disgusting act of vomiting in front of her drowsy husband into a suitable container. This had the positive effect of decreasing Martinus Caius' longing for morning sex. In the last few days, her general condition had improved a lot, and the morning sickness also had turned into a weak malaise, combined with a healthy appetite. And so far as to vomit every morning, Julia's need for purposeful theatrics increased as the need to empty herself vanished slowly.

She found it therefore necessary to fight the man's grazing hands. Since Julia knew quite well how to manipulate men – she had gleaned some knowledge about that topic from her mother –, it wasn't such a big challenge.

Martinus Caius muttered something, left the matrimonial bed, and stumbled toward the wash. The cup was half-emptied on the floor. Julia swung her legs out of bed and looked at herself in the mirror, which was placed next to the sofa. A pleasant fire lit the couple's bedroom. Outside, she heard the bustle of the house slaves preparing a breakfast.

Actually, she was doing quite well, at least that what she wanted to convince herself about.

Martinus Caius burped, sniffed and scratched himself extensively between his legs.

But really only *quite.*

12

"Some people are talking only because they don't want to be silent. How seldom does it happen that someone is silent where it would be better if he talked."

Malobaudes looked somewhat irritated at the Bishop of Milan.

The clergyman with the crooked pair of eyes smiled indulgently. "General, I know you're in a difficult situation."

The General didn't know what the Bishop was talking about. He might refer to their current place of residence, a house along the Lutetia road to the south, toward Italy, not far from the border of the Northern-Gallic province. It was more like a big hut, a bit windy, and the whistling wind inspired an uncomfortable atmosphere against which the lit logs in the fire place could do very little. Outside, hidden behind the building, were horses and the companions of both men, the latter bent over a camp fire. It was unpleasantly cool for this time of the year, a relapse into winter, and Malobaudes looked into the cup of warmed and spiced wine he held in his hands.

He was a king and a general, but that didn't mean that he had a great understanding for cryptic utterances, especially when there were much more important things to discuss.

"I'm sure you can be more precise."

Ambrosius nodded.

"The events have taken an unpleasant turn because of the Goth's betrayal. I feel that our plans are accelerating."

"There was no betrayal. Valens is dead."

"Did you find his Gothic confidant?"

The general moved restlessly on his chair. The question was obviously unpleasant to him.

"No."

"You're still looking for him?"

"Carefully."

"Carefully?"

Malobaudes sighed. "If I order my people to search too openly and with all means, people will ask me why and what is so terribly interesting in a Goth. And then, honored bishop, many things will indeed accelerate in a very unpleasant manner."

"Ah." Ambrosius smiled. "Good. I deserved that. Nevertheless, the incident with Valens and the lasting threat by this Gothic youth is a sign of the fact that we shouldn't busy ourselves with too many preparations. The time for action is now coming nearer."

Malobaudes felt colder than the weather and room temperature required. It is one matter if you kill someone who had long been dead. It is another one to overthrow the ruling Emperor – and in doing so his blood will inevitably be shed.

"We ... Maximus is ..."

Ambrosius waved dismissively. "Maximus is introspective. If it would be for him, we'd be waiting for months. But we don't have these months any longer. And now there is a Goth around who has a story to tell."

"No one will believe him," the General interjected.

"Anyway. He represents a risk. We also have to keep in mind that the time-travelers around Rheinberg dig deeper into the structures of the Empire. They are now talking about building an officer's academy, in which the leaders of the legions are to receive a one-year intensive training."

Malobaudes nodded. "This is one of the good ideas of our enemies."

"Of course, it's a good idea – and this way a very loyal, professional officer's corps will be created, which will be very difficult for us to influence if we hesitate for a long time. Do not forget all the other reforms! The state budget is about to be consolidated! Did you know that the income situation of the Imperial court has started to improve over the last few weeks, especially since all tax breaks for the large *latifundia* owners and the Church have been canceled? If this continues, noble general, Gratian will be able to continue to expand his network of influence and power, because he now has the money to do so! And if he even achieves military successes, even with a great insurrection, it will hardly be possible to overthrow him – and the heretical and gloomy machinations of the wanderers will finally be unstoppable!"

Malobaudes nodded. Ambrosius had spoken in rage, as almost always on such occasions. He himself had little sympathy for heretics – but above all, he was interested in becoming the Magister Militium of the new Emperor Maximus.

That's why he was part of this.

"Good," he said in order to say anything at all, and to put a stop to further excitement of the clergyman. "So if I understood you correctly, you see the time to act. I don't contradict you in regard to the speed with which the influence of the time-wanderers spreads. But I know that Maximus' troops are not yet ready. We must produce more of the weapons designed by our German so that we can lead a successful campaign. We make progress if the reports are to be believed. But it still will take time."

"How much?"

Malobaudes raised his shoulders. "Ask Maximus!"

"What is your opinion?"

"Six months."

"Then the summer is over, and we can wait another year."

"The cannons work even in winter."

"No!"

The Bishop hit the table with his fist, and the General winced. Ambrosius liked to talk a lot, and he was quite embarrassed and emotive.

"I can only judge from a military perspective," Malobaudes said, almost apologetically.

"There are, however, other points of view than military ones," Ambrosius snapped.

"For sure."

"And there are other strategies than military."

"I know what you think of."

"Only in part."

Malobaudes listened. It had been agreed that at the time of the insurrection he should be near the Emperor and put an end to his youthful life. Ambrosius expected that he would do so quickly and painlessly. The General, who had neither friendship nor hatred for the young Emperor, had apparently taken this part of their plans without emotional attachment. People died in such actions, and this included an emperor if necessary.

As long as his retreat was covered, he had no objections. But Ambrosius had apparently planned further.

"It is not sufficient to kill Gratian," the Bishop said, as if addressed the unspoken thoughts of the General. "His most faithful generals must also be removed."

"They will be with their troops if they don't dwell at court. We need to place agents everywhere. It will take more time."

Ambrosius moved his hand. "If the Emperor is dead, the most important dignitaries will be at court, I think here mainly of people like Theodosius or Arbogast, and the rest will fold under the storm of events. Many officers will feel the wind blowing, and join us. Many will want to save their careers. But the most important thing is to beat the heads of Hydra."

"The time-wanderers."

"Rheinberg and von Geeren are high on my list. At Ravenna, in the new German village, some more. I'd like to spare the man named Dahms, as he might be useful to us. Renna must die, there is no doubt about that. And if all other allies of the wanderers are harmed, I will not complain. Symmachus and Michellus, the senators, are on that list."

Malobaudes fell silent. The lists of death-warrants became constantly longer. For him, that was less an ethical problem than a logistical one. If a plan becomes more and more complex, the likelihood of errors also increased. It has always been his principle to keep things as simple as possible. But in one thing, the Bishop was right, of course. Rheinberg, the Magister Militium, had to die. "Rheinberg is guarded almost as well as the Emperor," the General remarked. "Our last attempt failed. The problem is that he can defend himself very well."

"Yes. But I have a second plan. This has also recently suffered a setback, but I haven't given it up yet."

"Enlighten me."

"Now I will, because I need your help, General. You have to have use your connections with the court and have somebody introduced."

"Be more precise."

Ambrosius rose and opened the door. Outside, the group of his companions waited, eager to join the warmth of the fire. He called someone, and Malobaudes couldn't understand. A slightly smaller figure emerged from the group and entered the hut. The Bishop closed the door and pointed to a free chair. "Sit down."

The figure threw back the heavy hood. Malobaudes' eyes moved. "A woman!"

And, as he added in thought, a very charming one.

"This is Aurelia." Ambrosius introduced the woman who sat silent. "Until recently, she was a slave of Rheinberg. I have offered her over a middleman to Renna, and he has given her as a present. The idea was that he takes her to live with him, and she kills him there. Unfortunately, it didn't happen."

"Rheinberg has smelled the plan?"

"He freed me before we could get so far," Aurelia said, with a deep, smoky voice. "I didn't get him to bed. He didn't seem to like the idea of fucking a slave."

Malobaudes shrugged. He was well aware of the strange views of the time-wanderers on slavery. "So what's the new plan?" he asked.

"Aurelia is of the opinion that in any case Rheinberg is quite smitten by her."

The young woman smiled. "He behaved like a little boy in my presence."

"And so?" the General asked.

"Aurelia is free and a woman of great education. Give her a position at court. Rheinberg obviously wanted to do that too, but the lady simply disappeared after her release."

The woman gave the Bishop a calculating look. "I didn't want to proceed without new instructions."

"That was the right thing to do, my dearest," Ambrosius replied gently.

"Be that as it may, the core of my plan remains. Aurelia is free, and she should get a meaningful position. Thus, she is no longer unapproachable for someone with the moral ideals of Rheinberg. She will approach him, he will fall victim to her, she will kill him at a suitable time and disappear."

Malobaudes looked at the Bishop for a moment. Then he nodded slowly. "This will be done. How shall he die?"

The Bishop gave Aurelia a look. Without any facial expression on her face, she drew a dull, shining blade, thin and sharp, from her garment. The weapon lay securely in the woman's narrow hand, and the General, at the sight of the assassin, was reminded of a deadly serpent. The eyes of Aurelia were unfathomable. She let the dagger disappear without comment and looked at the Bishop.

"Aurelia will accompany you incognito back to Treveri," Ambrosius said. "Do what you can, but do it soon. It won't be six months before we are going to attack. Three maybe. But not more. Do you hear me, General?"

He didn't like what he heard, but he could hardly pretend not to be attentive. He nodded again.

* * *

It was half an hour later, when Aurelia left the hut. Her face was hidden under the wide hood when she mounted her horse and waited for the General to give the signal for departure. She had said nothing else during the further course of the planning session.

When the horses fell into a light trot, her thoughts wandered to her mission. Ambrosius had once promised her freedom, a great reward, a house, and her own slaves. Who would have rejected such an offer? This was worth more than the life of a single man.

And as she thought about it, her right hand wandered unconsciously between her breasts. There, wrapped around her neck, lay a flat leather pouch, and her certificate of liberation, officially sealed and signed.

Signed by Jan Rheinberg, a man who was already dead without knowing it.

And not by Ambrosius, Bishop of Milan, man of promises.

She did not even notice that she nearly crushed the document through her clothes.

13

"Well, he's keeping all his promises!"

Neumann looked up and smiled at Köhler. It didn't take another minute, then Behrens and Africanus also appeared in the courtyard of the house. It was an early morning, the day of her departure to Aksum, and the NCO's commentary was in regard to the caravan, which was ready to take the guests to the Aksumite imperial court.

"I wouldn't have dreamed that our luck would turn so quickly," Africanus said, as he looked at the numerous mules. Guided by their drivers, carts were loaded with bags and boxes. They were packed not only with the goods brought by the Romans to Adulis, but also with provisions for the voyage, tents for camping in the open, and a chest with gifts for the Emperor. As they had been assured, it was a choice of commodities, which would be well received by the Emperor and his entourage. In the chest were various wooden boxes, all richly decorated and provided with the name of the receivers. Not all were destined for the Negusa Nagast but for other influential figures at court. Neumann had opened the casket for the Emperor and found in it fine jewelry, made of Nubian gold, and of excellent craftsmanship. This gift would definitely make an impression. The Governor had required only a few of the Romans' valuable commodities for exchange.

In addition to the men in charge of the mules, they had also been given a guide. In essence, this was not necessary for the orientation of the travelers. Aksum was accessible by a constantly-traveled and well-developed road that couldn't be missed by anyone. But the guide, an elderly man who conveyed the impression of an experienced traveler, was at the same time carrying the seal of the Governor, which would enable them to make use of official assistance on their way to the capital. As far as the Empire was concerned, there was no more comfortable and safer way of traveling. Mules with simple saddles were also provided for the Germans. In the thin air of the high plateaus, which had to be climbed, and to overcome the height differences, mules were more suitable than horses. They were slow but strong and persistent.

The stay in Adulis had been very pleasant in the last days, despite being filled with travel preparations. The Roman delegation had not been involved too much in those. Their quarters were comfortable and clean, they had plenty to eat, and they had visited the city and familiarized themselves with the history of the Empire. Any attempt to take part in the preparations for the trip had been rejected as a violation of hospitality. With such activities, they had been told, they didn't have to deal with; there were servants who knew exactly what they had to do. Now that the four men had seen the well-equipped, ready-to-go caravan before them, they had to admit that their hosts had been correct. It was to be doubted that they would've arranged a similarly professional effort. Besides, the days of rest had done them good. Since their arrival, the Germans had had little opportunity for idleness and relaxation, especially on the leadership level. From this point of view, the city tour through Adulis and the hospitality of the Aksumites had been a pleasant change. Neumann, Behrens and Köhler were now again ready for action, and even the Roman officer didn't want to complain too much about the little vacation he enjoyed.

"We can depart, can we?" Behrens muttered, looking somewhat confused at the guide as well as the muleteers, who in turn looked at the guests. There was undoubtedly a communication problem.

After all, Africanus could understand Greek. It became clear, however, that their Aksumite friends wouldn't be overly prolific conversation partners on the long journey.

The orderly chaos of the preparations for the trip now dissolved as the caravan formed. The four travelers were just about to mount their animals, when a group of men entered the courtyard of the house, and in their midst the Governor of Adulis. He had apparently come to say goodbye to his guests.

"I would like to express my gratitude for your hospitality," Neumann said after greeting him politely. "We felt very comfortable in your city."

Berhan smiled dismissively.

"Don't thank me too much. Your reception was not very hospitable at the beginning, and I had to make amends. In addition, it is important for me, as the governor of the most important trading hub of the Empire, that the relations with our powerful neighbors remain good and friendly. Rome is of central importance in the world, and Aksum is a friend of Rome."

"Have there been any new insights about the murder of Latius?" Africanus wanted to know. The facial expression of the Governor turned dim. Regretfully, he made a gesture.

"I'm very sorry," he said. "Though I have ordered my people to give this tragic affair great attention, they have not yet advanced. I hope to know more once you return to Adulis. I suspect that he has become the victim of a normal robbery. No glory for this city and for me as a Governor. For now, therefore, it is my goal to do everything in my power to bring those responsible to justice."

The Governor made a sincere impression. Africanus let it go. The departing guests exchanged a few polite words with the dignitary, and then they received the best wishes for a safe journey. They mounted the mules with difficulty, and when the caravan was finally ready for departure, greetings were exchanged for a last time. Then the animals set in motion, without any great incentive by the muleteers required. They trotted out of the courtyard to the busy street. Shortly afterwards, they reached the main street of Adulis, which stretched from the harbor across the center to the western end, and left for the capital city of Aksum.

They advanced well and had passed the outskirts half an hour later. In front of them, the mountainous regions of Aksum were visible. They assumed that they would reach the capital after seven strenuous days, if nothing happened.

On the evening of the first day, they arrived in a village that lay directly at the road. It was a relatively barren region, and the situation of the villagers seemed to be difficult, judging by the smell that struck them when they entered the only large building of the settlement and asked the village chief for a night camp. The seal of the Governor showed its hoped-for effect, and the travelers brought their own supplies and thus didn't require food from the poor villagers, which was quite welcome. Outside, close to the mules, bonfires were lit, for the men caring for them would spend their time outdoors with their animals.

After a simple but satisfying supper, Neumann joined Köhler, who stood outside the door of the house and looked into the night sky.

"We need to think more about how we want to proceed once we have arrived in Aksum," the Doctor finally said after a few minutes of silence.

"I think our approach is quite clear," Köhler replied. "We ask the Emperor for permission to look for the coffee bean. Or, better yet, someone at court knows the plant already and just didn't know what to do with it. Then we talk about the cultivation and make a contract – and next year we will start the first Roman coffee-making industry."

"You always think practically, Köhler," Neumann replied smiling.

"But this is not just about our longing for caffeine but also about politics. I have discussed this with Africanus. It will not be so easy."

"What did you learn?"

"The current Aksumite emperor is an old man and hasn't left his palace for years. Everyone knows his probable successor, a young man named Ouazebas. I didn't find much in the Captain's documents on the Aksumite history, so the name tells me little. The fact is that Ouazebas is gaining power every year and is already speaking at many occasions for the Emperor. He is the one with whom we must in any case speak, aside from the old man."

Köhler shrugged. "Good, we do that."

Neumann smiled and shook his head. "Many want to get in touch with him and get his favor. Even among our gifts is a large box with its name. Adulis, too, wants to be his friend."

"And?"

"He who has such power also has enemies. If the Emperor, on the advice of his predestined successor, is graciously accepting our petitions, we automatically turn the whole project into a part of the political play that takes place here – especially when he is behind it, especially in light of the considerable financial revenue we are expecting and with which we will vigorously advertise our plans."

There was no doubt for the time-travelers that a drug like caffeine should have a strong appeal in the Roman Empire. In contrast to alcohol, the moral reservations would be rather small, not even the otherwise critical Church could argue much against it. If production and distribution were well thought-out and organized, they were faced with a gigantic business that would enable both those who worked in it and the state to generate various revenues. If he wouldn't have been convinced by this perspective, Rheinberg would never have given his consent to this expedition.

"So we have to be careful," Köhler concluded.

"Very careful. It is also about the relations between Aksum and Rome. The people here are not stupid. They know who we are. Our reputation is at stake. And that we are closely linked to the Emperor, has certainly already become known. Whether we want it or not, we're playing a diplomatic role here." For a moment, the doctor grimaced and looked silently into the flickering fires of the muleteers. "That's why it's so tragic that Latius is dead. It was precisely because of these diplomatic considerations that his advice would have been of great value. Now we have to act like amateurs, and I don't particularly fancy that."

"This thing with Latius ..." the NCO mused.

"... I don't like the smell of it."

"There is more not to like."

"No, no, you get me wrong. I think we should have been more concerned about the matter. Neumann, while you have been considering great policy issues, Behrens and I have moved through the streets in the evening. Many people in Adulis can talk Greek because it is a trading hub. In the taverns, we asked quite innocently for Latius. He was, after all, an important businessman and only in second as a diplomat."

"And what did you learn?"

"Nothing definite, so we didn't bother anyone. Latius was probably considered to be a trustworthy business partner. But there was one thing that made us listen up: Someone told us that the business interests of the Roman were not always consistent with those of the officials here."

"Any details?"

Köhler raised his shoulders. "Unfortunately, no. But who are the officials in Adulis? This is especially the Governor! If he is the one with whom Latius has crossed the line, I can only take the story of his regret and serious concern for finding the murderer half as seriously."

Neumann nodded thoughtfully. "If there's something in it, we should consider it." He sighed. "Of course we don't need to do anything about it now – but we should check back on our return to Adulis. Perhaps with support of the court ..."

"I'm saying it because I've heard that Latius had good contacts at court, and spent several weeks in the palace every summer. We may be confronted with the murder story again. In fact, we may be the ones who bring this news to the Emperor."

Neumann could only respect Köhler's practical intelligence. He put a hand on the shoulder of the bullish man and sank back into the sight of the clear starry sky.

There were many issues to think about.

14

"There are a good five thousand men. More than five thousand actually."

"This is probably only a modest unit for the Huns."

Volkert lay on the heights of a hill and stared down into the plain. It was cool but dry, and the weather was clear. One could see far. The camp of the Huns, from this distance, looked like a single creature, a distant clutter, in which subtleties couldn't be precisely determined. Beside Volkert, Secundus lay on his stomach. The Decurion had excellent eyes. He had made the estimate.

The German looked left and right. Hidden in bushes and behind trees, more men crouched. There were not only Roman soldiers, but three of the German infantrymen had joined the scouting command. And, as he could see, they had, of course, oversized binoculars, with which they could make out the details of the Hunnish camp. As soon as they had withdrawn, one would certainly learn more from the observations of the army soldiers than even the sharp-eyed Secundus could contribute.

Volkert wanted a pair of binoculars now. Optical machinery, he knew, was on the long list of Engineer Dahms – a list that they probably wouldn't work off for years. It was by no means impossible to have the craftmanship and the tools required to grind optical glasses, and to produce at least crude lenses, preferably to be used in telescopes, as they were quite common in the seventeenth century. But as urgent as such an instrument was for military purposes, it was not very high on the list of priorities, and as long as the time-wanderers had a number of these wonderful instruments at hand, there was no immediate need.

Still, Volkert would've liked to have one now.

He regarded the billowing mass of warriors standing between their horses and tents as a threat, which was all the more dangerous because of the fact that this feeling of threat was apparent even despite the vast distance between them.

"We're retreating," Secundus hissed, and they slid backwards on their bellies down the hillside, rising when they were no longer in line of sight, then ran to the horses. The scouting troop consisted of thirty men. Volkert still made sure to stay apart from the Germans. On the other hand, they would most probably not recognize him anymore – in Roman uniform, with a beard and weathered, and certainly not being expected. They climbed on their animals and disappeared toward the common camp of the Roman and their allies. The ride lasted about an hour, then they were called by the advance guards. Only a few minutes later, they joined Luvico and Sedacius, who were already expecting their report impatiently. Fortunately, the Centurion took over the talking, so that Volkert could keep himself in the background. Tightly hung in a frame was a large parchment, sketched on it a very rough map, which a soldier now began to supplement, according to the reports received. Through that they got a pretty accurate picture about the strength of the opponent. Volkert's estimation was correct, they had to deal with a good five and a half thousand warriors.

Finally, the Tribune nodded and looked at the son of the King. Volkert had only met him rarely but had gained a positive impression from discussions. The man looked at them pensively, and once he spoke he used frugal gestures.

"We'll start, as soon as possible." Sedacius stepped beside the map. "The Huns seem to be preparing for something. It may also be that they rest, for we have heard that they have burned two villages not far from here. The time-wanderers have discovered a delimited area in the enemy camp where slaves are held, mainly women and children. This is a good opportunity to catch the entire enemy force in one place."

He pointed to the nearby hillside on which Volkert had hid a few hours ago. "From here, the Germans have a good field of fire for their miracle-weapons. We need to coordinate our attack so that we can drive the Huns straight into the Iron Fire."

Volkert nodded. If a mass of cavalry men rode into the concerted fire of the machine guns, both the bloodletting and the psychological effect would be considerable. Thus, the Goths had been broken before Thessaloniki, but with the difference that most of the work at that time had been done by the guns of the *Saarbrücken*.

But these were fewer opponents. And they were certainly not prepared for the kind of surprise they would encounter soon.

"We're going to attack from here," Sedacius explained. "The enemy will meet us, as the Huns normally do. In this way, they have to cross the plain in this direction ..." He pointed to an angle with his finger, obliquely in direction of the group of hills. "With this, the riders enter directly into the target range of the time-wanderers. Once they have done their part, we will do the rest the good traditional way."

Sedacius looked around. No one had to offer a comment, so the Tribune continued in explaining his plans.

"We are inferior in numbers, and we cannot overcome the cavalry of the Huns directly, as the reports of past battles indicate. I'm not a cruel person and appreciate a good horse like any of us – but we have to shoot the animals so that the Huns can't use their tactics with the archers like normally. The central advantage of our opponent is the combination of speed with the use of a perfectly controlled remote weapon, the arc fired from the animal's back. If we diminish a vital component of this equation, the Hunnish warrior is still a determined fighter, but far more likely to be hurt and overpowered than before." Sedacius turned to the present representative of the German troops, who had listened to him in silence. This was mainly due to the fact that he was surely still struggling with the understanding of Latin. Volkert resisted the urge to translate into German to make sure it had been understood. Sedacius had spoken slowly and tried to demonstrate his plan on the map.

The infantryman nodded, and hopefully not only out of embarrassment.

"Good," the Tribune concluded. "Once the guns have done their part, we are attacking in two closed formations. We have no time to combine our troops to a well-functioning army, therefore our allies and the Romans will operate according to a common plan but separately. The legionaries will leave their horses behind and march into the weakened Huns in a closed formation. In close combat without horses, the enemies are vulnerable and can be beaten. The time-wanderers give us fire protection until shortly before the battle commences. Our allies remain on horseback and attack from here ..." Sedacius showed something on the map. "They are pushing the Huns to the positions of the German weapons, so that they can choose their targets with care. I expect that the enemy will break at some time. It's the task of the cavalry to drive a wedge between the Huns and their camp. We don't want them to return to their loot. It's our aim to liberate the slaves, as far as our allies are concerned, and to capture as many of the others alive. All loot shall also be given to our friends, with the exception of coins; they are for us."

Sedacius nodded to Luvico. The tribesmen, if Volkert correctly remembered what he saw of the camp, would return home richly laden. The fact that the Tribune thought only of coins, which were much easier to transport, was cleverly considered.

"One last point," Sedacius concluded. "I'd like to have one or two of the Hunnish leaders alive. We are here to collect information, and we need appropriate sources. Anyone who brings me a high-ranking enemy who can still talk and who is feeble enough to fear torture will receive a bonus of ten denarii. Spread this to all men. Ten and liberation from all duties for the rest of this expedition, if he is a simple legionary. Everyone should know."

The assembled men nodded. A small fortune and laziness upon return, that was a tempting offer. The men would eagerly look for enemies who seemed to give orders.

"The plan is now roughly explained. Now we'll take care of the details ..."

Volkert suppressed a groan.

He moved on his stool and tried to concentrate further, although he felt a strong tiredness.

The Tribune, without any sign of exhaustion, began to give each of those present exact commands.

This session would take a very long time.

15

The truth wasn't that Godegisel didn't want to look back.

In fact, everything in the young Goth was longing to look back. He knew Pina was standing in the doorstep of her hut, and he also knew she wasn't crying. Someone who had grown up like this daughter of a poor man had by no means forgotten how to weep but kept it for the really important tragedies of life, and her standards were very high in that matter. If a man left for whom one had high hopes, whether justified or not, and who had sworn love to her the night before, only to announce at the same time to leave the next day ...

No, that was no reason to cry.

It might contribute to her embittered view of her own life; it added a further nuance to the hopelessness, which she had felt after the death of her father, but tears for this man, Godegisel, a Goth, she wouldn't shed.

For Godegisel, this was just as well.

He wasn't sure if he would had gone so far as to leave Pina if tears had flowed. The warrior had been the lover of many women in his life, and at the time when his position as a nobleman had still had any value, he had been a promising candidate for marriage. But this young woman here wasn't a foolish thing falling for a handsome fighter. She was also not a marriageable property, moved from one family to another for the purpose of forging political relations. She hadn't been trained in singing or beautiful embroidery to please a husband of status. Pina was a working girl, her hands already scarred by the countless burns that she had endured, and her eyes weary of sleepless nights of her vigil. Her beauty, in spite of her youth, seemed to fade away already, eaten by the deprived life she had lived, a flower that faded quickly, and now that she was alone again, one that would whither even faster. Sure, she would try to keep herself above water, but she couldn't inherit her father's property. Her greatest protection was the seclusion of her life, the fact that for years she had done all her errands and sales for her father, and no one would miss him for some time.

Godegisel could have offered her to go with him. He had been close to say the words a few times.

They could have sold a lot of the belongings and the last charge of charcoal, which would have made a nice travel allowance.

But he hadn't said it. And Pina hadn't asked.

Godegisel knew why he hadn't extended an offer like that. It had been because of fear, especially that Pina, the hopeful, the exhausted, would have been drawn, through him, into a political vortex that would have meant her death, or at least the complete disappointment of all her desires and dreams. Yes, he left her behind, but not because he didn't want her to be with him, but because he was not sure whether he wouldn't lead her to oblivion.

He could have stayed easily.

He hadn't agreed. Pina had offered it to him several times.

It wasn't even that he didn't want to take over the family business. The young man made himself familiar with many a craft and had learned a lot on his long journey, escaping from the Huns. But there was that face which made him smile in his dreams, that of Valens, the emperor of Eastern Rome, and then the body of a fat, bloated, old legionary who, without hesitation, gave his life to the old emperor, knowing that this sacrifice wouldn't change anything. And then with certainty that Valens' death should not remain without any meaning, God had not led him to this place so that he could now stay hidden and avoid the coming storm. Godegisel played a part, he felt that strongly, though he didn't know exactly which one.

Once he had played his role, he thought, he'd come back to Pina. Perhaps fulfill her dreams.

He didn't promise anything. She wouldn't believe him anyway. Pina wasn't a woman who trusted the promises of a worn out Goth. She thought practically. She didn't cry.

He was crying.

Also a reason why he didn't want to turn around.

And so he marched a good hour through the tramps of the forest, until he came to a road that went south. He wore dry clothes that had once belonged to Pina's father. Firm boots, a little too big, also from the possessions of the deceased, a bag filled with few supplies. He hadn't wanted to take it, though he could have taken anything without her giving a fight.

But he really intended to return.

Even if the woman had perhaps already banished him from her thoughts at this moment.

He didn't want to forget her, he owed her so much. He felt bad.

The tiring and monotonous march along the road didn't improve his mood. Godegisel had already experienced a lot for his age. He had killed many people and was not proud of every fight. He remembered a Roman centurion of the bodyguard of Valens, whom he had struck down without hesitation, almost an eternity ago. He still saw his surprised face, the suddenly destroyed hope. It had been the same face as made by Belucius, also fallen for his emperor. Godegisel had obviously changed a lot in between meeting those two, who were similar to each other. The death of the centurion now appeared to him in another light. He felt something like a bad conscience. He didn't care much for that feeling.

But that was nothing against what he felt when Pina crept into his thoughts again.

He would've almost turned around. Almost, almost, almost.

But relentlessly, his steps led him southward, on a mission which he couldn't explain to the woman, who now dominated his thoughts.

The young Goth wasn't a happy man, just a very determined one.

He heard behind him the sound of a cart. He paused, looked around, saw a rickety vehicle with an equally shaky-looking donkey in front of it, and a bewildered figure on the driver's seat. As ungainly as possible, he raised his arms, signaling a request.

The cart stopped. The collapsed figure looked at him from the depths of a hooded hat, said nothing, pointed to the empty place beside him. Godegisel smiled, nodded, swung himself up and crouched as well as his host.

He was as silent as he was helpful. For Godegisel that was just right.

16

The trip to Trier had been long and troublesome. During the entire journey Rheinberg had had a lot, perhaps too much time to think about everything. Because of a new outbreak of cold weather, the journey on horseback had been uncomfortable. The climate didn't behave as the German knew it from the Mediterranean. It was cooler and drier. Therefore, it wasn't surprising that the harvest yields fell and that they were heavily dependent on deliveries from northern Africa. Rheinberg didn't know what was wrong with the weather, but it didn't seem completely out of the question that the unusual cold and dry climate had a connection with the decline of Rome at this time. With all its power, the Roman Empire was ultimately merely an agricultural state, and its ability to support itself depended heavily on the farmer's performance. And so two developments coincided and mutually strengthened each other: The end of expansion and the few campaigns outside the borders slowly cut off the influx of slaves, so that the labor force diminished and the dry weather's negative consequences on the harvest, could only be compensated for by an expansion of the cultivation areas, which wasn't possible due to lack of population.

Rheinberg tried to increase production by means of the gradual abolition of slavery, but this could ultimately only be accomplished by a land reform. For this, many of the big landowners were not yet ready, even those who were otherwise regarded as supporters of Gratian. Rheinberg couldn't afford to push this unnecessarily without considering the risks. Instead, he saw an opportunity in the mechanization of agriculture. Steam power offered good possibilities, especially for comprehensive irrigation systems, as well as for the effective use of hydropower. Dahms worked day and night, opening up new areas of knowledge, which he hadn't yet dealt with as a naval engineer. He was surrounded by an ever-growing number of clever Romans, many from Alexandria, the scientific center of the Empire. His ideas were contagious to gifted contemporaries, and he did everything to spread innovation. Dahms skillfully worked with potential, as Rheinberg found out. Where he discovered potential in his group of disciples, he encouraged it. Anyone who made suggestions for improvements, which the engineer failed to see himself due to his lack of knowledge about the already existing technologies, was highly appreciated. Collaboration in working groups was something that was new to many Romans, even those with previous education. Rheinberg merely hoped that the engineer would not be bogged down in too many projects – or that his own stamina would find its limits sooner than later. During his visit to the "German village," he had also been able to see that the dry dock for the *Saarbrücken* had been completed. Putting the cruiser on keel and scratching it was one of the plans that was on Dahm's fully overloaded desk. Rheinberg wished to have ten men of the engineer's ability. Oh, twenty. Hundred. Archimedes had once said that if he were given a fixed point for his lever, he could lift the world. Dahms was such a lever, and here, at this point, was the point at which he came into action, although he would probably describe himself differently.

Thinking of the engineer belonged to the more pleasant subjects that roamed inside Rheinberg's head. The burden of all those challenges was sometimes hard to bear for the young man, despite all the help he got. He was about to change history, and there were these moments when he was frightened by the scope of his plans and the boldness of his project. Rheinberg wasn't a man who suffered permanently from self-doubt, but it was this feeling of being overburdened that sometimes made him hesitate.

Strange that he always had to think of Aurelia, the former slave girl, at such moments. Was he feeling lonely?

At the latest, every time he asked himself this question, he tried to think of something else. Rheinberg had never been raised to selflessness, but his father had imparted to him a sense of duty, and sometimes he felt beaten by it. He had self-discipline, perhaps sometimes more than was good for him. And he had duty, and so he managed to hold himself in an iron grip.

If only traveling wasn't so exhausting and time consuming. And it was actually not that far from Ravenna to Trier.

A steam train, made of bronze ... that was also on Dahms' list.

Ah, even a hundred Dahms wouldn't be enough, Rheinberg concluded. He needed at least a thousand.

Arriving in Trier, an unpleasant cold awaited him, which didn't remind him of the supposedly dawning spring. The duties of a General consumed him at once. Development of new military doctrines, based on new weapons technology, was only a secondary aspect. Before the new weapons were available in sufficiently large numbers, it was of little use to deal with the preparation of handbooks. Instead, Rheinberg had to realize that in times which were relatively peaceful, the Roman army was ultimately a bureaucratic monster who threatened to drown its leader in a multitude of documents. Again, Rheinberg made parallels to the German Empire: Not only were monuments and statues greatly valued in both epochs, no, the love for extensive administration was evidently already rooted in antiquity as well. The Magister Militium had colleagues, who had noticed quickly that their superior wasn't very happy with paperwork, and therefore only concerned him with the most important documents, but they were still more than enough to make Rheinberg quite moody.

On the third day after his return to the present capital, after a tiringly long meeting with a number of officials, who would gladly have convinced Rheinberg to meet more and longer, the General wandered without ceremony through the expansive palace of the Emperor, that was also the seat of his office.

He was looking for a document. It was about a garrison in the east, in the potential incursion area of the Huns, and he had to know something about an incident with a breakaway group of that people, which had been in this region for a while. In a report, he had found a cross-reference to another report, and to increase the confusion, it was obvious his secretary hadn't been able find it right away. It had been a reference to the marauding Huns, which had appeared

97

in some border regions where these warriors hadn't been observed so far. It was late, the sun had already gone down, and Rheinberg, who had a backache from all the sitting, strolled toward the archives to use the services of the few attendants still working. On the way there, he had planned, he would stop by in the palace kitchen to take a little refreshment. In the meantime, he knew quite well which of the typical Roman dishes he liked and which he preferred to renounce.

When he entered the small dining room, in which food of the workers in this part of the palace was provided, very few guests were present. The palace was working around the clock since important decision-makers often met until late into the night, or even receptions and parties continued until the morning hours. Only the mass of bureaucrats and staff regularly went to bed, the higher ranks and their agents often worked longer.

After a short snack, Rheinberg entered the archive a few minutes later. He was almost alone in the room, and the few other guests were aware of him only from afar, with respect and distance. He couldn't hope for an occasional chat.

Nobody "chatted" with the highest general – except maybe the Emperor.

The premises were not as large as one would have expected from a real Imperial Archive; in fact only current documents were kept here, and "current" was by no means unambiguously defined. Many older documents, so far as they were preserved, had been stored in Constantinople, or in Rome itself, but very many, if evidently no longer needed, were destroyed after some time. Parchment was often reused; for this purpose, the top layer was scraped off during processing. Still, a report from a garrison dated sometime the last year should be available, at least this was Rheinberg's hope.

Rheinberg took a moment to find a clerk who listened to his request. It was an elderly man with a carefully groomed beard, digesting Rheinberg's request with a head slightly turned sideways, before he frowned.

"I think it's an interesting task for our new staff."

Rheinberg looked critically at the old man. "I would be happy to gather the document tonight."

The man flashed a smile. "Of course, of course. I will watch over it myself. Follow me."

Rheinberg did as he was told. The shelves, which were often placed on top of each other, looked like square holes in the walls, into which rolled parchments could be arranged. They were often grouped together in regard to topics, marked with signposts cryptic for the German. The archive was packed densely and gloomy, only lit by occasional oil lamps, carefully placed in metal boxes or installed in niches in the walls to reduce the risk of fire.

The German wanted to remind the clerk in regard to the urgency of his order, when they approached a slender figure, who copied a document hunched over a desk.

"Aurelia," the old man said. Rheinberg's heart made a jump.

The young woman raised her head and looked directly into the eyes of the German.

There could be no doubt – it was his former slave!

Rheinberg sensed the way he turned red. Fortunately, this was not particularly noticeable in the generally bad lighting – at least that was his hope.

The old man looked attentively at the reaction of the two younger ones.

"I ... it seems to me that ..." he began.

"Yes, we know each other," Aurelia said.

"Yes," Rheinberg exclaimed more croakily.

The old man cleared his throat. "Well, the General here needs a document. We will look for it together. Try to remember my lessons from this morning. Then you should be able to show us the area where we will find it."

Aurelia lowered her head. "Yes, Master." Without taking a further look at Rheinberg, she turned and walked along the shelf wall. The two men hurried to follow her. When they reached her, Aurelia already held a bundled document, which she handed over to Rheinberg with the hint of a smile. Before this could take it, however, the hand of the scribe, who was about to examine whether the paper was in fact the one they were seeking, interrupted the gesture. For these few seconds, which he needed to unroll the parchment and to examine its content, the eyes of Aurelia and Rheinberg met.

The young man was hypnotized. He didn't say a word. Then the scribe held out the document.

"It's the correct one. Well done, Aurelia."

"I … thank you," Rheinberg said, who didn't want to remove his gaze from the former slave. He scolded himself. She was free. Now he could … He cleared his throat. "Maybe – it's late, and it …"

"Sure," she replied.

He looked at her questioningly.

"You want to know whether I will accompany you to a late meal," Aurelia said, smiling. The scribe looked at her, both in alarm and shock. Such disrespectful behavior in the presence of a high-ranking man was not only unusual for a young woman, it was also rude, even outrageous. It was clear that he didn't know what to do first – to scold Aurelia or to apologize for her to Rheinberg. He didn't have to choose either.

Rheinberg raised his hand and nodded toward the old man. "That will be all."

The man understood, muttered a farewell, and withdrew himself. Aurelia's smile seemed to illuminate the gloom of the archive.

"Your document, master," she pointed to the paper in Rheinberg's hand.

He looked at it as if he was seeing it for the first time, then pushed it back into a shelf. "This can wait," he said, still a little hoarse. Aurelia didn't complain.

17

"Yes, I've heard of that."

Neumann leaned forward. "Really?"

Their guide was an elderly man with a narrow, tanned face that had been exposed frequently and for prolonged periods to the weather. He had been a caravan leader for more than twenty years and had already directed commercial expeditions into the remotest corners of Aksum. When Neumann had heard this, his eagerness to get into conversation with the man had been spiked.

In fact, he had explained him about an Aksumite legend that didn't exist yet. The legend of the origin of the coffee bean was told in such a way that a goat-shepherd who one day had noticed, in the Kaffa region, how his animals, after tasting a certain plant, had awakened and jumped up and down all night. This he told a monk who had followed the case and had confirmed both the existence of the plant and the invigorating effect of the coffee bean. And so coffee – the plant from the Kaffa region – was spread around the world.

As it was with legends, when exactly and who discovered the coffee plant and, above all, its stimulating effect, had been hidden in the darkness of history. Neumann knew, however, that the preparation of the bean by roasting had not started until the 15th century in the Arab world. Thus, the triumphal conquest of coffee had been initiated by the cultural history of another region.

This didn't mean, however, that there were not those who had previously been confronted with the plant but without considering its effect.

And it seemed as if this old caravan leader was such a person. His name was Gebre, and he had patiently listened to the Greek of the physician, a language in which he himself was only somewhat conversant. But they had time to talk to each other in the tents or houses where they had been accommodated, and therefore time to find a common basis of communication. Finally, with patience, paper, pencil and his graphic talents, Neumann succeeded in describing exactly what he was looking for.

Gebre had studied the drawing intensively. Neumann had explained what color this plant had, dark green, with red fruits, and shrubby.

"I've never seen it myself," the man said, holding the paper with a certain awe. It took him a moment, and then Neumann realized that the attention of the Aksumite was less on the drawing but of the paper itself. Parchment was probably known to him, albeit of low quality. But real paper, if only from a normal drawing block Neumann always took along, was, of course, unknown – not to talk of the pencil with which the doctor had drawn the sketch.

"But?" Neumann urged cautiously.

"But I've heard from other muleteers that they came across this plant in the highlands. Some have tried to chew them. It wasn't very tasty."

Neumann knew that was true.

"Others say they've tried to cook them in water. That wasn't very tasty as well, but one could drink it in cold nights. Afterwards one would become more attentive to guard-duties."

Neumann nodded. To make a simple mixture with hot water was certainly the most primitive form of processing, and the result would be less satisfactory. The next step was to roast and grind in order to achieve an experience of taste that came closest to modern enjoyment of the drink. But to do all this, it was necessary to grow and harvest sufficient amounts. The purpose of this expedition was not only to find the coffee plant but also to convince the Aksumite ruler that cultivation and sale of the coffee could prove to be highly beneficial to his empire.

In addition to the temptation of money, Neumann had prepared another argument, with which he tried to convince his distinguished interlocutor: In his luggage was the last pack of roasted coffee, which could have been found on board the *Saarbrücken*. The doctor had secured it in time and kept it safe, in spite of the covetous glances of others – and despite of his own withdrawal symptoms. Together with the coffee, he had also provided a small pack of sugar – although this could be replaced by another sweetener, and he expected to find milk in Aksum as well. And then he would invite the Emperor of the Aksumite Empire to a nice cup of coffee.

If that didn't work, Neumann knew no better way.

And even if the ruler of this empire didn't prove to be a friend of this drink, Neumann, Köhler and Behrens would at least once again enjoy a good cup of coffee after a long break.

And that was already worth something.

"That means the plant is well-known?" the Doctor said.

"No, Roman." Gebre had never bothered to understand what Africanus differentiated from the other travelers and what these time-wanderers really were. For him, his proteges were all Romans. He knew Romans. He frequently led trade delegations to Aksum. They were there, as a rule, welcome guests. No need to know more.

Neumann had no intention of changing his somewhat one-sided view of things. Ultimately, the Germans were Romans, as Gratian had given them full civil rights.

"Some like me have heard of it or know the plant," Gebre continued. "Just those who travel a lot. Nothing that is really exciting. Is this plant worth all this trouble?"

Neumann nodded. "As a matter of fact, it is. Whoever does this right can become very rich."

Gebre might be old and a simple man, but the sparkle in his eyes made it clear that he knew quite well how to imagine "very rich."

Neumann had never intended to make a secret of the potential benefit of coffee. The more they spread the word, the more likely there would be potential producers. And when the product hit the market, the market would be big enough for everyone. And the Germans would develop an excellent economic base – not to mention the good reputation that the drink would bring to them, in contrast to brandy.

Neumann concentrated again on Gebre, who still turned the paper in his hand with great fascination. He took an empty block from his backpack and put an unused pencil on it. He held it to Gebre with a smile. "Tell me, Gebre, these other caravan leaders we were talking about now, will we be able to meet some of them in Aksum?"

The journey to Aksum took no longer than a week. They rose at first sunlight and let the mules march constantly. Although sometimes stubborn, the mules were very persistent and received enough water and food during breaks, so they maintained a steady pace. The road to Aksum was quite well developed despite the differences in altitude, and the weather also played along; it was cool but remained dry and largely windless. When, at the end of the week, they saw the suburbs of the imperial capital spreading before them, Neumann realized that Aksum might not reach the size of Rome, but the imperial charm of the metropolis couldn't be overlooked. It seemed remarkable that the city, in contrast to the great Roman settlements, had no city wall. Although the Aksumites waged wars, these took place usually far away from the capital, and Aksum itself had never been seriously threatened militarily. Neumann knew from the records that it would remain so for a while. And if the calculation turned out to be true that the export of coffee would also contribute to the prosperity of Aksum, it could even be that this empire would develop differently than in his own history. The breakdown, the long period of internal wars between different nobles, the resurrection in the Middle Ages until anewed disintegration – not everything might develop differently, but with a new economical basis perhaps one or the other event could be avoided. Perhaps it would make Aksum a powerful friend, who also needed Rome in the long-term to survive on its own. It was not good to have enemies everywhere.

For a moment Neumann remembered the position of the German Empire shortly before the departure of the *Saarbrücken*. He had never said it openly, but he had never been so convinced of assured victory as outcome of the "inevitable" war, unlike most other officers. Above all, and this may seem paradoxical, he had always had serious doubts about the massive expansion of the German Navy that the Kaiser had so favored. He was by no means certain whether the Navy would play the central role that Wilhelm II obviously attributed to it.

Well, the small cruiser *Saarbrücken* would certainly not make any contribution, as long as no second miracle happened.

Once arriving, the escorting letter from Adulis, as well as a corresponding letter from the Roman Emperor and the Egyptian governor, were legitimate enough to receive accommodation in the guest house of the imperial palace. Here, the load of the mules was stowed on a covered storage area. Gebre and his men said goodbye to the travelers without a major ceremony, while the caravan leader had promised Neumann to look out for those who had heard of the coffee plant. It was agreed that they should report directly to the guest house. Neumann wanted to make sure he got all the necessary information on time.

Although they were regarded as respected guests, and their importance was by no means slighted, the Aksumitic court had its own ceremonial arrangement, and the Negusa Nagast worked on a tight schedule. The governmental system of the Empire was based on the emperor, as well as on the regional chiefs, who often had a respectable degree of autonomy due to the geographical conditions. This didn't change the fact that it was the Negusa Nagast who had the ultimate power of decision-making. Since the current Aksumite emperor was an old man who had already crossed the zenith of his abilities, it was no easier to get an appointment for an audience. In fact, it was heard that the old man usually didn't have more than three or four hours a day in which he was seriously engaged in state affairs, and especially in the last few months the habit of sleeping had a great deal. Therefore, it took a few days to get an invitation to a formal dinner at the court. This was quite an honor, since this opportunity was normally reserved for the highest nobles and dignitaries. This would also lead to the possibility of getting rid of the presents.

The fact that visitors from afar had come only to meet the Emperor, possibly also connected with the exquisite luxury goods from Rome and Adulis they brought, definitely hastened the process as much as possible. Everything would be handed over to the Imperial

Court, either for its own use or for resale. The joy of this had been clearly visible on the officials' faces as they heard of it, and some experts would be sent to assess the value of the goods. Neumann and Africanus had both insisted on carrying only items of real value and not trying to blind the Aksumites with rubbish. This decision turned out to be very wise.

In the evening before the reception, the expeditionists had gathered around their own dinner in the guest house's dining room. The Aksumitic cuisine was food for workers, heavy, with many pods and cereals, spicy and sweet sauces, as well as a tasteless dough, which was used instead of cutlery for eating. This combination led to the fact that even small portions were quickly filling and the diversity of the dishes offered couldn't be enjoyed at all. Often enough, after the first passage through the large and flat bowls on which variations had been arranged, they were completely saturated. As tomorrow's supper would consist of several courses, Neumann had impressed on the friends, warning them that he wasn't going to dig in at the very beginning, and that they should be prepared not being too hungry, in order to control themselves. Köhler and Behrens, both of whom were regarded as gifted eaters, had at first dismissed the warnings of the physician, but with every new round of Aksumite cookery, the deep wisdom of the advice became more and more apparent. This evening, before dinner at the Negusa Nagast's table, was, in a way, a rehearsal. They had agreed to chew on some food for prolonged time, and endure eating toward the end of the meal, no matter how much had already been consumed.

They had just assembled when a dignitary entered the room. He behaved politely and bowed, but led four soldiers, which gave him a certain authority. He couldn't say exactly, but Neumann recognized by his clothes that he might be an officer of the palace guard.

The man spoke perfect, carefully articulated Greek. "I have the obligation to examine the gifts," the man said. "I have heard that you will give valuables to the Negusa Nagast and other leaders of the Empire tomorrow evening."

"That's our custom."

The officer smiled. "Nothing can be said against this tradition. But in Rome, as I have heard, one also pays attention to the danger that a gift might be associated to an evil purpose."

Neumann bowed his head. He could only agree. As far as he understood, the balance of power between the various regional princes in Aksum, as well as in relation to the Emperor, wasn't always so smooth that no one would attempt to remove a Negusa Nagast by force. This hadn't yet reached the same proportions as in Rome, where, unfortunately, it was now customary to appoint any successful military man to become emperor, in order to clarify the actual power relations later in a long-lasting civil war. Things went more quiet in Aksum and according to the established protocol.

Neumann nodded to Africanus. The other expedition members stayed behind. Together with the soldiers, they strolled to the covered storage area, under which the goods brought along were packed in crates and bales.

If the doctor had assumed that the soldiers would submit the gifts only to a superficial investigation, his error would soon have become obvious. With conscientious thoroughness, the men opened every single pack. They searched the materials they had brought in, looked into golden cups, and opened boxes. They were careful in this, as they were aware of the value of the goods. Neumann had the impression that these men knew exactly what they were doing and had a certain experience in it.

Finally, only the small, richly ornamented wooden boxes that the Governor of Adulis had given them remained. One of them, with the most elaborate embellishments, was intended for the Negusa Nagast and another for his probable successor, Ouazebas. The officer ordered one of his men to carefully open the containers. The soldier took the first piece, meant for the Emperor. He searched the contents briefly, then nodded to his superiors and closed the container again. Then he took the crate for the Crown Prince, opened it, and looked into it. Neumann looked over the man's shoulder, for he didn't know the contents of this casket. He saw a medallion made of gold, in the middle of which was placed a remarkable gem. The soldier looked at the beautiful work with obvious admiration, then closed the box again and placed it carefully on the flat table from which he had picked it up.

Thus, the inspection was apparently finished. The soldiers were satisfied with the result and said their goodbye politely.

Neumann and Africanus wandered back to the dinner, which was already in full swing.

They recognized, however, with a glance that there was still enough food left to put their endurance, as well as their ability for culinary time-management, to the test.

And so they sat down.

18

And so Thomas Volkert – Thomasius – sat on a horse ready for the first cavalry attack in his life.

Actually, "ready" was too strong a word.

Volkert sat on his beast, which patiently stood before the men whom he commanded, together with the Centurion. He knew what they intended to do, and he had seen the confidence in his comrades' faces. He also knew that a good part of this confidence had to do with the almost naive belief in the marvels of the time-wanderers, who had already gone into hiding on the chain of hills where Volkert had been active as a scout. It was by no means that the young German had doubts about the abilities and determination of the infantry, but he was the one who had been shaped by the attack of the Sarmatians. If this mountain people were a measure of the boldness and brutality of the "barbaric" enemies of Rome, Volkert could believe in a victory of their alliance against the legendary Huns, but not with much confidence.

Sedacius himself rode in front. His men loved him for it. From a tactical point of view, it was nonsense. In the midst of the turmoil, the Tribune wouldn't be able to keep an overview and risked possibly becoming a victim of poor coordination. But Volkert had thought long enough about the words of his friend Secundus to see what prompted the Tribune to lead from the front – he needed the necessary military glory, proof of manly bravery, if his probable plan to become an emperor should bear fruit. He couldn't appear as a timid commander. Sedacius risked a great deal, as his high-flying intentions could as well end with an arrow in his throat.

Volkert, therefore, didn't know whether he should admire or condemn the Tribune. He contented himself with simply being afraid and using all his strength to not show that too openly.

There were men who were much less eager to keep their emotions under control. Bertius, for example, the special protege of the German, radiated his displeasure about the fact that he had now actually to go into a fight. The unambitious legionary was sitting miserably in the saddle, constantly examining the shield, behind which he no doubt sought to hide as much as possible. Volkert didn't expect Bertius to be a valiant fighter, but he didn't envisage him to be coward as well.

To resent the attitude of the legionary turned out to be difficult for the Decurion. If Sedacius would call off the attack here and now, also Volkert wouldn't be very sad.

Sedacius, however, apparently had no such intention.

It was very early in the morning. The sun was just above the horizon.

The cavalry was ready. Their allies seemed to be quite pleased with the prospect of fighting with the Romans. In any case, Volkert saw many eager faces in the dim light. Horses snorted and stamped with their hooves, as if they were as impatient as the warriors. Above all, there was an unreal atmosphere, as if it would be inthinkable that a deadly massacre was about to begin in a few moments.

Sedacius made a sign. The Quadians then broke away from the troop and began to ride along the hills sideways to prepare the planned maneuver. The Roman cavalry remained behind. Since they were not too many, Volkert suddenly felt left alone. He hoped their allies would do their part as planned.

They waited for about half an hour. There was something stirring in the Hunnish camp. Of course, the movements of the attackers had not escaped the enemy. Through the clear air one heard excited shouting, orders were given.

"They've woken up," Secundus murmured. "It's time." He was right.

Sedacius had the cornicen blow into his horn. And then, like a slow but unstoppable avalanche, the Roman cavalry moved into the direction of the Hunnish camp.

Not too fast.

The enemy should feel provoked, leave the camp and storm toward the attackers, in order to get exactly into the firing range of the German infantry, presenting a target that couldn't be missed.

Despite the cold air, Volkert was sweating. It was a cozy trot, with which the Romans descended the hills. Sedacius gave a cry of war, which was answered from behind. Then he motioned the men to laugh out loud. It must sound like the ultimate insult in the ears of the Huns.

The first part of the plan seemed to work.

From the camp, a large cavalry movement was discernible. Volkert had now already moved too far on the plain to have a full overview, so he couldn't guess whether it was all of the Hunnish warriors, or whether a unit had been left behind in the camp itself. Their allies would find out about this early enough. But even if the Huns held back a defensive unit, it would be numerically in a disadvantage compared to the Quadian cavalry.

The risk was calculable. Hopefully.

The war cry of the angry Huns was clearly audible. The hoofs of their small fast horses, almost like ponies, made the ground tremble. Sedacius once more laughed contemptuously. Volkert followed, although he felt anything but contempt for the wave of angry warriors. He had at least respect for them and certainly also fear.

But the Huns were furious now.

And rage was not good counsel in any battle.

The Roman discipline held. The riders turned out, everyone had raised the shortsword, no one accelerated beyond measure.

The Huns reached the death zone.

The sun now threw her clear light over the scenery.

Volkert only heard the familiar buzzing and crackling of shots fired. There was nothing to be seen, hardly a flash from the well-chosen coverings of the infantry. Volkert identified the MG position with a practiced eye, but death came if not silently, then invisibly to the enemy.

At first, they didn't notice it at all, when, on the brink of their advance, a horseman was swept from the animal as his skull, pierced by bullets, burst without reason. Then the horses cried.

This shouting of the animals was what Volkert was most concerned about.

The wide, sturdy breasts of the animals exploded into blood and bones. The riflemen on the hills couldn't miss. The closer the Huns came, the better did those precisely matched bursts of the riflemen who, with mechanical tact, spread death among the barbarians – merciless, invisible, effective.

The Huns noticed something.

The shouting grew louder, orders were heard. Restlessness shivered through their advance.

Sedacius gave the signal.

The riders ripped their horses around, galloped back to the hills.

Sure, the Huns saw this, but they were busy looking for the actual enemy. Disorder broke out, yes chaos. Fear, panic had taken the warriors. Individual men broke out of the crowd, tried to flee, died in the shower of bullets, clearly visible to everyone.

And the horses. Their screams sounded almost human, like children's.

Volkert couldn't shake off these sounds penetrating to his heart. Too much suffering at once.

He stayed in the formation and didn't look back, but one didn't have to use his eyes in order to see what was happening.

The infantry didn't let go. The machine gun spoke in short, steady bursts. It was about using the ammunition sparingly. Efficiency was the goal of the men. Efficient and effective.

They were both.

"Stop!"

The Roman cavalry stopped.

"Dismount!"

Volkert followed the order with mechanical obedience. Here, on the hillside, they were closer to the infantry. The shots were more clearly heard, the regular bursts of the machine-gun especially. Volkert looked down, recognized complete dissolution, confusion and panic.

"In formation!"

The legionaries, most of whom were grateful to be able to be foot soldiers once more, stood up, shield to shield, sword to sword, and the NCOs, like Volkert, in front of them.

Then silence.

No, the horses were still shrieking their pain, but the shooting had stopped.

The work of the German infantry had been done, the cruelty ended for now.

The order was given.

Rome marched toward the Huns, the old, the tried and tested way. Normally the foot soldiers would have been an easy prey to the mobile cavalry, but in this condition, with hundreds – thousands – of dying and wounded animals on the ground, injured and thrown warriors, disoriented and shocked, it was different.

Volkert's palm, which clasped the shortsword, was sweaty.

The first Hunnish warriors shouted something, pointing to the legionaries marching in stoic resolution. Then further shouting, this time from farther away. Volkert guessed it more than he saw it; their allies had commenced their carefully coordinated deployment, and apparently were already quite busy in the Hunnish camp.

Was the leader of the enemy fallen or injured? The Hunnish warriors had finally disintegrated into chaotic circles. But then those reformed, who were still sitting on their horses. Since the invisible death was apparently over, and the infantry had no intention of accidentally killing Roman legionaries, or even their new allies, the Hunnish cavalry, which was still active, wanted to effect the traditional strength of their kind of warfare. Yes, the enemies were decimated, and many of them were really shocked, but courage apparently hadn't left all of them.

Unfortunately, as Volkert found.

And then everything happened fast. Decurion Thomasius was still marching in front of his unit, and they were already among the enemies. Huns, even without horses, were determined fighters. The warriors had got rid of their bows, which didn't help them in close combat. Now they were swinging two-edged longswords. These weapons had a much larger range than the Roman ones, but they were more unwieldy and could rarely be used for direct stabs, which were very effective in close combat. The longswords could be used in a swinging fashion and could be, if fighters were packed too tight, easily been catched or deflected. Nevertheless, the Huns were practiced in the use of this weapon. Preferably, they used the swords from the back of their horses in pursuit of an enemy. However, they were quite capable of wielding them in this rather unfamiliar situation. Still, as Volkert remarked as soon as he avoided a long sweep, and instead swung his sword straight forward and sank it into the throat of a shouting warrior, the Huns were in this battle – man pitched against man on foot – clearly in the disadvantage.

His adversary gurgled, dropped his blade, and instinctively touched the gushing from his neck. Volkert drew his sword back, the movement followed by a surge of blood. The Hun staggered, his bladder and his intestines drained, and he fell dying to the ground. Volkert stumbled briefly, which saved his life. A blade passed over him so close that he could feel the displaced air. The young man threw himself forward, rammed his shield into the body, then the sword spoke again, this time a clean push directly into the chest.

Volkert forgot time and space. The formation of the legionaries dissolved somewhat, many individual battles developed. A centurion shouted an order. A legionary beside Volkert sank silently to the ground, one of the brutally powerful Hunnish arrows in his forehead.

More subconsciously, the Decurion made sure that he remained close to his comrades. Nothing was more dangerous than being cut off from the main body. As a single fighter, there was no chance of survival.

Out of the corner of his eye, Volkert recognized how Secundus got rid of an enemy. The Roman fought with an almost unaffected cleverness. Volkert swung his sword with the same force, but not half so precisely and not so coldly and distantly.

The stench of intestines swelling from people and horses mixed with the metallic smell of blood. The bodily fluids, of man as well as of animals, made the battlefield slippery. Approaching, Volkert relieved a horse of his agony, lying on the ground and suffering from severe pain. Then he had to face a Hunnish warrior who had pulled his long-sword through the side of a careless legionary and roared triumphantly.

His triumph transformed into a cry of pain once Volkert's blade hit him cleanly into the chest, and glided through his ribs in full length across the body. The German swiftly pulled the sword out. To get stuck in the ribs and be hit by a falling body was one of the dangers of this weapon.

"Decurion!"

A warning cry.

Volkert looked around with no orientation, felt the danger more than he directly perceived it. A blade went into his direction, and although Volkert raised his own to push it aside, he knew at the same time that he would react too late. As if in slow motion, he looked at the beardless face of the enemy warrior, distorted in concentration and exertion, his eyes directed precisely at his target, the German.

But then somebody intervened. Volkert was pushed, stumbled out of the striking arc of the attacker, almost fell to the ground. He struggled on his legs, staggering, then saw the man's sword pass through another man's forearm, separating him neatly from his elbow. Volkert watched the chopped half-arm fall to the ground, accompanied by a surge of blood. Then the body of his already unconscious rescuer followed.

It was Bertius!

Secundus stepped up from the rear, pierced the attacker with the shortsword, another precise push through the chest. Volkert threw his own weapon aside. He acted like hypnotized, grabbed the stump of the unconscious Bertius, then tore at his own tunic until he held a firm strip in his hands. With hasty movements, he tied off the arm of the fat legionary. His action was diligent, his training in first-aid had been thorough. Then Volkert thought of the paramedic whom the Germans had brought with them, and who, together with two Romans, had opened a kind of field-hospital on the other side of the hills. This was otherwise not the habit of Romans, whose most important method of treatment in cases of severe injuries was usually to redeem the injured quickly from their suffering – permanently.

Neumann had been the first to push for reform. And it seemed as if the commander of the Roman forces, Rheinberg, had surrendered to these plans with joy.

"Thomasius!"

Secundus's voice tore him out of concentration. The Decurion held out his sword. It seemed as if a bubble of relative tranquility had formed around them for a moment, for no enemy attacked. But that wouldn't last long. Volkert took his sword and stood up. He waved a legionary, who already had several bleeding cuts, and a bad-looking but probably harmless forehead injury.

"You!" Volkert shouted. "Take this man to the field hospital. You've had enough for today!"

The soldier didn't even try to oppose the Decurion. He put his sword away, grappled Bertius under his shoulders, and began to pull him backwards through the ranks of the Romans. By order of Volkert, his comrades closed around him, guarding his retreat.

The young man turned around, half expecting to face another fighter, but had to realize that the focus of the battle had shifted, more toward the camp of the enemy.

"Formation," he yelled. "Formation!"

He saw with satisfaction how the men around him fell in line.

"Forward!"

The goal was clear – the Quadians were now in the most violent struggle against the Huns, who evidently were doing everything they could to protect their camp. The Roman legionaries had to move forward to help their allies. Soon the Roman and allied attackers would meet in the middle, and with some luck divide the enemies among themselves.

It became clear that the Huns indeed began to rally around their camp. And the Romans saw, as they came closer, that they were too late. Luvico's men had already overrun the loosely encircled area. There was still fighting going on. As far as Volkert could see, the slaves had already been liberated, and while the battle was raging, their allies were disciplined and began to guide the frightened slaves out of the camp. The Romans and fellow Quadians among them

116

would soon be liberated and released as agreed. All the others would exchange only one master for another.

The Romans entered the camp into a jovial crowd, uncoordinated, and evidently some already jubilating. In spite of all the losses, about 2000 Hunnish warriors were encircled here, weapons ready. And no one would ever be able to reproach a Huns without a fight.

The Romans therefore entered the camp, and the fighting began anew. When the Huns had noticed the arrival of the legionaries, they left no doubt about their intentions. They raised their weapons against every enemy who stood in their way.

Again, the formation of the Romans, divided by fences, tents, huts, and large camp fires, dissolved. Volkert, too, found himself, with a few legionaries and Secundus, facing a group of Huns; these evidently had separated two horsemen from the main body. The Huns knew how to deal with horses, and their longswords killed the terrified animals with practiced skill. When they collapsed, they buried one of the riders. Desperately, the man tried to get rid of the horse's body, but then he was hit by a stroke of a long-sword.

The other rider had more luck. He jerked off the falling riding horse, whirled through the air with acrobatic skill, and landed safely on the ground on both feet. The Huns seemed to be grunting their respect, before they turned against the single man.

Volkert jumped forward. His men followed him without hesitation. As they roused the attention of the Huns, more enemies invaded them from all sides. Finally, Volkert caught a closer look at the acrobatic Quadian, who was currently fighting against two opponents at the same time.

It was Luvico, leader of their allies.

Volkert struggled to his side, killed one of the Huns on the way there, and received a superficial cut on his own upper arm. With aching muscles and an angrily pulsating wound, he stood next to the young man.

They said nothing.

It wasn't the time for conversation.

The coming minutes became a wild crescendo of a concerted and relentless struggle. Volkert moved like a sleepwalker, without conscious consideration. It was repeatedly evident that young Luvico was perhaps a good acrobat and an outstanding rider, but in the sword-battles he was clearly inferior to the Huns. Only Volkert's shortsword kept him safe from deadly attacks by one of his opponents. It was a narrow fight, with changing foes, and on this corner of the battlefield, numerical superiority was a fluid state.

Volkert lost all sense of time. Finally, his arm slumped. A deep exhaustion seized him. As a last enemy approached, the German only lifted the sword arm tiredly. But the warrior stepped aside and lifted a lethal blow to Luvico, which he got out of balance with a heavy foot kick.

Instinctively, Volkert stumbled forward, rammed the Hun with his right shoulder. The blow went wrong, hissed casually through the air. The warrior turned to Volkert with a furious face.

And there, in his left hand, the long, slightly curved knife.

Volkert saw it well. He turned aside, in any case wanting to avoid the slow, agonizing death caused by a stab into the stomach, a painful inner bleeding. He succeeded.

The attack went into his left chest.

The pain was sudden. For a second, Volkert felt light in his head, staggered back, staring consciously at the handle of the dagger that protruded from his chest. He didn't even notice how Secundus had jumped to his aid and sent the Huns to the ground with his throat cut open.

Decurion Thomasius followed him, gratefully embracing darkness.

"Julia," he stammered. How silly.

He was all alone down here.

How nice to finally feel no pain at all.

19

Was the trip uneventful?

Godegisel had experienced so much in his young life, he couldn't answer the question without hesitation. He didn't know exactly how old he was, but the estimates of his relatives were all around 23 to 25 years. The escape from their homeland, the suffering at the Roman frontier, the campaign at Thessaloniki, the trip to Britannia, the flight from there – so many things, an almost hectic sequence of events that made him recall the quiet moments in his life much easier than those in which something happened. In fact, he felt that the calm and restful phases, especially his time with Pina, were more consciously in his awareness than the supposedly revolutionary things he had witnessed as a bystander as well as a participant.

From this point of view, his journey was poor in events. He was lucky if he could ride on a cart, or, better still, with a river boatman, especially when he stopped to take him as a worker and paid a few small coins beside food and lodging. He also thought he was happy every time he had a roof over his head at night, a crackling fire, and nice company. He was out of luck when he had to make long walks with an empty stomach, and had to make camp in the open at mostly quite cool temperatures. He seemed to look run down enough to not appear a worthy victim for any robber, but hadn't yet come down enough for others to regard him as a threat. He found occasional work, here and there, mostly for some bread and soup, more rarely for money, occasionally for a worn-out pair of trousers or old sandals, when his own fell apart. He learned to be submissive and respectful to people who, in his opinion, didn't deserve it, and then to courageously and bravely seize an opportunity. He kept himself from legionaries and avoided larger cities. Perhaps they didn't look for him. Perhaps they did.

He didn't want to take any risk.

He rarely thought of Fritigern and his people, settled in the east of the Empire.

He often thought of Pina and wondered if he was paying too great a price for his strange commitment to a dead emperor.

But, in the end, and this was the most important thing, he was moving fast, rode, walked and drove tirelessly, didn't allow himself to rest longer than necessary, and took every chance to advance faster than on his feet. And so, despite all deprivation, he reached Italy within three weeks. Fortunately, Ravenna was located in the north and the base of the time-wanderers in the immediate vicinity.

It was an early afternoon, when a filthy, gaunt figure crossed the border to the settlement of the Germans. It was a city quite different from all that Godegisel had ever seen. The residential quarters still reminded well a Roman settlement, although the tenement houses made a more stable impression. The young Goth also noted that the distances between the houses were larger than usual, and he saw runoffs streaming along the road edges through which water flowed. The streets themselves were paved. Toward the sea, however, the appearance changed noticeably. Large halls had been built, impressive structures with chimneys. A small port closed the settlement to the coast. From the edge of a fountain that Godegisel had climbed, he could see the outline of the ship that had brought his own defeat before Thessaloniki. Everywhere there was a hustle and bustle. Metallic noises sounded from the workshop; here, everything was duly executed whatever the time-wanderers had planned. A shipyard was to be seen, in which a ship was built, as Godegisel had never seen before. Out of the wooden hull protruded a mast, but for a sailing ship the vessel seemed to be of a strangely compact shape, and the mast was made of a metal. And then, in the port itself, the Goth made out a second ship of this kind, apparently already completed. Fine steam clouds rose into the blue sky. It had to be a completely new ship construction, initiated by the time-wanderers.

Godegisel was no friend of the sea. His interest in those vessels immediately vanished again once he saw the massive, low stonehouse that stood directly on the quayside. He had been told that the leadership of the time-wanderers, if they were not on their iron ship, had found quarters there, guarded by a troop of legionaries.

How could he get in? He knew that the settlement of the time-wanderers attracted not only curious craftsmen and but also young men and women who wanted to learn things in the schools of the city that no one else taught. Charlatans, dubious figures, crazy and fanatical fools came here.

Some of them strived for the favor of the strangers in order to realize absurd ideas, which they themselves considered to be ingenious, and others wanted to join them, like a religious sect, because they considered them divine envoys. Others had planned to kill them as quickly as possible, assuming they were the exact opposite of divine. And then there were shady businessmen who were trying to make money from the technical achievements, and better without asking those responsible for these achievements for their permission. The city of the Germans, it was said, was a magnet for thieves. Safety measures had been tightened up everywhere, there were patrols day and night, and the most important buildings were illuminated throughout the night with those new charcoal lamps, as well as traditional oil lamps or torches.

Godegisel, by the way he looked, would be considered a madman, a fortune-teller, or simply a thief. He had to improve his appearance and hope that one of the Germans would remember the man who had killed their leader Becker – and that memory wouldn't cause him to be discarded as someone who couldn't be trusted.

Luckily, there were many opportunities here to transform himself into a quite respectable human being again, as workers were constantly being hired. The wanderers had employed slaves, but their reluctance to use them was now widely known. Wherever financial resources were available, free workers were hired. The wages were not impressive, but as some training was provided at the same time, the jobs were in demand. It might also help that everyone who worked in this settlement became part of a special atmosphere of change, a departure from the old times. There were many people who wanted to be a witness of this process, whether consciously or unconsciously.

After some questioning, Godegisel found a foreman, who saw through the man's torn clothes, recognized a powerful and young body behind him, and got him a job as a harbor worker. The conditions were very decent, there was half a wage as an advance and workwear made of a thick, double-woven fabric, which was to protect against abrasions. After the young Goth had washed and changed, he even got a proper shave. In his simple but clean work-clothes, he immediately made the impression of someone much more trustworthy than before.

He was almost tired of having to deceive his employer right from the start of his professional career. But he hadn't come here to haul boxes at the port.

As soon as he had convinced himself that he was making a human impression, the young Goth headed for the squat stone building in which the wanderers lived. It was generally known that the Captain of the iron ship was at court in Treveri. The command was in the hands of Magister Dahms, who was something of a genius in crafts. Godegisel wanted to see him.

As expected, this was easier said than done.

The two bulky legionaries, who stood guard already a hundred yards from the entrance of the building, didn't seem to take any risk. It took some minutes before Godegisel had convinced the men of his harmlessness. It was helpful that he had allowed himself to be briefly searched by the soldiers. Since he had no arms at his disposal, nothing more than clothes on his body, he didn't seem to be very threatening.

A second, more thorough search took place at the main entrance of the building, again by legionaries, who took their duties very seriously. Then he was led into a unadorned room, where another Roman was sitting, no soldier this time. He evidently had the task of deciding whom to allow into the presence of the time-wanderers and who not. It was a young man – the strangers seemed to employ a considerable number of younger people –, and he made a cultivated impression on Godegisel.

"Your name is Godegisel and you're Goth?" he began, not even unkindly.

"That's true."

"I've heard of a Godegisel. An aristocrat of your age, who fought in Thessaloniki." The young man smiled. "I'm from Thessaloniki, and have joined the time-wanderers after our salvation from your people. My name is Marcus Diderius Praetus."

"I greet you."

Praetus nodded. He didn't say anything else, but looked at his visitor.

"I'm that Godegisel. My sword felled Becker, one of the leaders of the time-wanderers."

If the Goth had now expected the young Roman to be frightened or even angered, he would've been quite disappointed.

"Whether or not that is true," Praetus replied calmly, "important is that you are open about it, a fact that speaks in your favor."

Godegisel, now seated on a stool, moved uneasily. "It's me, I assure you. I cannot say that I deplore the act, nor that I should be proud of it, for ..."

"Uninteresting," Praetus interrupted. "All the Gothic warriors have enjoyed amnesty after the end of the hostilities and the signing of the treaty. This is also true for those who killed in battle, whether you are among those or not."

"Dahms knows me. Also the one called Neumann. Both were very angry at me. They will definitely remember me."

Praetus nodded again. "Who else of the time-wanderers did you meet?"

Godegisel had been expecting the question and braying his brain to recollect the sometimes very strange names. What he stuttered thereupon might not exactly match the actual name, but the young Roman listened and didn't seem unimpressed. Godegisel took some courage. This turned out better than expected.

"And your concern? What is the purpose of your visit?"

"I convey a warning."

"About what?"

Godegisel hesitated. He didn't know how far he could trust Praetus.

123

On the other hand, the man was obviously the guardian of any access to the time-wanderers. "It's about a conspiracy," the Goth finally said.

Praetus raised his shoulders. "The Empire's fabric is composed of conspiracies. I think that has been going on for several hundred years."

Godegisel forced an understanding smile. Praetus wanted to be clever. The young Goth took a deep breath. Anger wouldn't help him now. "It's a serious issue. Otherwise I wouldn't have come here, especially as a man who had once been an enemy of your masters."

"That's why I'm talking to you and you haven't been sent away by the guards. But you have to be a bit more convincing."

"I'm not sure how far the conspiracy goes."

Now there was something like interest glimmering in Praetus' eyes. "You mean you don't know if for example I belong to it?"

"I didn't want to ..."

"But you did." The young Roman rose. "You're afraid."

Godegisel was about to shout something, but after a short pause, he accepted that the man's remark wasn't totally off the mark.

"You came here from the East?" Praetus asked, still standing. He looked down on Godegisel and wanted to show his authority. Godegisel smiled imperceptibly. He had watched the Emperor of the East crying behind a bush, burning his butt with nettles while taking a dump. Authority had gained a different meaning for him. Praetus couldn't know. The Goth came to the conclusion that the Roman presented a well-studied drama. The best thing would be to play along. So Godegisel raised his head a little and looked up at the Roman. "I'm from Britain," he finally said.

A remarkable transformation took place with Praetus. It was the well-practiced image of the Roman bureaucrat who shifted to sudden activity. He turned around, went to the door, glanced at Godegisel, then left the room. It took less than five minutes, then a legionary took the guest along, led him up a flight of stairs. At the end of a long corridor, from which many doors went off, he was led into a large room dominated by a simple but gigantic desk. Racks on the walls were dotted with drawings and sketches, as well as the desk itself, which seemed to be buried under the weight of innumerable papers and scrolls. Godegisel knew the man behind this chaos, at least from his appearance: He had met him during the peace negotiations after the battle of Thessaloniki. It was Magister Dahms, the one who de facto ruled this settlement when Rheinberg wasn't present. Godegisel knew that there was another high officer on board the iron ship, commanding the cruiser itself; but the organization of the new city lay on the shoulders of the man in front of him.

The time-wanderer didn't show whether he recognized Godegisel, but the Goth had no doubt. Godegisel was assigned a stool beside a small table, then Dahms sat, wiped papers aside, and looked at the Goth.

"Praetus!" Dahms finally shouted.

The factotum stretched out its head.

"A meal and wine for my guest," Dahms ordered.

"And for you, Master?"

"Nothing, thanks."

Praetus' head disappeared again.

Dahms looked at Godegisel. The Goth found the older man looking tired. Yet his gaze was attentive, even searching.

"I remember you, Godegisel," Dahms finally said, after a servant had set a tray of bread, cheese, some fruit, and a cup of diluted wine before them.

"I know."

"You killed Becker."

"That's true."

Dahms nodded. "I'm listening. Speak."

"I come from Britain."

"Praetus told me this. Far from the settlements of your people, Godegisel."

The young nobleman took a piece of fruit and held it undecided in his hands.

"I don't know where ..."

"At the beginning."

Godegisel looked confused at Dahms.

125

"Start at the beginning. I feel like you have an exciting story for me. And eat. It doesn't bother me."

Godegisel nodded slowly.

And then he told his story, from the beginning. Master Dahms didn't interrupt him even once.

20

Mehadeyis, Negusa Nagast of Aksum, King of Kings, was an old man and wouldn't last much longer. Neumann estimated him at the end of his fifties, which in these times was indeed a most blessed age. The Emperor of Aksum had once been a very handsome and powerful man. Underneath his gown, uncovered arms protruded, and although they were now knotted and frail, they gave a hint of how muscular they had once been. For his old age, the Negusa Nagast sat remarkably straight. He rested on his throne and looked into the large auditorium. In front of him, a long table-top lay, without feet, directly on the floor. He resided at one of its brows. The plate offered enough space for about 40 guests sitting directly on the flat and carpet-covered ground. To the right and left of him were warriors. They weren't purely ceremonial guards. They watched the incoming guests closely, especially when they approached the Negusa in a long line, to bow down before him and receive the greeting of their sovereign.

Mehadeyis would only be able to work relatively short periods of the day, and he didn't seem to be particularly active or strong this evening. But Neumann didn't miss the fact that the monarch looked at each of his guests. He spoke little and rarely moved, but knew exactly what was happening around him. Since the whole ceremony of salutation took a good half an hour, it was clear that the Emperor intended to get over it while exerting as little energy as possible.

He was wide awake, however, once Africanus stood before him to present the delegation. He listened patiently to the introductory words of the Roman officer, then opened his mouth to a reply. When he spoke, in a low but steady voice, there was silence in the room. Everyone wanted to know what the Emperor had to say to the somewhat strange visitor.

"I greet the time-wanderers," the Emperor said.

Neumann bowed deeply. Apparently, the Negusa was well-informed.

"I've heard very strange stories about you," Mehadeyis added. "Some say you are demons or worse, if that seems possible."

Neumann dared to look up but said nothing. They had agreed that Africanus would speak for them.

"Strange they are, sir," Africanus replied. He and the Emperor conversed with each other in Greek, which the old man mastered perfectly. "But I cannot confirm that they are demons. It is, however, difficult even for them to explain how they came to us at all."

"I can imagine that," the Negusa said with a gentle smile.

"I don't think everyone in Rome knows even now. In regard to many questions, there is no agreement among the learned."

Mehadeyis looked at Africanus with a slight expression of doubt. "You speak openly about the inner turmoil in Rome, dear guest."

"You are well informed anyway, I suppose," Africanus replied. "Why should I lie to you, then?"

"Indeed, we hear a lot."

"Much of it won't please you as much, as it doesn't please me."

"Quite possible. But this also depends on why the time-wanderers thought it necessary to make a long journey to Aksum. Now it suddenly concerns me a lot." The old man's gaze rested on Neumann and Köhler, who stood directly behind Africanus.

"We're bringing gifts."

"Of course you bring gifts," the Emperor said with a deprecating movement of his hand. "Everyone is giving me presents. And everyone wants something for it. A princess here, a position for a righteous man, a posting for the son, the cousin, the brother. This auditorium is like a market square, Roman. And I'm not sure whether the favor that I am expected to do is worth the gifts I'm given. I'm usually pulled across the table in these matters, I believe." The old Emperor grinned. For a second, he looked so young that the many years seemed to fall from him.

Africanus smiled back. "This will not be the case with us. The favor you can give us will benefit you as much as it will benefit us."

"Ah, is that so? And who exactly is *us*?"

"The Aksumite Empire and the Roman Empire."

"A noble answer worthy of a Roman officer. Allow me to suppose that for me as well as for you personally, some additional profit is probable."

Africanus bowed his head. "Oh yes, noble Negusa. Additional rewards are most welcome."

"Most? I am old. My greatest pleasure is to get up in the morning and not feel pain for a few minutes before the tortures of the day begin. The highlight is when I can piss without problems."

"There's something we have for you."

"Bring it then."

Of course, all this was discussed in front of the courtiers. Two officials had carefully observed how Köhler, with ceremonial seriousness, had prepared the coffee brought along in the kitchen of the palace. And then they had tasted. Their faces were absolutely immovable, so Köhler couldn't even guess how the drink affected them. But they were still alive, which was the most important thing.

Africanus waved. Behrens had taken over the job of the waiter. He stepped forward with a tray, on which stood two steaming, earthen cups of coffee, one with milk and sugar, the other black.

The Aksumite emperor leaned a little forward and looked suspiciously at the drink. "I'm not sure if that's too helpful. For a long time I have only be able to taste very spicy food, the rest ..."

Neumann nodded. It was known to him that the feeling of taste diminished with age and tended to react only to extremes. He had added four spoonfuls of sugar.

"This variant is natural, without any additions," the doctor said politely.

"The black one?"

"Yes. The other contains milk and is sweetened. Strongly sweetened."

The Aksumite emperor smiled broadly, and exposed darkened teeth with large gaps. "I like sweets, wanderers!"

Without further hesitation, he took the cup with the milk coffee, gently blew on the steaming drink, and took a deep sip.

Everyone in the hall looked at him curiously.

He took another sip, then another. He rolled the coffee in his mouth, closing his eyes. After another ten seconds, he had emptied the cup.

He opened his eyes, set the container down, and looked at the second cup. He took it, drank again, and though he obviously didn't quite enjoy it as much, the Negusa Nagast obviously had every intention of carefully investigating the whole matter.

Then, after he also dropped the second cup empty and Behrens, with a mischievous grin, bowed like a good servant, the Emperor took a deep breath and looked at Neumann. "I feel animated, wanderer."

"Yes, Your Majesty. This is indeed the most important effect of this drink. Many don't like the bitter taste of the pure form, but there is a remedy, as you've seen. Everyone appreciates its quality as a means to stay awake. Those who work a lot at night, such as your guards, will find the ordinary drink very helpful in preserving their own attention."

The Emperor nodded. "I think I understand very well the value of the drink. Well, why is it a matter you have to bring to my attention? I should sleep less?"

Neumann cleared his throat. "In our time, however difficult this concept may be, this beverage is widely known as coffee. It is ultimately a bean-shaped plant growing on shrubs. It is planted in various parts of the world, including the country, which is called Ethiopia in our time and is currently known as Aksum."

The Negusa's eyes narrowed.

"Tell me," he replied softly. "In your time, so far in the future – and yes, I can only try to understand this miracle –: How is my country?"

Neumann had only superficially dealt with the history of Ethiopia. He knew that the Aksumite empire was slowly collapsing from the 7th century onwards, and that it wasn't until the twelfth century that the Empire of Ethiopia was reborn. Then followed a very changeful history, with civil wars as well as phases of great unity. He didn't want to go into too much detail here.

"At the time when we were sent here, Emperor Melenik II ruled over the Empire."

Mehadeyis tilted his head. "He is a direct descendant of mine?" Neumann hesitated for a moment, but saw no great purpose in lying.

"He's assuming that officially, yes. The direct succession, however, goes back only to Menelik I, who will be the first Emperor of what will be named Ethiopia in about 600 years from now."

The Negusa Nagast smiled. "It's quite neat, this time-traveling."

Neumann smiled as well. "There are only a few royal houses, noble Majesty, which can be traced back to such a long and illustrious line like the one in Ethiopia." He didn't mention that the Ethiopian emperors had been marionettes of strong and mutually warring noblemen for long periods of time.

"We must talk about it in peace," the Emperor said, which Neumann had secretly feared. The historical documents that Rheinberg had presented in his private library had been very sparse on this subject. He knew very little and might not be able to answer the Emperor's questions.

"Well, I've forced you to digress," Mehadeyis said again. "We talked about this plant – coffee is it's name?"

"In our time it is known that your Empire is probably the place of origin of this plant."

"Aksum?"

"As a matter of fact. We assume that we'll find the wild form of the plant in the Aksumitic highlands."

The Emperor nodded. "And once we found them, what then?" Neumann's Greek was not perfect, but he had been listening carefully. The Aksumite ruler had said "we."

"It would be to our advantage, if Aksum could decide to plant the wild beans in plantations and export the harvest. We are hoping for a joint project, as our goal is to make this drink popular in Rome and thus to make money. While Aksum would receive a sum of that money for cultivating and harvesting, we would organize further processing in Rome."

"Would you?" Mehadeyis' expression suddenly had something

lurking. "Now let's assume, my Roman friends, that a bag of the coffee you have processed costs a golden denar. Only as a basis of calculation, just an assumption."

Neumann suspected where the Emperor wanted to go. He smiled and nodded.

"And how much of this denar would arrive in Aksum once a Roman citizen bought this bag of beans on the market? Let me reckon. There would be transportation costs, which would surely come to book. And the cost of processing – which looks exactly like what?"

"Essentially it's the roasting of the bean and the subsequent grinding."

"Like flour?"

"Yes, quite comparable."

"Good, so to roast and grind. The transportation. Then maybe costs involved in order to make the drink popular, yes? And I suppose the distribution in the Empire would be added. But then there would be the possible profit by selling the product to other countries. The Persians may also like the drink."

The Persians will love coffee, the Doctor thought, but said nothing. He tilted his head.

"I understand where you're aiming at, your Majesty."

"Do you?"

"Yes. Look, no matter what agreement we are going to make, no one can and will prevent Aksum from roasting and grinding the coffee itself. The procedure is not particularly mysterious, even if we wouldn't explain it to you, there are enough intelligent people in your realm who might find out quite soon by eager trial and error. And there will be enough traders who would be willing to buy the roasted coffee directly from the source. Since the coffee comes from your realm – it grows and flourishes and is harvested here – Rome cannot claim any monopoly. We are at best able to be the first and to gain a significant position in the trade before the competition arises. It's about an early start for a new business opportunity, if you want to see it like that. But it will never be a monopoly."

Mehadeyis nodded, leaned back on his throne, and closed his eyes thoughtfully. "So what are we going to do now?" he asked into the silence.

"We ask for your permission to look for coffee. Or at least your assurance to look yourself for this plant and then consider the cultivation. Furthermore, a trade agreement between Aksum and Rome, with a purchasing guarantee. The price could be negotiated. We will, of course, start with small quantities. We also have to experiment with further processing. Our knowledge is only theoretical."

Neumann stretched. He felt that he had been very tense, almost cramped all along. Diplomacy strained his muscles.

"But the basic prerequisite is to find the plant."

Mehadeyis opened his eyes again. "I'll think about it, time-wanderers. Perhaps we will come to an agreement." Then he leaned forward and clapped his hands. "Let us dine!"

Neumann took a step back and pointed to the gifts that the staff had built up in a corner of the room. "Your Majesty, we ..."

The Emperor pointed to a still young, vigorously built man. "My good Ouazebas, please take care of it."

When that name fell, Neumann turned around involuntarily. The only information he had had was an incomplete and questionable list of the Aksumite rulers, from which he had ascertained that the tall and self-assured nobleman who had now stepped forward and stood before the ruler would indeed become the next emperor. The governor of Adulis, of course, was very certain of this succession, since he had made a valuable gift expressedly reserved for this man. It was therefore important to secure the benevolence of Ouazebas, especially if a long-term trade relationship was to be established.

Neumann gestured toward the man. "I've heard a lot about you."

The heir apparent presented a wide smile. His tone, however, was somewhat sarcastic. "That pleases me. I'm sure Berhan of Adulis had only good things to say about me."

The Doctor hesitated. Evidently, the relationship between Berhan and the future emperor was not quite as heartfelt as the Governor had wanted to make them believe. "In any case, nothing negative has come to our attention. All spoke of you with the highest praise."

133

Ouazebas smiled wider. "This is also advisable, as everyone seems to expect that I will be Negusa Nagast."

"What do you mean, my friend?" the Emperor interrupted. "I am old. I cannot drink nearly enough of this coffee to live a lot longer."

Ouazebas bowed before the Negusa. "Lord, you are in good health and not so old yet. There is still a long and blessed rule before you."

"Ah, that's adorable," Mehadeyis replied, laughing. "You have been chosen with wisdom."

"I serve you."

"And to my satisfaction. After the meal, the gifts. You know my taste. Take the rest. Put the goods into the magazine. Notwithstanding my suspicious nature, it is clear that the Emperor of Aksum has absolutely no objection to amass a certain wealth."

"Your Majesty, I'll get at it immediately."

The Emperor nodded contentedly and clapped his hands. "Let's do it! Enough of trade and politics! I am hungry, and you are all as well."

Hectic activity broke out. All the guests sat at the table, on which gigantic, flat bowls were placed. Distributed on these plates and similar containers were all sorts of food, which was taken using soft bread and eaten. Servants hurried around. In honor of the guests, Roman wine was served, all of which consumed with obvious enjoyment. Conversation filled the hall, which soon included the Roman delegation. As the first round of the wide plates slowly emptied, there were already servants with more food ready.

Neumann sighed softly, which, as he had learned, was not considered as particularly rude. He knew why he had called the training session the night before.

This would be a long evening.

21

"We are ready!"

Klasewitz looked with great satisfaction at the series of cannons, which had been arranged on massive, wooden racks in the spacious workshop. It was the pride of the artillery officer who spoke through him, less pride for the tireless effort of the numerous tradesmen who had worked under him and had suffered much.

Magnus Maximus looked at the twelve guns, which were in exact alignment, the pipes shining, and presented by their five-man crew. The men were exhausted. For days they had practiced with the unusual weapon, and the German had been an unrelenting drudger. Maximus, however, had deflected every complaint, for although he had no idea about the workings of this miraculous technology, he recognized an expert when he saw one. What kind of errors the renegade wanderer might have had, he surely was proficient in his area of expertise. And he was ready to share this knowledge.

Each of the gunnery-crews, which consisted either of loaders or shooters, was supported by a whole squad: those who were responsible for the transportation of the pieces, then two projected observers per cannon, who were to provide information for the targeting, and a group of legionaries who were supposed to take over the protection of the otherwise helpless artillery crew.

Maximus looked around. For the short time of the presentation, the work had been temporarily suspended. As soon as the Comes had taken the cannons in, and thus officially announced the inauguration of the first Roman artillery company, the production of more guns would begin immediately. The time to begin the insurrection against Emperor Gratian was drawing closer and closer, and it was his declared goal to have at least two additional companies at his disposal.

"What are the prospects?" Maximus asked quietly as the men walked slowly along the row of the pieces, as if they were examining them. "Can we do it?"

Klasewitz knew immediately what he meant. After all, this question had been asked to him before during every visit.

"Since we've got a certain routine and confidence in the production process, the speed of our work has increased significantly. It was the prototypes that gave us headaches for some time. Now we know how to proceed, and only minor problems remaining."

"It would be nice if there were none at all."

"Have all the other arrangements advanced sufficiently?"

Maximus hesitated briefly. However, the question of the German was quite justified. A lot depended on the guns, but not everything.

"Our allies in Gaul say they are ready to strike. My own legions are also well prepared. The most difficult thing now is to coordinate three events in time."

"The murder of Gratian and the beginning of our attack and ...?"

Maximus smiled. "Not quite. We will give the signal for the murder of Gratian with the beginning of our attack. But it is also clear that the death of the Emperor alone will not suffice. Rheinberg isn't a fool, despite all of his mistakes, and he has also gathered capable officers around him. Even Gratian's death wouldn't prevent him from organizing an effective defense."

Maximus stopped and looked at the nobleman.

"In our case, the hydra has two heads, which must both be cut off."

Klasewitz nodded. "I would have liked to do it myself, but Rheinberg's death is certainly inevitable."

"Both of them have to be dead, and at the same time our attack has to begin," Maximus resumed the conversation as well as their inspection. "I hope the confusion will be strong enough to give us victory. Ambrosius has promised to place the Church on our side, as far as his influence is concerned. A few public protests should be enough to show the other Generals that it is better to make me emperor rather than allowing a civil war against the expressed volition of the people."

136

"I hope this plan will work."

Maximus made a dismissive gesture. "No plan is perfect. We will be careful and make decisions once they are necessary."

The Comes ran his hand over one of the pipes. They had arrived at the last cannon.

"These guns will help us advance to Treveri. We have heard that parts of the time-wanderer legionaries are in in the east, in search of the Hunnish host. A good opportunity to attack now. But the greatest challenge will be Ravenna. And the iron ship."

Maximus looked penetratingly at von Klasewitz.

"Even if we put these guns in position, the iron ship will destroy us."

The mutineer nodded. In a direct confrontation with the *Saarbrücken*, they wouldn't have any chance. Even a nightly attack, as he had planned one with his mutiny, couldn't be implemented at the moment. It was well known that the cruiser was well guarded. And the crew was loyal, as the nobleman knew from bitter experience. Not to talk of the new "Roman recruits," who were now serving on the ship as well.

"We have to choose another way," von Klasewitz said.

"What do you suggest?"

"I've given it a lot of thought, and I've come up with an idea."

Maximus motioned to the waiting soldier to signal that the presentation had ended, and made an emphatically pleased face. Only a few moments later, hectic activity commenced in the hall. The production of more cannons was in full swing.

The Comes pulled von Klasewitz aside. "Speak!" Maximus ordered tightly.

"We will only be able to control the *Saravica* if we can weaken those who defend the ship so that they won't be able to perform their duties. If no one is able to use a cannon, it's not a threat anymore. Besides, I don't want to damage the cruiser at all, it could be quite useful for us."

Maximus nodded. "So?"

"We must poison the crew."

The Comes looked on, thoughtfully. But he didn't dismiss the idea right away. Then he mustered the traitor with an encouraging smile.

"Our agents report that the *Saravica* crew is fed in two ways," von Klasewitz said. "Those who fulfill duties on land have a canteen where they are provided for, organized by the cruiser's cook. There is also food prepared in that canteen for those who work on the ship itself. The kitchen of the ship has been largely mothballed to save fuel. Therefore, if we succeed to smuggle a proper poison into the crew's food, we should be able to affect within one day everyone on duty. The only risk are those who either have no current duty that day or carry out tasks far away from the cruiser. But that should be a very small number."

"It has to be a good poison," Maximus murmured. He seemed quite impressed with the idea. "It must be relatively fast, but not effective directly, so that people are not immediately warned."

"That's the hurdle to take. And it would be good if people didn't die in the end. If we want to use the *Saravica*, we will need the bulk of the crew, otherwise the ship will not be operational."

"You have many wishes at once, time-wanderer."

"Our victory is one thing, Comes, the other is to maintain the power to rule and to expand. Notwithstanding our joint rejection of the current Magister Militium, Rheinberg is correct in one aspect: The Huns represent a real danger, as does the entire big migration caused by their appearance. The Empire will need to use every means to avert this threat."

Maximus grimaced. "One task after another. First I become emperor, then we take care of all those barbarians. Keep it up, Klasewitz. I'm going to inquire about the poison. The Picts and Scythians are good in poison. I'll tap some sources on the other side of the wall."

The German made a bow as the Comes turned and marched away. Von Klasewitz tried to keep his facial expressions as neutral as possible. Maximus wanted to be emperor, that was correct.

A very thin smile appeared around the mutineer's mouth. He wasn't the only one.

22

When Volkert awoke, he felt hot.

In front of his eyes, only shadows were visible, and it was obviously dark. When he breathed in, he felt a stinging and burning pain in his chest, which involuntarily lead to painful cough. The pain became more and more intense, and he immediately lost consciousness.

When he woke up the second time, he recognized the contours of a person beside him. He remembered the pain and tried to breathe very shallow. It was tolerable. Then he felt a wet, cool cloth on his forehead. He relaxed involuntarily. The image in front of his eyes became clearer.

"Quiet, my friend," a voice muttered. "Do not get excited. You've survived the worst."

Volkert recognized the man. It was the medic of the German unit. He didn't make an overly anxious impression.

"How ... what ...?"

The paramedic looked at Volkert comically, then leaned forward and took the wet cloth from his forehead to wring it, moisten it, and to put it back.

"A Hun got you in the chest," he said. "You were carried from the battlefield, unconscious. We took care of you in the field-hospital. You have lost a lot of blood, but the internal bleeding was limited. You were unconscious for a long time, and you had fever, but refused to die. The good news is that I suspect you have no infection and that everything will be okay. The bad news is that you will never have the same power in your lungs like you had before. You will have to live with it."

"Ah, shit."

The paramedic looked at Volkert again quite strangely, then nodded.

"It will still be painful for a long time. I have hardly any drugs I could give you. Some morphine is still available. But there are other legionaries with more painful injuries, too, and I want to ..."

"No problem," Volkert groaned. It was very difficult for him to speak, and it hurt. But he had seen himself with what kind of injuries legionaries were carried off the field, still alive. If the medic was able to save some of these human lives, then surely under great pain. Volkert longed for relief. Morphine seemed to him like a promise, and he almost wanted to take his rejection back, but before he could open his mouth, he was again completely exhausted and fell into a deep slumber.

When he awoke for the third time, everything was still there: the pain, the burning, the difficult breathing – but the rest of his body felt quite good. His gaze, too, was clearer and no longer so vague. He noticed that he was lying in a building, a wooden hut, and not alone. Beside him, he realized, Bertius rested with his arm-stump. The otherwise well-nourished and healthy man had a pale face and lied motionless with his eyes closed. Volkert couldn't see whether he was asleep. But he breathed deeply and regularly, and there was no sweat on his forehead, indicating that he wasn't suffering from any fever. To Volkert, it seemed as if Bertius would survive.

He knew why the man was down. He remembered it very well.

He had been mutilated because Volkert had made sure that he took part in this expedition.

And he had been mutilated because he had saved the life of his Decurion.

Involuntarily, Volkert felt the need to get up, but urged himself not to. The fact that he had survived this injury was a miracle. But he knew that he owed Bertius something and that the man had done more than he had expected from him. The gratitude he felt mixed with shame. He would have to do something about that, sooner or later.

Someone stepped beside his deck. It was Secundus, his comrade, who had fought with him when the almost deadly blow had come.

"Well, Thomasius, how are you?"

"Everything sucks."

"That sounds good. You have been lying around for long enough."

"How long?"

"Did no one tell you? You were in delirium for seven days. We hardly got any water into you. Then the fever subsided. You've slept for almost another twelve hours, and now I have the order to give you water, and, if possible, a decent broth."

Volkert suddenly realized that he felt a burning thirst. Secundus handed him a cup and supported his head with his hand. Volkert drank deliberately slow and felt almost immediately quite animated.

"What's the situation?" he croaked.

"Oh, a lot has happened. The Huns were, of course, beaten. You saved the son of the King, which led to some interesting developments."

"What?"

"On the one hand, Sedacius seems to have gained an external ally for his political ambitions."

Volkert closed his eyes.

"Then there is the fact that the Tribune has promoted you to centurion."

Volkert looked at Secundus again. "You, as well, it seems, my friend."

The man looked at the insignia on his breastplate. "Oh, I haven't even noticed yet! Damn it! How could this happen?"

Volkert shook his head gently.

"Sedacius is still waiting for a few days as the captured Huns are being interrogated. They will not survive as long as you. Then we leave and go home. Our Tribune has great plans, and that includes you, my friend. As soon as you're up and kicking, he'll talk to you."

Volkert was not sure whether this was a good prospect or not. In the next few minutes, Secundus was busy pouring a hot broth into his friend. Although this process was associated with pain and some clumsiness, Volkert felt very comfortable after the procedure, the first time since he had awakened. The pleasant warmth of the soup spread in his body, and the part of his pain that he only now identified as being hungry disappeared. "So we'll be back soon? Did the questioning of the Huns give us anything?"

"These are hard boys, I can tell you," Secundus murmured. He looked down for a moment.

Volkert suspected that he had been involved in the torture and was remembering. Torture was an absolutely legitimate and normal method of obtaining information in the Roman Empire. It was used against Roman citizens as well as against external enemies. Rheinberg had begun to ask the moral question. While assisting in the abolition of slavery, and making progress quickly, the discussion about the abolition of torture had mainly caused consternation, even within the Church. Volkert was grateful not to have been entrusted with these interrogations, although he had bought this "liberation" from duties with a life-threatening injury.

"In any case, we have a clue as to where the Hunnish main force is. It is still a good distance away, but not as far as we would have guessed from the historical data of the time-wanderers. We still have a grace period, but it seems to be shorter than expected."

"Yes, but the idea is not to let it come to this attack on our borders in the first place," Volkert replied. "The defense at that time was only possible because of a combination of very happy circumstances, if I gathered it correctly. And the main part of the military burden hadn't even been borne by Rome, so much the Empire had already been diminished."

"So I've heard. In any case, we will continue to work the prisoners for a while, and there will be little left of them. As slaves, they will be no good, and many have not been caught anyway. They fought like the devil."

Volkert nodded. He felt that he was slowly getting tired again, and Secundus must have noticed this too, for he put a hand on the German's shoulder and smiled at him.

"I'll be back tomorrow, then you should be a bit more approachable. Sedacius will be glad to be able to talk to you, maybe he will be faster than me. Oh, you didn't have the information about your promotion from me. He wants to tell you. The King might also come along. A little ceremony at the hospital bed."

"Tell everyone that I am dying."

Secundus grinned, shook his head, and left the room. When he had disappeared, the paramedic came back, gave Volkert a long look before he began to care for the other wounded in the hut.

Volkert closed his eyes and tried to relax again. *Damn it!*

He opened his eyes and stared at the ceiling.

What a great, indescribable fool he had been!

Now the memory crawled up inside him, and he knew what he had to fear more than anything else, more than any infection.

Mentally delusional caused by pain and disorientated by feverish delirium, he had made the mistake twice, as he remembered now. Twice he had said something to the paramedic.

Volkert now felt cold sweat on his forehead.

Twice in German.

23

"How very, very cute!"

That Lucia, the strict wife of the respected Roman senator Michellus, was capable of such an utterance at all, left Julia with no small surprise. When her mother clapped her fleshy hands against each other and took a step toward the crib to circle around it, she found it very hard not to shake her head. The delightful singing, Lucia elicited for the crib where the little one was supposed to sleep, consisted not only of words, but a mixture of delighted cooing and the expression of deep, even triumphant, satisfaction. The belly of her daughter, bulging, the nicely done crib, everything was confirmation that she had been able to carry out her will, and that her frustrated and frustrating daughter was finally, at last, where she belonged.

For a tiny moment, Julia allowed herself the most unfavorable imagination of how her mother would react when one day she found out whose child this actually was – or when she learned that Julia had succeeded and purged her unloved husband to live her life with the man she had chosen.

Julia forced a smile. That event hadn't yet come. For the time being, it wasn't advisable to destroy Lucia's benevolence.

"It's sooo cute," her mother assured her with a loving voice that Julia had never noticed before. "Adorable! Simply adorable!" She looked at her pregnant daughter. "Did Martinus Caius build it?"

Julia wanted to give a harsh and contemptuous reply, but then she remembered her intention, and she forced herself to produce a polite paraphrase of reality.

"He's very busy, mother. Since we've married, he has become very interested in his father's business. He is well aware that he now has to look after a family. But he gave the carpenter exact instructions."

Lucia made another of those cooing sounds, her broad face radiated pure happiness. She began to circle the crib again.

The sudden interest of Caius in the business of his father was, as Julia knew, only temporary, until the great load of newly arrived Greek wines had been dispatched to the cities of Gaul, and he had personally convinced himself of the high quality of the goods. Furthermore, the carpenter had received his instructions from Caius, but they had only consisted of the sentence "Do as my wife says!" Julia had a beautiful crib made for her child. She had the desire to spend the money of her husband as well and comprehensively as the situation allowed. She guessed that her future life with Thomas Volkert would be marked by deprivation. Until then, she wanted to take all the luxury offered to her, enjoying it as long at it might last.

So deep in her thoughts, she hadn't even noticed that her mother had approached her again. Lucia put a hand on her daughter's belly. The unborn child took the opportunity to kick. Julia smiled happily. There was already a deep emotional bond between her and the child, and they shared the same sentiments.

"You are fine, yes, my daughter?"

"All is well," Julia answered truthfully. In fact, the midwife was very pleased with her. She developed superbly through the pregnancy, and the ever stronger and persistent movements of the child testified that it was doing well and obviously looking forward to see the light of the world.

"You don't have to worry about delivery," Lucia said gratefully. "It is certainly not easy, but it is the most proud moment in a woman's life. It is the fulfillment for which we are born."

Julia offered her mother a smile. Lucia had fulfilled many things in her life, and the short moments of the delivery of her two daughters were certainly not among the most important. Julia had her own theory of what her mother was doing, and it was by no means a particularly flattering one.

"I have no fear," she replied truthfully. "I have a good midwife with great experience."

Here, too, she had invested her husband's money with prudence. The midwife, in fact, had an excellent reputation and was rewarded well for her services. Above all, Julia was on a daily check-up. She enjoyed the conversations with the educated woman, having light wine and the wonderful little cookies she always brought from the market.

For a moment, Julia thought of the layers of soft flesh which began to develop in parts of her body, and which had little to do with the bulge of the growing child. She glanced at the massive figure of her mother and frowned. Lucia bore her numerous pounds with aristocratic dignity, but suffered particularly during the summer months, which generally set her in a worse mood than she normally displayed.

Perhaps she should refrain from the cookies for a while.

Lucia patted her forearm.

"If you need anything, just say it. You belong to your husband's family now, but our bonds are strong and persistent, and you can always turn to me."

"Where is Father? I haven't seen him for a long time."

"He keeps himself busy at the court in Treveri," Lucia said with a certain reluctant acknowledgment in her voice. "He belongs to the Emperor's close circle of advisers. I have heard that he is to be given the position of procurator once a vacancy is available."

Julia didn't know if that was good news. For Lucia, this equaled social advancement and even more wealth. Her father would certainly not be averse to such a challenge. But as much as Julia despised her mother's attitude, she loved her father very much, and it would be hard to bear to not see him for years, especially if he were to be employed as the administrator of a very remote province.

"When will he be back in Ravenna?" Julia asked.

"I don't know. But it is said that the Emperor would like to visit the city of the time-wanderers to convince himself of the numerous technical developments. Surely your father will accompany him."

"Please tell me once you know more."

"Of course, my dove."

It took several minutes until her mother said goodbye and Julia remained alone. As a rule, Julia preferred this condition. Her husband's family was an almost more unbearable company than her own. The mother of Caius, whose task was to take care of the highly pregnant daughter-in-law, was so timid and withdrawn, that Julia was hardly able to see her. And even if she appeared, it didn't lead to any pleasant conversation.

Julia stepped onto the balcony of the splendid villa. From here, she had a good look at the hectic bustle of Ravenna. The city had been blessed with an unprecedented economic upswing by the arrival of the time-wanderers. Immigrants from all parts of Rome wanted to be close to the strangers, from curiosity as well as with business-interests. Ravenna had never been a poor city, but now it transformed itself into the richest in the whole Empire.

The child kicked her, as if it wanted the mother to remember something.

Julia sighed softly. In recent times, dark moments had piled up, putting her determination and confidence to the test. Volkert was far away, and she couldn't even be sure that he was still alive. And it was said that the women of the East, especially those of the barbarian peoples, were particularly skilled in embracing a young man who was rather naïve in love affairs, and to let him forget home and family.

No, she couldn't think of that. If she lost confidence in her Thomas, she could at once resign herself to the unhappy life with an unpleasant husband, like so many of her age and from her class.

Julia took a deep breath. She wasn't to succumb to depression. At the moment she was on her own, without confidants and without friends. But that would change if she only believed in the destiny that had so far filled her with sufficient confidence.

She hesitated for a moment.

She left the balcony and called for her body-servant. The unborn child kicked boldly.

It was high time for a walk.

24

"The Emperor is inspecting a few fortresses north of Treveri. He will soon return. We should inform him about this beforehand. Rheinberg must know as well."

Langenhagen stared out the window. The Roman glass had defects in the cast and showed indeficiencies, but he could look from the top floor of the administration building down to the port. The gray body of the *Saarbrücken* was sharply distinguishable in the bright sunlight, and the officer didn't feel for the first time the longing to simply strip the burdens of his office and to be just the servant of this beautiful old lady.

"He must know as soon as possible," Langenhagen confirmed. "But we should have a plan that would allow us to answer Gratian's questions. After all, it is indirectly our fault that it has come so far."

Dahms frowned, rose from the chair behind his desk, and joined Langenhagen. "Our fault?"

"Klasewitz is the best artillery expert we have. He crossed over to the enemy. We should have watched him better."

Dahms snorted. "Of course, it would have been good to take von Klasewitz as prisoner once Rheinberg became captain." Here, without publicity, they allowed friendly confidentiality among themselves. Only out there, in front of others, they kept their etiquette. "But seriously, the fact that the man would be so insane as to start a mutiny no one really could've foreseen."

Langenhagen shoved his shoulders forward, seemed to make himself small. Dahms looked at the young man anxiously. Both had visibly aged in the year since they were lost in this epoch. Deep rings under Langenhagen's eyes testified to the iron discipline with which he was driving himself, and the lines that had deeply buried themselves in the actually youthful face spoke another clear language. But after all they had heard, there would be no opportunity for relaxation in the foreseeable future.

"This Godegisel seems to be trustworthy," Dahms said.

"I'll have his information checked, of course, but ultimately we depend only on his word. Tennberg's statements confirm everything, though. There seems to be a coherent picture."

"It smells like von Klasewitz and fits into what we know. Gratian is in great danger. I fear the worst."

Langenhagen tore himself away from the sight of the *Saarbrücken*. "We have done all this to prevent the great civil war that would weaken Rome decisively. So decisively that the Huns would give death to the Empire, even if they didn't win. And now? Now, one of us is concerned to trigger exactly such a civil war – and a far more brutal and modern one than that in our timeline."

"And years earlier," Dahms said.

"That too."

Langenhagen's face reflected his concerns. Dahms had the command over the city. He himself commanded the cruiser. The ship was his highest responsibility.

"Johann, I would like the *Saarbrücken* to be placed on an increased readiness. It costs us fuel, but I want it to be constantly under steam."

"This works out. We have received large quantities of high-quality charcoal, and we are expected to be able to get hard coal, albeit initially only in small quantities. We don't touch our old supplies. The charcoal should be sufficient for readiness. We have to shove the stuff from the quay to the *Saarbrücken*, that's all, and we have the manpower available by now."

"Please also reinforce the security measures. I wouldn't be surprised if the attack would commence in several places at the same time."

"How could that happen? Maximus is in Britain!"

"And we picked up Tennberg in Alexandria. Our opponents have contacts everywhere. They cannot coordinate it in time, but it is already enough if their allies start a round of insurrections after a certain activity has functioned as the agreed signal to carry out targeted actions – also here and now against the *Saarbrücken*. We

149

are important in our role to protect Gratian and ..." Langenhagen frowned. Then he went on. "Klasewitz wants the cruiser, Johann. He considers himself to be a gifted officer, born for this role. It will be his prize for providing Maximus with weapons technology. At least. And that means he will be targeting the cruiser, but not wanting to damage it. He wants to conquer the ship, and to command it afterwards."

Dahms nodded. "Yes, I agree."

"Sit down with the other officers. Look how you can increase security. What about the weapons for the legions? Klasewitz has focused on cannons. What do you have in mind?"

Johann Dahms looked down. "I have to be honest, Klasewitz did it right. He has undertaken a single project and has consistently pursued it. We here have too many building sites at the same time. Our biggest achievement is the bronze steam engine. But otherwise ..."

"No. That's not it. We have taken these decisions together in order to provide the biggest possible foundation for the development of Rome. An industrial revolution. But this is something quite different from creating a special product for a special purpose. We may have failed to set priorities, but otherwise ... So what do we have?"

"I can offer you a total of three Valentinian-class ships within four weeks, all equipped with light hand guns and steam catapults. We have made progress in the development of explosive devices, although I don't know how to solve the problem of reliable impact detonators. But once the three ships are ready, they will have the necessary ammunition."

"That's good, but it's not enough. This war will take place on land, Johann, not at sea. We have a small advantage with maritime superiority, but ultimately we are dependent on a base, and that is currently only this city. Our little advantage stands and falls with this settlement, the workshops, and the workers who live here."

"I'll do what I can."

Langenhagen nodded. "Johann, I want the *Saarbrücken* to be ready to sail at any time. We must have Rheinberg's back. He cannot even care about the ship, he has other worries. The cruiser must be safe."

"As I said, the coal ..."

"No. Everything. Duty roster. Provisions. I'd like to be able to leave as soon as a situation arises that makes it inevitable to make our operational basis mobile. This also applies to the ships of the Valentinian-class. We should be able to get as many of them ready to leave as we can."

Dahms looked searchingly at the officer. "You really think it will be so bad? We have the whole apparatus of the Empire on our side! And then there is the infantry. The company alone makes up for a legion, if not more."

"I've talked about it with von Geeren. We divided the company already in too many small pieces. Two units are stationed here, about half of the men. One is now spread over half the Empire: Some protect our newly emerging iron industry in the Saarland; some are on an expedition to the east to find the Huns; some of them belong to von Geeren's staff in Trier. We have moved men to Trier, in order to make a presence and to signal that the Emperor is protected."

"Not to mention Rheinberg."

"Yes. But the biggest problem is not even that we have distributed the men. At the moment, ammunition is still quite plentiful, but it won't last forever. Thessaloniki has already drained our supplies. I assume that the men in the east, who have taken two MGs, won't be able to get away without any shooting. On the one hand, the psychological advantage is diminishing with every further use of the weapons, on the other hand, we cannot replace the ammunition – or is there news?"

Dahms raised his hands. "Steel, my friend, steel! Give me a working puddle furnace and a smart mold foundry, then I can start making cartridges. Not quite as good as we know it, but good enough to get the belts of the MGs filled up."

"How far are you with the furnace?"

"We're almost ready. I think we have solved the biggest design problems. I have the first real test run next week, then we will see if we can reach the necessary temperatures. After that, it is only a matter of time before we can produce steel in at least small quantities."

"How long?"

"A month. Two."

"That's not fast enough. I'm afraid that's *really* not fast enough."

"The insurrection will begin in Britain. Even if it's going to be completely smooth, it will take a while before he arrives. Until then ..."

"I don't believe, as I said, that we are dealing with only one opponent from one direction. We should not be too pessimistic, but it's necessary to be prepared for everything."

Dahms sighed. "Good. How should I proceed now? We need to focus."

"I'd like you to prepare explosives at all the important production facilities, including your furnace, for the worst case. Even the ships must be blown to smithereens if we cannot take them with us. Klasewitz will be able to use any technical equipment immediately against us if he conquers it. We must not give the enemy such an advantage."

"I'll get it done. Von Geeren has a few pretty skilled firecrackers in his troop. They will know what to do."

"Very careful, Johann. If we cannot stop the enemy, it is necessary that they cannot lay their hands on all this." He saw Dahm's painful countenance, and smiled joylessly. "I don't like giving such orders. Here is a lot of our heart invested in material and people, especially from you. But we must be prepared. It is of no use if we allow material in the enemy's hand with which he can one day use to end to us."

Dahms lowered his head. "When we are already at terrible scenarios – there are at least two more questions: What would do we do in case of an evacuation with family members? I don't refer only the families of our Roman recruits. You know that many of our crew have now found brides. I hear that children are already on the way. The men have begun to strike roots."

"That's why the steamers have to be prepared, too. We must have them ready. In addition to the crew, they can transport the families who will make it to the port in the event of an attack. You should also work out a plan for this, preferably together with Joergensen."

"Good."

"And the second question?"

Dahms took a deep breath. "Let's suppose the worst happens and we have to go."

"Yes?"

"Let's suppose that we can prepare all the ships and take them with us. Our own little flotilla."

Langenhagen nodded. He knew the engineer's question already.

"Then the central question remains: Where are we going?" Dahms looked at the officer.

He shrugged. "I'm open to suggestions, Johann. I have absolutely no idea."

"Let us hope that Rheinberg can give us an answer when it's time."

25

They were awakened, very early in the morning.

The dinner with the Emperor had lasted well into the night. Nobody had dared to say goodbye before the old man had declared himself too tired to attend any longer. Neumann and the others had not been able to take another bite at that time.

Exhausted and expecting digestive problems, they had fallen into their beds after midnight. They staggered accordingly, as furious screams, the crashing opening of doors, and the grip of hard fists tore them from their slumber.

But they were soldiers, all of them. Even with little sleep, they had been trained with iron discipline to function properly. When they were threatened with blades and dragged into the yard in a row, still in their night shirts, each of them was already very awake.

And extremely confused.

Many soldiers had gathered in the courtyard of the guest house. They were threatening, even hostile.

Ouazebas, the heir to the throne, came forth from their midst. Behind by this dangerously calm demeanor, a volcano was hidden, ready for eruption. Neumann exchanged a look with Africanus. The Trierarch nodded in mute communication, raised both arms, and stepped forward.

"What happened?" was his simple question, not challenging, but seriously interested.

"My brother is dead," the Aksumite said in a low voice. "My four years older brother, the pride of my father and one of the best officers of the Aksumite forces, died last night. He died a cruel death, rolled for minutes in his own excrement, with foam in front of his mouth and wild eyes. His pain must have been unbearable. Then he was dead. Torn from life. Just like that."

154

Africanus looked at Ouazebas, recognized more than anger and indignation in the arduous self-control of the man, above all a deep, burning grief, an honest feeling, nothing played, no charade. The pain was deep in Aksum's heir.

Africanus did the right thing.

He lowered his head and knelt.

On Neumann's sign, everyone followed his example without saying a word.

Then the Trierarch spoke. "Royal Highness. The news of the cruel death of your brother grieves me. But you see us at a loss. Why are we so obviously connected with this incident?"

Something close to Africanus hit the ground. It was the casket in which the gifts of the Governor of Adulis, had been stored. The one for Ouazebas. Now it was empty.

"The brooch, Romans, your gift. It was poisoned. The poison, I suppose, was intended for me."

"I suppose so, yes," Africanus replied, raising his head. "But we didn't place it there. This gift, like many others, was chosen and made available by Berhan, the governor. We have assumed in good faith that it would be a serious expression of appreciation."

Ouazebas's eyes narrowed. "Berhan has given you this item?"

"He did."

"And what other presents actually come from him instead from Roman hand, not provided by you?"

Africanus felt hot and cold. If the special jewelry had been poisoned for the heir ... "That for the Emperor, too. A similar box."

Ouazebas' face turned ashen. He pulled Africanus up. "Follow me! The rest will wait here. Do not let them go until I'm back!"

Africanus staggered to his feet. Two soldiers took him into the middle and dragged him along.

The other men remained behind. A large section of soldiers stood with motionless faces before them, the swords drawn, spears directed at them. But it didn't seem to bother anyone when they talked among themselves.

"Where will they carry him to?" Behrens asked.

"To the Emperor. Ouazebas suspects that the present for him has also been prepared with deadly poison," Neumann surmised.

"Preparation for a coup?" Köhler murmured, pointing out that he had gathered his wits quickly.

"I guess so too," Neumann replied. "Berhan has abused our confidence in settling bills at the imperial court – and made us look responsible. He probably thinks that no one will believe our assurances of innocence. After all, we are aliens – and quite strange."

"What will happen now?"

Neumann raised his shoulders. "It depends on how much the family of Ouazebas is pushing for revenge, and whether the Emperor is a little bit offended. In the latter case, I don't want to make any big bets on our lives. But we get a chance, we must try to strengthen the suspicion of Berhan's responsibility."

"There must have been previous incidents and hints, things like this don't happen without a long story or out of the blue," Behrens said thoughtfully. "There must have been more to it we are not aware of."

"I agree," Neumann said. "There is a history or at least a clear picture of Berhan and his ambitions, otherwise our words would've been dismissed right away. On the other hand, Ouazebas, despite his grief for his brother, doesn't appear to me like a man who immediately falls victim to the first conclusion and isn't ready to think beyond the too obvious."

"Quite hopeful assumptions, aren't they?" Köhler interjected. He looked at the phalanx of the soldiers and lowered his head. "Even if Behrens and I had our pistols in our hands, they would chop us into pieces in no time."

"We will not provoke anything," Neumann said. "We are peaceful and docile. What is important, is the Emperor's reaction – and his current condition. Our fate is essentially dependent on his. If he is dead, we are, too."

* * *

The darkness just before dawn. Africanus could barely orient himself, but that didn't matter anyway. The strong hands that led him belonged to men who knew every inch. When they finally reached the imperial palace, the news of their arrival seemed already to have spread. Everywhere, torches had been lit, and troubled guards hurried to meet them. Africanus overheard an excited exchange between Ouazebas and an officer, after which the haste continued. It took no more than five minutes until they had reached the Emperor's private quarters. There were once again violent discussions with body guards, which were terminated when someone brought the opened, gifted cup from the emperor's sleeping chambers. Ouazebas became agitated, pushed the bodyguard aside, and rushed with his men through the doors.

Mehadeyis of Aksum sat in his bed, watching the newcomers with great relaxation. Ouazebas, visibly relieved, fell on his knees before the Emperor and seemed to explain what brought him here.

The Emperor's eye fell repeatedly on Africanus. "Good, my friend, thank you," the old man finally said in Greek. "I am fine. I have back pain, flatulence, and I have to pee too often without anything coming out, but that has nothing to do with any poison."

"I thought ..." Ouazebas began.

"I know. I opened the present and nothing happened to me. What does that tell you, my friend?"

The heir to the throne had by now regained his self-control. He rose and sat down on the bedside of the Emperor. "I was the target," he said.

"And you alone," Mehadeyis confirmed. "I am old. I don't need much encouragement to die. Sufficient to let nature take its course. If, however, the Romans had the goal of causing Aksum to be stirred up or weakened in the long run, then this goal would be served well by preventing a strong and dynamic future emperor."

Ouazebas looked at Africanus, who gazed at him quietly.

"But where is the advantage?" the Trierarch finally asked. "Aksum and Rome are friends, but quite far apart. We have different interests. And Rome has really enough to do with other challenges."

157

"Name anyone who could profit, we are willing to listen to your opinion," Mehadeyis said with a hypocritical naivete.

Africanus lowered his head. "It is not for me as your guest to interfere with Aksum's inner affairs or to voice suspicions."

"Bullshit," the old emperor said. "I'm sitting in my bed, not quite frightened. Ouazebas here has lost his brother, and we stand around like idiots. Everyone is tired and angry and irritated, and I am also very thirsty."

A chambermaid stepped quietly out of the room.

"Let's leave this diplomatic nonsense. Roman. Speak out!"

Africanus looked slightly helpless at Ouazebas. The successor to the throne seemed not to be surprised about the nature of the Emperor's language.

"Berhan is an intriguer, we know," Ouazebas said instead of the Roman. "And he has influential friends, provincial nobles like him. It has been rumored for some time that he himself wants to raise claims to the throne."

"It's a matter of simple rumors, my friend," Mehadeyis said, straightening in his bed. "He has ambition, but he's not stupid. And his friends defend him. He is a danger primarily to you, Ouazebas."

"He is a danger to the Empire!"

"Nonsense! Aksum will also do well under an Emperor Berhan. Ouazebas, I love you like a son, but you are astonishingly stupid in some aspects!" The Emperor laughed. His heir seemed not to resent criticism. He probably didn't hear it for the first time. "An Emperor Berhan would be a man of influence and one who had been born into intrigue, harassment and political strategy, that is exactly what is needed on the throne. We'd have a wonderful emperor in him!"

Ouazebas snorted, but said nothing.

"But there are some disadvantages," the Emperor continued. "The people find him terrible, especially his penchant for cruelty. And everyone knows that he is a thief. Just as he has many friends, he attracted many enemies. Ouazebas, however, may have opponents, but the least of these are real enemies. He can involve them through his personality. A post here, a nice campaign for loot there, it can be done. If Berhan is emperor, there will be slaughter."

Africanus looked at the heir. He now recognized that the Emperor was only repeating a conversation which he and Ouazebas had surely already had several times, but now summarizing it again for the Roman's benefit. But he didn't know what was going to happen.

"Did I mention I'm thirsty?" Mehadeyis asked, his voice raised. A moment later a servant appeared with an amphora and a chalice. The Emperor watched as the wine was poured.

"Your time-wanderer-drink would help now," he said as placing the cup to his mouth. Africanus nodded.

"You are asking now why we want to believe you that it is not in your interest to kill the Aksumite emperor, Africanus."

"I'm still waiting for enlightenment, Your Majesty."

"Ah, now he's cheeky. We have been too nice to him, Ouazebas." The heir forced a smile. Mehadeyis got serious and nodded.

"Your brother was a good man. He couldn't leave his fingers off the wives of other men, but he was a good man. A good Christian. May the Lord accept him. We will all pray for him, Ouazebas. But we both know that you should not direct your anger against the Romans and their strange new friends."

The prince lowered his head. "I know. But ..."

"Yes, I understand your rage. But we want to remain friends of Rome, right? And I want this coffee."

Mehadeyis looked at Africanus.

"Tell your friends that your expedition to the highlands will be delayed. We'll go to Adulis tomorrow. I'll hold court."

Africanus straightened, unsure of what to say. He knew, however, what role they were supposed to play.

"I will be the judge and you will be witnesses."

"Witnesses to what, Your Majesty?"

"Witnesses to all that I demand of you."

Africanus met the Emperor's gaze. Everything made sense. The old Mehadeyis wanted to take the opportunity to settle the bill with Berhan and secure the legacy for Ouazebas before he died. He really didn't care if the governor was actually guilty or not, even if everything spoke for it.

This was about politics.

"When the trial is over, and Berhan has been judged upon," the Emperor continued, as if he had read Africanus's thoughts, "I'll give you permission to look for coffee, and I will plant the seeds and make sure that Ouazebas will not only be a favorable but also a filthily rich Negusa Nagast."

Africanus lowered his head. "Your wisdom is immeasurable, Your Majesty."

"The only thing that is immeasurable is the strength of my urge to pee, Roman!" The Emperor laughed again, and drained the cup, then nodded to Ouazebas. "Prepare everything, my friend. We depart at dawn. I will not hesitate. The coastal winds will do my old bones good. And I have to break an enemy's neck, who would otherwise and sooner or later bring you much trouble."

Africanus could not hold onto himself. "But how can you be sure that it was not us who had the poison ... I mean ... you'd never know with ultimate certainty! Neither would you, Ouazebas. Our word against Berhan's! This may well sound politically feasible, but will the future Aksumite emperor not be suspicious of all the Romans, since he will always suspect that Rome is behind the death of his brother?"

Ouazebas and Mehadeyis looked at each other. Both smiled. Africanus looked highly confused from one to the other.

"Roman, you are certainly a good soldier. A good officer. A clever man. But as a politician you are completely incapable. I'll use you and your friends, and for that we had to knock you up," the Emperor said relaxed. And Ouazebas still smiled.

"But ..." Africanus didn't understand a word. The Negusa Nagast clapped his hands.

It took only a few moments, then two men entered. One carried a simple garment, the other the armor of an Aksumite soldier. Both of them looked amused when they came before the Emperor and bowed before turning to Africanus.

"This," Ouazebas said, pointing to the soldier, "is my honorable brother, one of the bravest officers of the Empire of Aksum. He will one day roast in hell, for he covets the wives of others, and this repeatedly and with endurance. But the time of his judgment has not yet come."

The man, a few years older than Ouazebas, and looking almost identical, raised his hands. "You convey a completely false picture of mine, brother."

Africanus looked bewildered at the man. Then his eyes wandered to the second. He knew him.

His name was Haleb, governor Berhan's factotum.

"This man here ..." Ouazebas began, but then Africanus raised his hand.

The heir fell silent.

Africanus looked at the Emperor, and he didn't know what came upon him when he said aloud to the Negusa Nagast. "The most accomplished intriguer of Aksum, Your Majesty, is undoubtedly you."

Mehadeyis laughed and raised his empty cup.

"I'm thirsty! Hello? I'm thirsty!"

26

"And what did he say?"

Secundus' curiosity was just as intrusive as it was understandable. He had directed his horse to move beside the wagons for the wounded, or rather the column of three carts pulled by donkeys on which those who were still too weak were for riding independently rested. Volkert was half-erect in the middle cart, supported by a pillow of rolled blankets, and with every rumble and shaking, pain passed through his chest. For a week, the wounded had been nursed, and the paramedic had done miracles. Volkert had known his name – Florian Feldmann – and had since only spoken to him in Greek, which the young man was more likely to understand without further suspicion. No word had been said about the mistake the deserter had made, and Volkert was not sure whether Feldmann had ever reported the faux pas to his superiors.

Secundus' question was asking for another conversation.

Volkert grimaced, as the truck rumbled through a particularly deep furrow. Two more wounded, sitting next to him, cursed. The man on the harness pulled his shoulders together. He could do nothing about it, but he remained the appropriate target for his passenger's insults.

"Sedacius made me centurion."

Secundus waved him off. "Yes, yes. What else?"

"The king of the Quadians thanked me. His son is doing well. He also thanked me. Look!"

Volkert took something from underneath his tunic. A golden necklace, decorated with precious stones, a beautiful and valuable handwork. A gift from the King. For the value of this piece of jewelry, he could buy a piece of land if he wanted. If he would ever have the opportunity.

"Fine!" Secundus cast a professional and greedy look at the chain. Volkert didn't hesitate to show it to him. On the one hand, Secundus was a gambler and a crook, but he wasn't a thief, and he thought of Volkert as a friend. Apart from this, Volkert was certain he had surely "found" something of this and that in the enemy's camp which someone else had "forgotten" during the gathering of valuables.

"But what was said?"

Volkert probably knew what the equally promoted Centurion really wanted. It was about the Tribune's plans to become an emperor. The successful expedition had increased the fame and financial resources of Sedacius, and he had once again told Volkert that the aspiring officer could face a brilliant future if he only supported him in his endeavor. Volkert had asserted to be faithful to Sedacius, who would continue to help him. The German knew he could use any protection that was offered. Especially if one day the suspicion would arise that he was not the one he pretended to be.

Volkert leaned toward Secundus and made a covert hand movement toward the other wounded. The curious comrade understood. Nobody could know who was in favor of Sedacius' plans and who probably opposed them. It was better not to talk about these things in public.

After a few more words, Secundus spurred his horse and left Volkert to himself and his thoughts. There were some things he wouldn't tell his friend even in confidence. For instance, that the Tribune had taken him, the deserter, into his closest circle of advisers, into his general staff, if one wanted to call it that. Volkert was not sure whether he had deserved this kind of promotion, but he saw no reason to reject it. What exactly that meant for him in the future couldn't be estimated.

Again the cart jerked and the chest ached. The caravan paused every two hours, during which the paramedic cared for the wounded, changed bandages, and spoke to the men. Volkert simply longed to have some quiet.

"Centurion."

Volkert looked to his side. Bertius shared this cart with him. His neat arm-stump hung down at his side. The blade of the Hun had been well sharpened, and Bertius had survived the loss of blood, his face color was almost rosy again.

"What will happen to me, Centurion?"

Volkert groaned, as he turned to the legionary and looked him in the face. "What do you think?"

Bertius made the impression of being somewhat lost. "I've spent my entire life in the legion. I know. Though I have never been particularly successful, the legion was my life."

"You've proven yourself sufficiently to me, Bertius."

The man nodded and smiled. "Thank you, centurion, but it might not have been very smart."

"I have to contradict that."

"I believe you. But with this injury, I cannot return to active duty."

Bertius was right. Even with a good wooden prosthesis, the manufacture of which was definitely not beyond the abilities of Roman artisans, and which Volkert had undertaken to commission immediately upon his return, Bertius could no longer participate in combat. And a legionary who could not fight wasn't useful to the legion.

"You've been doing duty for several years," Volkert said. "Sedacius has announced that all seriously wounded, who cannot return to Noricum to the fortress, will be given an honorable dismissal, as well as the promised land and gratuity."

Bertius shook his head. "What shall I do with land? I'm not a farmer. I cannot work any land."

So no difference to his life before, Volkert thought to himself. It was only that Bertius now had a better and, unfortunately, a permanent excuse.

"I've grown up in the legion," the man added. "I don't know anything else to do."

Volkert nodded. He had feared something like that. And he knew that he had to pay a debt to Bertius. In the past few days, he had devised several ways to do this, and this conversation led to the solution most feasible. "I am now a centurion, Bertius."

"Yes, and congratulations are in order, sir."

164

Volkert didn't know about the seriousness of this praise, but he dismissed the issue right away.

"In addition, Sedacius called me into his staff." Why he revealed to Bertius what he had not wanted to tell Secundus, he didn't really know.

"Congratulations again, sir!" Now there was something like respect in the legionary's voice.

"In my position, I have the right to a soldier who takes care of my personal affairs – erect my tent, keep my things neat, cook my food."

Bertius' face brightened. "Yes?"

Volkert knew he would regret this one day. Bertius could build a tent, yes, but he was messy and a miserable cook. Yet ...

"If you want this position, you can stay in the service." Bertius smiled gratefully at Volkert and nodded eagerly.

"It'll be great, Centurion! It'll be wonderful!" Volkert closed his eyes and feigned fatigue. Yes, he would regret it.

There was absolutely no doubt about that.

27

A summer morning, dry, a little too cold for the season, but it was a time he couldn't have chosen any better.

The sound distrust in von Klasewitz in regard to the Romans' naval abilities was almost as much a part of his habit as in his distrust of any other construction the British legions had prepared upon their planned crossing of the English Channel. He knew that the Romans had succeeded in carrying out a successful invasion to the island, and he also knew that the captains of those large-scale transport vessels knew the occasionally wild weather conditions of the canal. The sailor in him also recognized that the waves were low, the breeze at best a lukewarm and everyone radiated great confidence and serenity.

Comes Magnus Maximus, the future emperor of Rome, who was in full armor with a polished helmet, stood next to his officers and watched the loading from an ascent.

Von Klasewitz had to admit that the Romans were experts in handling their primitive equipment. The officers had a good grip on the whole process. The legionaries themselves were, as expected, disciplined and entered the landed transport galleys in long rows, setting sail directly afterwards in order to transfer the heavy ships to Gallia at a slow pace. Many of them had already made this crossing several times, some even in the worst of weather conditions.

They had avoided using one of the established ports. Instead, they had accepted an arduous work of loading and unloading. They didn't want to make it easy for the Emperor's spies. However, a certain redesign of the loading equipment had been necessary, and von Klasewitz had been able to add to that with his expertise.

The main concern of the nobleman was that his by now 36 bronze cannons, divided into three artillery companies, constituted not only the core of their insurrection army, but also posed special challenges in shipping. Three particularly large and sturdy transport galleys had been provided for the three companies, and the dismantled guns, the heavy tube first, were hoisted on board with the aid of pulleys. Von Klasewitz himself had designed the construction of the crane. If a pipe fell into the soft sand of the coast, worst of all under the water level, it would not be just a difficult job to get it out again, it would be exposed to corrosion much faster than the other guns. So the German was almost feverishly attentive with every piece, while the Roman soldiers put it on the ships.

And it all worked out perfectly.

The nobleman had to admit a few days ago that he had underestimated the Romans in some respects. Perhaps, he had come to the conclusion, they were not as primitive and underdeveloped in everything as he had assumed. Above all, he had had to realize that some of them were very eager and willing to learn – even from someone whose teaching method could best be described as raw.

Von Klasewitz, of course, had not resigned himself to praising his men for their energy and dedication. But the fact that he had every day less reason to scold and complain spoke in a certain way for itself. Likewise, the man had begun to delegate many tasks to subordinates without fear of failure. He still couldn't really suffer any of these people, and certainly none of the soldiers felt much sympathy for him. But on some level a mutual and professional approach to their work had developed, the existence of which the time-wanderer couldn't deny.

"It won't take another hour, then the loading is finished," Maximus said, as he joined the German. "The weather is quite favorable. We are also expecting emissaries of our Alanian allies. They have already eliminated any guards at our landing site, so there will be no early warning. We will form our troops before the military leaders of Gaul will know. And there will be only *limitanei* to oppose us, and they won't be too eager. With a little luck, we'll be able to convince their commanders to join us."

"Luck?" Klasewitz raised his eyebrows. Maximus grinned.

"Of course gold has already changed hands, and promises have been made in regard to promotions and better conditions of duty. It is always useful to help fortune a bit."

"How many Alanians will join us?"

Von Klasewitz had met the tribe. A troublesome folk, that was his first impression. A group of almost 100 chiefs, who were roughly equal to the rank of an officer, had been acquainted with the cannons and their way of operation. Their task was to prepare their own people at least theoretically for the new weapon and, if possible, to avoid panic when the three companies fired their first volley. The barbarians had been deeply impressed. The German didn't know whether the hours of teaching had been fruitful. In any case, they had made a positive contribution to the stability of their alliance with Maximus.

This fact had not escaped the Comes.

"We have been assured of 20,000 warriors," he answered the German's question. "We ourselves have 15,000 legionaries from Britain available. In Gaul, as I suppose, we will be joined by a another 15,000 border troops, perhaps more. Then we need a decisive victory, and the neighboring provinces will subsequently turn away from Gratian. But precisely because the time-wanderers are widely regarded as wizards in military matters, many will wait until such a preliminary decision emerges. And your cannons play the central role in this matter."

"I'll do anything not to disappoint you."

"I expect nothing less."

Maximus smiled knowingly and turned away as an officer approached him. Von Klasewitz didn't know how to interpret the last remark of the Comes. Was that a proof of confidence in the abilities of the traitor? Or a clue to von Klasewitz' dependence on the Comes, especially in regard to the consequences the deserter would have to suffer if their plans failed and the opposite side won the day?

Von Klasewitz hoped for the first explanation to be valid, but he had the indeterminate feeling that the second would probably get closer to the truth.

"Everything is on board!" The Roman legionary, who had been given to von Klasewitz as his official factotum, pointed to one of the great ships.

The German nodded. It was the last of the three, which had been especially prepared for the cannons, and it was only waiting for him. The time for departure had come. He gave himself a jerk, followed the legionary down the hill toward the ship. A long walk made from wooden planks led him, though somewhat wobbly, directly to the ship, on the aftdeck on which a bearded man stood, "captain" invisibly tattooed on his forehead. As von Klasewitz navigated the slightly slippery deck, he looked over the railing at the sea, and he felt what he had missed in the last weeks and months. His sea legs came back again, and quite instinctively, he adjusted himself to the hardly palpable movements of the ship's hull. A movement went through the ship as the soldiers took his arrival as the right time to push the galley away from the shore. The waves grew stronger, but von Klasewitz had no problems to keep up.

"How long?" he asked the Captain, who evidently left the routine to his *gubernator*.

"In this weather? Two hours, no longer. The men are rested, we will have a good time. If there are no winds that blow us off, it will be two hours."

Von Klasewitz nodded. Then he walked along the long deck of the ship to the bow. He stared through the clear air at the distant shore of Gaul, which appeared indistinctly in the mist. Inspecting, he held his nose in the air, tasted the salty breeze, then smiled.

Two hours he was looking forward to.

Orders arose. Rudders were extended and lowered into the water. The tact was played.

With a gentle groan, the galley seriously engaged the waves.

The finality of their endeavor was now clear to everyone. Von Klasewitz also knew that they were now condemned to success.

Another thing he could look forward to.

28

"You are and will always be the most beautiful of all!"

Diderius had to exert himself a little to say these words, for the recipient of his praise might enjoy many advantages, but beauty was surely none of them. Flavia was more broad than high, her skin covered with all sorts of pimples and warts, and her coarse fleshy hands bore witness to the work with which she earned her meagre income. Her dark brown hair touched her sweaty face in an untidy manner, and her lips showed a relaxed and happy smile, as Diderius, his imagination fixed on a well-known whore, had done his utmost to satisfy Flavia's carnal needs.

Her smile showed that he had been very successful. He forced himself to lay a hand on a wobbly breast of hers and managed to deepen the smile on her face.

Surely, it was a happy coincidence that Flavia, in addition to beauty, lacked other qualities as well. Thus, she was, according to the conviction of the Diderius, devoid of all intelligence, of an almost impossible simplicity, and possessed the emotional depth of a dog. That was the reason why he had managed to sneak into the heart of the cook, had aroused her passion with simple, even clumsy compliments. Moreover, Diderius had received a certain budget for his work. Even after he had spent half the sum of money on himself, he still had enough to buy cheap goods for his "sweetheart," who without hesitation always reacted to them with bright enchantment, and the trinkets only seemed to deepen her passion for Diderius. That wasn't surprising. Flavia's most precious possession was, as her lover could tell, a large, well-cut butcher's knife, which, as he found, fit well with the woman. Diderius' attention had therefore to appear to her as gifts from the gods.

A few days passed, almost two weeks, since he had secured his position as Flavia's official companion and lover, but now he stood every day in the early evening beside the back of the large canteen in the German's village, a place responsible for feeding not only of the numerous employees of the administration and of the medical school, but also the crew of the iron ship. Here, simple Flavia had an important part to play, for despite all the limitations of her mental faculties she was an excellent cook and, in the last few months, had been promoted to manager of one of the shifts that provided the food almost round the clock. In the evening, smelling from kitchen waste, with a bright smile on her lips, she went into the widely spread arms of the young, handsome man, who for some reason was enraptured by her. Diderius had in the meantime taken a steady position, which enabled him to survive this powerful expression of affection without immediately losing his balance.

The evening usually ended in an inexpensive tavern, where Diderius invited Flavia to dinner, a walk across the market, where he bought her trinkets for little money, which she immediately described as "eternal recollection of our immortal love" until additional memorabilia were presented the following day, and this was the most difficult part, in the bed of the small dwelling that Diderius had hired in a tenement house, and which consciously showed modest prosperity without appearing to be pretentious. Every now and then Diderius flashed the denarii, which he kept hidden in a chest to impress Flavia. The lover was not sure if Flavia's passion for him had anything to do with the fact that he was the first man in her life who seemed to be willing to lie with a woman like her at all and, with the outlook on marriage, would raise her standard of living. Probably it was something of both, but above all the fact that Diderius showed any attention to poor Flavia, and since then had, as far as possible, delighted her with pleasures previously being completely unknown to her.

There were, indeed, the occasional short moments in which he felt almost sorry for her. The thought of the gold and a comfortable position in the administration of a province of his choice, which had both been promised to him, made such sentiments disappear very quickly. Even from sex with Flavia, surely a physical as well as a psychic act of willpower, he got a break, as he kept himself free for one evening a week, not only to forfeit the advances of the cook, but also to visit a woman, a whore of his greatest confidence, whose body and abilities calmed his nerves.

Furthermore, the long awaited messenger had arrived. The instructions given to Diderius had been clear: Wait for the messenger, or hear how far the uprising has already approached Ravenna, and react accordingly. Diderius was delighted that he was considered intelligent and farsighted enough to make this decision independently. He had safeguarded the two bags with the greenish-brown powder which had been given to him like his eyeballs, locked in a small chest, which Flavia had never seen during her visits.

The messenger had come. He had set off on the same day from Britain Magnus Maximus had started the trip across the canal. This had been four weeks ago, when the messenger, almost always on horseback and on river ships, had traveled to Ravenna to tell Diderius that it was time to make contact with another spy. He sat in the city's military administration, and was to pass on to Diderius any information about the progress of the insurrection so that he could judge when it was appropriate to enter the decisive phase of his plan which would make him a rich man and provide a comfortable life.

Everything else, to be honest, didn't matter to him.

The message also meant that his relationship with Flavia, carefully maintained and kept alive under considerable personal sacrifices, had to undergo its first real test.

"You know, my darling," he said lightly, caressing the soft mass of her voluminous belly, "your work is fascinating. You are responsible for the physical well-being of so many people – and so important people! So close to technical wonders that none of us really understands. It must be very exciting!"

Flavia's face reddened. She was embarrassed by his attention and praise. "But Didi!" He hated it when she called him Didi. "Didi, believe me, I'm just a simple cook!"

"A shift manager with considerable responsibility. Do you think the time-wanderers would really allow anyone in their vicinity? The

172

crew of the *Saravica* is fed by you! You strengthen the empire's backbone through your work!"

"Oh Didi!" she whispered, and at once fell silent, visibly ashamed. "No one has ever said that to me."

"Then it was due time," Diderius asserted, and began to gently massage the region below the abdomen. "You're not a Roman woman sitting at home and leaving all responsibility to the men. You are a strong woman who makes her contribution in a responsible position!"

"Oh Didi!" This time it sounded more like a sigh, which certainly had to do with the massage he had started to perform.

"They trust you, Flavia," Diderius whispered. "This is quite understandable, you are a very trustworthy person!"

Trustingly describes it better, he thought to himself, but was glad that Flavia turned red again. It worked!

"You even have the keys to the kitchen, don't you? Not everyone would be given the keys. The keys are important!"

The keys were indeed important. Flavia directed the late shift, timed from the early afternoon to the evening hours. In this position, she was obliged to make sure that the kitchen complex was properly closed in the evening. Diderius had assumed that she dropped the keys afterwards. It could also be that someone from the security team was responsible for the final check. It was time to find out more about that. The time-wanderers had introduced quite complicated mechanical locks. They were chunky, but far safer than anything the Romans had used so far. And very difficult to open.

"The keys I keep where you are as well, my dear Didi!" Flavia whispered, smiling. "I'm carrying them in a bag around my neck, close to my heart!"

Diderius made a delighted face, and this time he didn't even have to pretend while he was exerting soft pressure between Flavia's legs. The cook rolled her eyes and groaned, while her lover's gaze wandered over to the clothes, which lay carelessly on a stool. There, half-hidden by the patchy tunic, lay a small leather bag with a rolled collar. He had about the right size for one of the big, iron keys.

While Diderius continued his massage with automatic movements, and the massive woman was thus increasingly agitated, the next

173

step of his plan was formed in his head. He wondered how he would be able to remove Flavia from his calculation. To kill her would cause unnecessary suspicion, especially if the military threat of the insurgents approached. He had to make her disappear just before his intervention so that it didn't seem to be too suspicious – or even better: to manage it in such a way that she didn't realize what was happening with her key, would never miss, it and therefore exactly radiate the innocence, which would surely reflect on himself.

Flavia was trembling. "Didi, oh Didi. Don't stop!"

Diderius had no intention. He was ready for the climax.

29

When they arrived in Adulis, dusk fell. In spite of the arrival of the Negusa Nagast, there was a strange calm in the port city, as if everyone was straining to see what would happen. Officially, this was merely a visit by the Emperor to his estate, in order to be informed about the latest developments. The fact that the Roman ambassadors were laid in chains and tightened to their donkeys was only noticed by the observers who knew exactly who these men actually were.

Berhan saw it with satisfaction. For him, the fact that the Negusa came to him with the captured Romans was an indication that he considered them to be those responsible for the assassination. It was heard that Ouazebas, the heir to the throne, was bound to his bed with severe poisoning, and no one was sure whether he would ever recover.

When all this was over, Berhan assumed that he would have to speak with his poison experts about the dosage for future action. Ouazebas, a strong man in the flower of his life, did evidently need a higher quantity than expected. These were the small problems that could sometimes have big consequences. Nevertheless, the hope remained that the attack would still be successful.

Berhan himself stood before the gate of his residence as the Emperor's entourage arrived. The men were already carrying torches, and lamps had been lit. The Negusa Nagast, apparently driven by a proper rage about the cowardly assassination organized by the Romans, had only a relatively small group with him, not even fifty servants, and only about two hundred men of his bodyguard were accompanying him as well. Berhan had hurriedly provided the necessary quarters. Of course, the

Emperor had his own residence in Adulis, but it was only appropriate to give the old man every possible care and reverence.

Two servants helped the Emperor from his mule. In spite of his age, Mehadeyis preferred to forego wagons or litters. He came with a groan on his feet and looked around, until he saw Berhan. A friendly smile of welcome on his lips, the Governor hurried to bend his knee before his master.

"Arise, my dear Berhan," the Emperor said, with good will in his voice. "It is well."

The Governor did as he was told, and waved invitingly toward his residency.

"I've prepared everything for your reception. Refreshments are available. Rooms for you and all your men are at your disposal. No matter what desire you have, I want to meet it. Rely on me and my people!"

"Too kind, my dear Berhan, too kind. I'm making too much fuzz, my old friend. The visit came quite unexpectedly, I know. I won't be a burden for you too long. But there are certain things which are to be discussed, and which I'd like to tackle in person."

Berhan made a well-studied, worried face.

"I've heard the terrible news. I am dismayed, horrified. I myself ought to have done something against the Romans once their blood trail began in my town. But I have acted in good faith and didn't think that this official delegation had been sent to attempt an assassination. And now this! I am surely to blame for this disaster! May the Lord strengthen Ouazebas and give him the ability to survive this mean attack. I pray for him every day."

Mehadeyis nodded measuredly. "Your sympathy comforts me, my friend. Really, I appreciate it very much. And let's not talk about you being responsible. That's not true at all."

Berhan smiled and bowed deeply. Then he personally led the Emperor into the brightly illuminated audience hall, where his servants had prepared everything for a feast. He watched with pleasure how the soldiers rushed the struggling Romans, saw them stumbling and dropping to the ground, and smitten with evil curses.

The men looked torn and unkempt. They had certainly suffered greatly since the attack.

Berhan found that this was a good starting point for him. This could only go well for him.

"Do we want to deal with this waste during the meal?" he asked the Emperor, as the soldiers pushed the prisoners into the main hall. Mehadeyis looked worried.

"I'll have it done quickly, my friend, as soon as possible. I'm sorry for charging you and your house with this spectacle, but some things cannot be tolerated even by an old man like me."

"Of course, of course."

As expected, the Emperor sat on the elevated seat, which was normally reserved for Berhan. The Governor didn't show the slightest annoyance. Like an obedient underling, he took his place at the table, while the prisoners were ordered to stand on the wall by soldiers, who were beating them freely.

Mehadeyis made movement with his hand toward the miserably downtrodden delinquents. "Berhan, you spoke to them. What did they say?"

"Oh, they've obviously lied to me, and I've been tricked. I'm very embarrassed. They seemed to me like a trade delegation, who wanted to present certain offers to you. They carried all sorts of goods with them, but above all was their desire to go to your court."

"You have prepared mine and Ouazebas' gifts!"

Berhan looked sad. "Here the treason of my hospitality is so painful that it almost threatens to tear me apart. O Lord, I myself have chosen for them the right items for the taste of influential personalities at court, paid out of my own pocket to promote the good relations between Rome and the Empire. And these traitors have shamefully exploited my willingness to help by infesting these presents with poison, if I have understood correctly."

"Apparently, yes. And before that they killed their own ambassador?"

"It seems so, yes. My men are still investigating this issue; we have not yet concluded our efforts. Of course they denied everything. I also don't understand the possible motive. On the other hand ..."

"You have a guess?" Mehadeyis' gaze rested pleasingly on the man, and he felt encouraged to continue.

"Well, in the light of the latest developments, it seems as if the victim had perhaps learned about the sinister assassination plans and expressed his profound opposition. This in turn leads to the assumption that Rome itself is not at all aware of this plan, but that it has to do with the intentions of the time-wanderers, who seem to be very dishonest. I hear that even in Rome the arrival of strangers has not met with approval everywhere."

The Emperor nodded thoughtfully. "There's something to be said for your argument, Berhan. You have obviously given the issue some thought."

Berhan bowed, not least in order to hide his triumphant smile. "I'll serve wherever I can!"

Mehadeyis sank for a few moments into a deep and brooding silence. Quietly and efficiently, the servants prepared the dishes for the high guests. But until the Emperor would commence the meal, no one would touch any of the delicacies offered.

The old man raised his head and looked at Berhan.

His face was now hard and repulsive. The Governor was sure that Mehadeyis would probably order the torture of the prisoners before their eyes. It was obvious that the Emperor was most annoyed about the attack on his heir.

"Berhan."

"Your Majesty?"

"You must consider me very stupid."

"I don't understand ..."

Mehadeyis rose. He gave his soldiers a sign. These brought out the knives and cut through the fetters of the prisoners with fast, safe movements.

Berhan looked from the Emperor to the soldiers and back. He didn't grasp what was happening here.

One of the guards now stepped forward, he had hitherto been hidden in the shadows. He put down his helmet.

Berhan made a sound, involuntarily, like a wounded animal. Ouaze-

178

bas stood there, in all health, a little tired perhaps, but obviously not struggling with death.

The governor of Adulis rose tumbling. He didn't say a word. Now he realized that he was the victim of a charade. "I ... Your Majesty ..."

"You're really glad that I'm still alive, Berhan?" Ouazebas asked with a dangerous smile. He waved toward the time-wanderers, the Romans. Africanus and the physician Neumann stood next to the heir. The massive, older man, Köhler, joined them. Suddenly, they no longer looked so torn, exhausted and tormented.

"Of course ... I just don't understand ..."

"Ah, is that so? No problem. My friend here can explain everything." Ouazebas waved to the group of servants. A man detached himself and put his hood back. His face was motionless, without feeling, and Berhan knew it only too well.

Haleb. A traitor.

He responded quickly. Now that everything had collapsed, it was necessary to taste a last triumph before he looked forward to certain death. Berhan was not an old man, and he was a good fighter. As a man of high rank, he was allowed to carry a weapon in the presence of the Emperor, but he made no attempt to draw the sword. The soldiers would have been in between them before he could have done the first move.

A small dagger lay in his hand. A fast, dangerous and purposeful weapon, if guided by an expert.

Ouazebas shouted a warning. The prince was too far away. Soldiers pulled their weapons. Too late, too much distance.

Berhan whirled around, the tip of the dagger between the thumb and the forefinger, directed at the old emperor, who stared rigidly confronting his certain death. With a flowing, almost elegant movement, the Governor swung the dagger back, ready to throw.

Then a bang, crackling, loud.

An invisible fist hit Berhan, throwing him out of balance and forcing him to the ground. The dagger slipped away. He looked down at himself and saw blood that spilled from his chest. Then the pain. Then nothing more.

Köhler lowered his hand with the pistol.

For a moment, everyone stared at the Governor's corpse. Everything had happened so quickly, and especially for Berhan's servants the turn of events had been startling. The Emperor's soldiers were keeping an eye on the armed men. But the Lord of Adulis was dead. None of his followers even made any faint move to do anything foolish. It was even possible that on many a face a little relief appeared.

Neumann patted Köhler approvingly on the shoulder. He still held the pistol steadily in his hand, kept looking at the corpse.

Ouazebas and Mehadeyis turned to the shooter, their eyes full of respect, fear and curiosity in regard to the little handgun. Köhler did nothing to hide the weapon.

The Emperor broke the silence by sitting down and pointing to the corpse of his enemy. "Take that away!" he ordered.

Servants hurried to obey the order.

Then he looked at Neumann and at Köhler, who saved his life. And the Doctor, whom he thought was the speaker of the group.

"Coffee, yes, time-wanderer?"

Neumann smiled and bowed his head.

The old Emperor grinned and scratched his hair. "You've convinced me. I shall be soft in my old days."

Neumann said nothing.

The Emperor might describe himself in any way he liked. His own impression, however, was quite different.

30

Rheinberg wasn't present, and that wasn't good. He had announced his arrival for the day, coming directly from another exhausting inspection of the troops stationed in the vicinity of the city. He wanted to go directly to the Emperor, directly into the meeting, but so far he hadn't yet appeared, and although the discussion had begun, the group's unrest was clearly felt.

Klaus von Geeren sat in the circle of high officers under the Emperor's chairmanship and felt a little lost. He had immediately, once it became known that Maximus had initiated his first move, sent a messenger to Rheinberg, already suspecting that the newly minted Supreme Commander had long since received the news. But he had to do something now, even if it would only turn out to be a gesture.

The Generals Arbogast, Malobaudes and Richomer, the latter recently promoted to that rank, were sitting around the large table with some other officers. The current version of the Roman imperial map was hung up in a wooden frame, improved by German material, for the first time at least approximately true to scale and with correct distances between the marked places.

A duplicate of the map, freshly delivered from the halls of the draftsmen, lay spread before them on the table. Since no one wanted to say anything, they all pretended to study it intensively. Particular attention was given to the troops of Maximus, marked by small red pieces of wood, on the west coast of Gaul, where they were at least suspected to operate. They had, without doubt, landed in the same province, in which Treveri was situated, but still remained close to the water.

The *cursus publicus* worked well, especially the faster part of the system, the *cursus velox*, and especially well in transmitting bad news. The messengers, sent by the competent authorities in Gaul, had been on fast horses and moving without breaks. It still had taken quite a few days for the first warning to arrive in Treveri. They had no knowledge of what had happened since then. Almost every day messages were received, but all confirmed what they were expecting: Magnus Maximus had been in contact with Alanian allies, who had given him a large number of additional warriors, and it was already clear that some of the smaller garrisons of the *limitanei*, probably encouraged by threats as well as bribery, had joined the usurper in his uprising.

It was reassuring for von Geeren that none of the news so far showed that von Klasewitz had been able to add any of his special weapons to the attacking force. On the other hand, no one had ever thought of approaching Maximus' men in battle to find out. The military authorities of Gaul, so far as they had not immediately surrendered to the Comes, held back because they didn't have the manpower to intervene. This manpower was with the Emperor and his field army, in addition to what von Geeren might scratch together from his company of German infantry. At that moment, the preparations were made to depart with the legions to the north and confront Maximus. The provision of all the troops and the return of Rheinberg to Trier would coincide. They had until then to develop a plan how they would oppose Maximus.

And there was apparently no agreement about this.

Gratian rose and walked quietly to the narrow, high arched windows, from which he had a good view of the city. There was great activity, for the equipment of the legions had to be provided. Some people would make good business. It was always like that.

"We mustn't hesitate," the young Emperor finally said, trying to give his voice the necessary strength. "We can't wait and we can't waste time with unnecessary tactical maneuvers. We mustn't appear to be weak. If we hesitate too long, others will turn over to the side of Maximus."

He faced to his officers, more determined than ever.

"We have to make a quick and unambiguous decision in our favor. We can't allow ourselves to enter into an endless campaign with a multitude of battles and thus also devastation. None of us, Maximus or I, have great reserves. The armies of the East, after the invasion of the Goths, remain only a shadow of their own. I have the legions of the West, and I have only one chance. If the defeat of Valens before Adrianople taught me something, then that I shouldn't throw away my troops. But at the same time, too much caution will cost us victory. The dynamics of the current development are on Maximus' side. We have to take this up, and as soon as possible. Then we will have the momentum and we will end this civil war as quickly and as painlessly as possible."

Gratian looked around. No one seemed to want to contradict him until Richomer raised his hand. The Emperor nodded toward him and sat down again.

"Augustus ... I had the unfortunate task of leading your vanguard to Valens, and of witnessing how the whole of the East's army was going down."

"I know."

"I really want to push the preparations as thoroughly as possible. You are certainly right, that the army of the East is only reforming slowly. But if we act defensively, and gather at least those troops that we have in Thessaloniki, we would increase our chances of victory. Since Thessaloniki, these soldiers have known the way in which the weapons of the time-wanderers work. They will not be intimidated by the German legionaries, and even if the insurgents have guns, they won't react like panicky chickens. We can make good use of this hard core of experienced men, as they keep their nerves, and they are very loyal to the time-wanderers, and especially to Rheinberg. I therefore suggest that we move the Western troops to the East, that the units from Thessaloniki meet us halfway, and then we will seek that decisive battle of yours."

Gratian had listened to Richomer's speech with an expressionless face. It was, however, to be noted that everything in him felt contrary to the General's suggestion. Nevertheless, he dispensed of any immediate comment.

"I agree with Richomer," Malobaudes said. "We shouldn't jump to conclusions too fast. Whether we're going to march or not, the only thing we'll risk is that Gallic troops will join Maximus. This will increase his strength only insignificantly. Ultimately, if we follow Richomer's suggestion, we will be able to gain loyal reinforcements in the East, which will ultimately benefit us much better than a few *limitanei.*"

Richomer nodded approvingly.

Arbogast, on the other hand, as the only general who had hitherto expressed no opinion, seemed unconvinced. "I'm more inclined to follow the Emperor's suggestion in this," he said at last. No one would think of him as a toady, for he had already vehemently objected to Gratian on another occasion, and was regarded as respectful, but also as someone who had his own head. "We increase Maximus' strength, indeed. And that is not all. We have reports according to which priests in various cities have spoken openly in favor of the usurper. They spread rumors that the Emperor had come under the ominous influence of witchcraft, caused by the time-wanderers, and is no longer the master of his senses. Those people are being reviled. If Maximus advances, and we don't contain him quickly and decisively, the words of the rebels will fall on fertile ground. When the people turn against Gratian in massive scale, we have a serious problem that can't be solved militarily."

Richomer uttered a curse and hit the table with his fist. "We owe this to Ambrosius and his fellows!"

Gratian raised a hand. "We don't want to draw premature conclusions. The Bishop has not explained himself. There are indications of his involvement, but there is no conclusive evidence. I know what this Goth has claimed, and I must consider it. But he is the one who has kidnapped my uncle and surrendered him to Maximus. I'm not sure if he's to be trusted. Ambrosius is nowhere close to the Comes in sight; he resides in Milan, and is concerned with affairs of the Church."

Richomer shook his head. "My Augustus, your Majesty, I'm quite aware that Ambrosius is an important and influential personality, but that is why he is so dangerous. He has made unmistakably clear how he thinks about our alliance with the time-wanderers, and we should take that seriously. Maximus is known as a faithful man, even a fanatical Trinitarian; he has always belonged to Ambrosius' camp. They know each other well. The fact that the priests now hold rebellious speeches and make accusations fits too well into a picture of a carefully prepared insurrection, it can't be a mere coincidence."

"That's true!"

All heads turned to the door. An exhausted, dust-covered Rheinberg entered the room, put helmet and coat aside aside, and stepped toward the table. Gratian just nodded at him. Rheinberg smiled at the visibly relieved von Geeren, then he leaned his fists on the table without sitting down. He looked into the round. "I guess you all have already discussed the right strategy for a counterattack."

"We are at odds. Richomer and Malobaudes favor a defensive strategy to gain time and strengthen our legions, Arbogast and I are for determined and immediate action," the young ruler summarized.

"You are the Emperor," Arbogast reminded Gratian with a slightly blunt tone.

"The Emperor would like to hear the opinion of the Magister Militium," Gratian replied, looking at Rheinberg.

"My opinion is clear: We must attack, and as soon as possible." He looked at Richomer and Malobaudes.

The younger man, freshly promoted, shook his head gently, but seemed to agree that the mood had shifted away from his proposal. Malobaudes, however, wasn't beaten yet. "With all due respect, Magister ... But you have not led a Roman legion into battle. You know little about our tactics. Your strength may be the superior power of your weapons, and I'm the last one to deny their advantages. But we're talking about a regular, traditional campaign, with proven strategic rules our ancestors ..."

"But the problem is that it's actually no longer a traditional campaign," Rheinberg interrupted him impatiently. "What the ancestors have taught is only of limited value. Maximus obviously understood this quickly and took the right measures by assuring himself of the services of the mutineers."

"We don't know that for sure," Malobaudes said. "Reports ..."

"Are full of holes and ambiguity. But we know with certainty that von Klasewitz is with the insurgents. I know him well. With all his faults, he is an excellent artillery officer with great expertise in his field. He will have given this special knowledge to Maximus, probably in exchange for the promise to return at least to the command of the *Saravica*. He can build cannons. That he knows. He has the necessary resources and materials. He surely has been cooperative. And if I were Maximus, I would have hid my weapons as good as I could, before I put them into action on my first battle – to accomplish that his enemies will underestimate him and his military power."

If Malobaudes was angry at the silent reproach contained in Rheinberg's words, he didn't show it. In fact, he seemed to be carefully considering this argument. After doing that, he finally sighed and laid the palms of hands on the table in a gesture of capitulation.

"Then it is decided," Gratian explained, and he obviously felt satisfied.

"When can we leave?" he asked Rheinberg.

"I'm not quite up to date. Klaus?"

Von Geeren had expected this question. "We have an army of 24,000 men at our disposal, the core of the field army. In addition, there are 200 German infantrymen with full equipment. On our planned approach to the north, we plan to collect a further 15,000 *limitanei*, so that we will end up with almost 40,000 men. The main force is ready to leave."

"I'll lead the legions myself," Gratian decided. "This is about me and my claim to the purple. I must defend it." He looked around. "You all will accompany me, except for Richomer. He remains in Treveri and sees how he can organize additional troops from the east. I would like to avoid the mistake of my uncle, and therefore have an emergency plan, if Maximus should be victorious. Richomer will rebuild a line of defense toward the direction of Ravenna; I will give him all necessary authority. We will try to get the enemies within reach of the *Saravica's* guns where they will be hit hard. Their cannons will have to fight an uphill battle."

Rheinberg bowed his head. He didn't believe in this duel. On the one hand, everything that von Klasewitz was able to produce was totally inferior to the modern guns of the cruiser. On the other hand,

Maximus would never allow himself to even get near the *Saarbrücken* without preparation. He had learned from Thessaloniki what effect the ship's cannons could have. He wouldn't take the risk, neither personally nor for his troops.

But he left Gratian this illusion. If they couldn't stop the advance of Maximus, he was certain that the *Saarbrücken* had only one remaining function: to enable them to run away.

While the generals began to debate anew about strategic and tactical details, the eyes of Rheinberg and von Geeren met. The Captain nodded to the Captain. It was clear that they had similar concerns.

Rheinberg tiredly closed his eyes.

31

Noricum had changed, Volkert thought. When the troops returned, the messengers had long since left the Legion's camp with the latest insights on the advance of the Huns to rush to Treveri. At the same time, messengers from the capital had arrived to confer what Volkert had secretly feared: The uprising Rheinberg had attempted to prevent had started anyway.

Volkert hadn't yet fully recovered, although he made good progress. He therefore observed the preparations for the immediate departure of men, who had just mastered the arduous return. Almost the entire legion had been ordered to Ravenna to serve as the core of a second defensive line, strengthened by units from the east. Volkert found the preparations equally disturbing and soothing, for on the one hand they showed that Rheinberg wasn't afraid to consider his total failure as a commander, and on the other, they showed foresight and a rational risk assessment.

In his new rank as a centurion, he hadn't simply been given additional responsibilities. As a confidant of Sedacius, he was increasingly involved in an inner circle of a conspiratorial group, who was to help the Tribune to become emperor. Although Volkert was aware that his fate was closely connected with that of this hidden, second usurper, he had strong doubts about his plan. He came from a time when the Emperor's violent overthrow would have been a completely inconceivable step, aside from the abstruse plans of some anarchists and communists. He had been a naval officer for the opportunity to fight with the elite of the Reich. Not being of noble birth, he had not had it easy, but in the end it was clear to him that his induction into the ranks of the fleet was a distinction of a special kind. Now to be involved in something which would lead to the fall of an emperor, filled him with deeply ambivalent feelings.

His conspirators didn't have these doubts. In current times, the violent overthrow of the current emperor "out of the barracks" was an absolutely normal and usual process. Since that time when Maximinus Thrax, the first soldier-emperor, had opened the way for this kind of political career planning, every military careerist was distrusted by reigning emperors. Men like Sedacius had to hide their ambitions carefully, because otherwise they would very quickly be the victim of countermeasures.

Countermeasures, which, as Volkert knew, would be initiated not least by Rheinberg as Gratian's supreme commander. If he did not want to do one thing, then it was fighting against his German compatriots. It was fortunate that Sedacius also tried to avoid this. The use of the infantry in the battle against the Hunnish camp had clearly shown him the military potential of only a handful of these men.

The Germans, so his conclusion, had to fight on his side.

The Tribune probably didn't know how to achieve this. In any case, Volkert didn't propose any promising strategy either. He stood in the courtyard of the fortress and watched as the soldiers were driven to prepare for their imminent departure. Volkert and a group of about 50 other injured comrades would follow as soon as they were fully operational again. They remained until further notice with a skeleton troop in the fort.

Among those who would leave for Treveri were the German infantrymen. The soldiers piled up their belongings. They were also not overly pleased to be faced with an additional military confrontation and its highly uncertain outcome.

Volkert was lost in thoughts. It was not until the man was almost standing in front of him that he came to recognize his presence. In the last few weeks, he had almost forgotten his stupid faux pas after his injury had been treated, but the sudden presence of the young man brought the memory back with force. He involuntarily straightened himself and strained his muscles, as if to defend himself against someone.

Private 1st Class Feldmann, on whom the hardships of the past weeks were still clearly visible, looked tired. He had saved many lives through his tireless commitment beyond his limits – and still had to concede defeat for just as many he couldn't help anymore. This was evidently his first experience in combat, and although he had kept himself upright with exemplary discipline, it was clearly visible how suffering and pain had afflicted him. Volkert saw that the man departing from here would be different from the one who had arrived – more quiet, more self-conscious, thoughtful. For the physicians of the legion, so far as the men could be described with this designation at all, Feldmann had become something of an idol, although he was much younger than most of them. Neumann's medical school had not yet been able to provide enough training for medical professionals in such a short period that the effect would have been felt throughout the Empire. That would take years. Feldmann's equipment and his understanding of the treatment of wounds, his efforts to keep clean, wherever possible, all of this was partly observed critically, partly respected. However, once a few wounded, who would otherwise have been relieved from their suffering as hopeless cases, were recovering – not least a certain decurion with a sword in his chest – the critics had gradually fallen silent. The more intelligent among the so-called physicians had come to the conclusion that it was possible to learn something here. And since then, they had not left Feldmann out of their eyes and assisted him wherever they could.

The time was now over. The medic would leave with the infantry-men and be integrated back into the company, as long as this unit would continue to exist.

Volkert looked expectantly at the man. If he wanted to say something, he wouldn't encourage him unnecessarily.

Feldmann cleared his throat. "You ... you are better?" he asked in Greek.

"Thanks for your help, yes," Volkert replied. "Otherwise, I probably wouldn't have made it."

Feldmann nodded. Volkert's gratitude had obviously not been registered by him. The question was only the prelude to the real issue.

"You speak German," he said suddenly, in German. He could

190

not bring Volkert out of balance if that was his intention. He had expected something like that.

He nodded measuredly. "I speak German."

"How come?"

Volkert looked at Feldmann's eyes. The young man had indeed been a witness to the events of the recent past, but perhaps he didn't have paid too much attention to the details of some of those occurrences. The mutiny had surely surpassed the desertion of an ensign who fell in love. However, it was just this kind of story which gave wonderful occasion for endless gossip.

"What do you think?" Volkert asked.

Feldmann looked down. "Are you one of the mutineers?"

Volkert had not yet gotten that idea. But perhaps it was only the officers who had escaped with von Klasewitz. And the infantrymen were ultimately still passengers, at least for many of the sailors. They wouldn't have told them everything. "No I'm not. I have nothing to do with the mutiny. Von Klasewitz is an asshole."

Feldmann nodded. "Then you are the enamored ensign." He had heard of it.

Volkert was struggling to make a statement. He tried to remain composed, appropriate to his status as centurion and Roman veteran. So he just nodded, gave the man a moment, then asked, "What are you going to do about it?"

Feldmann didn't have to think long. "I haven't told anyone yet."

"Why not?"

He pointed to Volkert's injury. "You're not a normal deserter. I've heard what you've done. You are not a coward."

"I hope not."

"You have fled because of the girl."

At the thought of Julia, a sudden stab passed through Volkert's heart. He pressed his lips on each other and nodded.

"You will be able to return one day," Feldmann said. "You are not like the former First Officer. They will pardon you."

"That doesn't solve my problem."

The medic grinned. "Another promotion, and you're a good match for a senator's daughter."

Volkert relaxed. It became clear that the young man didn't want to do him any harm.

And he realized that the man's utterance wasn't stupid at all! As a centurion, he was already a highly respected member of the military hierarchy and would be considered promising indeed, not least because of his youth. The old ban not to marry during the time of duty had long since ceased to be meaningful. Legionaries, which had been stationed for a long time in a place, had long-lasting relationships and families. For a senatorial family, a centurion was perhaps still somewhat below the social level that was acceptable; on the other hand, the gap has diminished considerably now, he was of rank and status, and a wedding would be much more easy, and another promotion would indeed bring him quite close to the status of a Roman noble.

"What are you going to do?" Volkert asked.

"I will keep it to myself."

"And then?"

"I will keep my ears open, and if it turns out that Captain Rheinberg is ready to pardon you, I will try to inform you."

Volkert looked at Feldmann in surprise. But there was no deception in the eyes of the young medic. He looked openly and honestly at Volkert. He seemed to be serious. "I ... do not know ..."

Feldmann shrugged. "You fought well and are a respected Roman officer. It may not be my business, but that's what I've witnessed, so I've decided to act accordingly. I have to live here for the rest of my days. At some point, the German units will be fully integrated into the Roman forces. We are already citizens of the Empire." He looked at Volkert grinning. "It cannot hurt to know someone in higher places who owes me something."

Volkert replied the grin. He understood this language only too well. With all the sympathy Feldmann had shown, a considerable measure of slyness was connected to it. Feldmann would be good friends with Centurion Secundus.

They chatted a little more, then the paramedic took his leave and devoted himself to his preparations. Volkert was about to turn away when he heard a raspy throat behind him. He turned and saw legionary Bertius. The man wore, with dignity, a wooden arm, masterly created by a craftsman of the fortress, with an extended, carefully carved hand at the end. So far, he had done quite well as his personal orderly, at least better than Volkert had expected. And the gratitude for this opportunity to remain in the service was apparent and persistent. It was indeed questionable what would have become of him, had he been dismissed.

"Yes, Bertius? What can I do for you?"

"That reminds me of what I wanted to ask you during my time at field hospital, but I have always slipped away into slumber before I could."

Volkert raised the eyebrows. "What would that be?"

"Well ..." Bertius cleared his throat again, then his gaze fell on the group of German infantrymen, who finished loading of their equipment. The legionary too had a very positive remembrance in regard to the medic. "How is it, o Centurion, that you speak the language of the time-wanderers?"

Volkert stared at Bertius in silence. Naturally. He should have thought of that.

Before he could open his mouth to an answer – or rather a bad excuse –, Bertius raised his healthy hand defensively. "No, I'm not really interested. I'm glad to be at your service, Centurion. You have a great career before you. It is good to serve someone who is destined for higher positions."

And so he turned away.

The legionary had simply understood what Feldmann had instinctively recognized. In these times, the only thing one could rely on was the relationship with other people.

And as long as you could be part of a good one, you didn't ask too many questions.

32

"I thank you for this proof of confidence."

Magnus Maximus held out his hand to the old centurion. The man had to be just before the end of his time of service, a strong soldier with gray hair, slightly bent forward. Although he had obviously polished his breastplate for hours, it looked repulsive and stained. Some years ago, the man's career had abruptly fallen into a dead end, either because he was not sufficiently politically linked, or simply because he was not capable of a higher command. From then on, he had been faithful to his service, despite all adversities. He looked like an honest man, a veteran of endless skirmishes with barbarian tribes, one who had witnessed many small victories and defeats. Von Klasewitz suspected that he had won the trust of his men, who shared the same resume and who had grown old with him.

The centurion wanted to bow, but Magnus put a hand on his shoulder.

"No bows, my friend. You have taken a great step, which will lead us all to further greatness. I am the one who respects you, because we could have faced each other as enemies. You chose Rome. It's not about me. Rome is at stake. And my respect is yours, Centurion. Return, in the neighboring tent wine and a meal has been prepared for you and your officers. Enjoy. I will join you at once."

The centurion smiled delightedly. He had obviously expected another treatment, more distant, a cool gratitude. But that was not the way of Maximus, as von Klasewitz had observed. It was especially interesting to him because it was not his way either. The strength of the Comes was that he looked after his men and was seriously interested in their well-being. If food was lacking, he gave out his own supplies. He ate what the simple legionaries were eating. In regard to wine, he shared it generously. If there were wounded, he visited them, each and everyone. If someone was brave and courageous, there was no lack of personal praise in front the assembled troops. When the most simple soldier had been noticed, had saved a life, held a tight position, he could be sure that he wouldn't be overlooked in the next round of promotions. The Comes didn't make any difference.

And so he had recognized what it meant to the old centurion, the commander of a guard post with perhaps 50 men, to join the insurgents. The gray-haired veteran was not a classical traitor, not one who was unfaithful to Rome, who looked at his short-term advantage. He simply wanted to survive until the end of his service, receive the promised gratification from his emperor, a piece of land, tax exemption, a peaceful life for perhaps another ten or fifteen years, die in his sleep as a well respected member of his community. A man of modest prosperity, of rank, with a glorious and honorable life, to which it was worth to look back.

And so the Comes had shown him due respect.

Von Klasewitz was sure that Maximus had not even pretended.

The usurper was not an insane upstart, no victim of megalomania, no one who wanted to gain power to realize irrational plans of grandeur. This was reassuring and disturbing at the same time for the German. And he didn't know exactly why.

The Centurion left the tent. Maximus watched after him for a moment, then sighed, and turned to the map, which showed Gaul and the adjoining provinces. Andragathius, the faithful general of Maximus, had been interrupted in his lecture by the appearance of the new ally. The fact that the Comes had gladly stopped the briefing for the commander of 50 tattered frontier soldiers spoke for itself.

Klasewitz' eyes were fixed on the map. It was an old Roman representation, in which the scales were not correct and distances between villages were recorded by marked lines. Important geographic features were also inserted, but their exact location was more estimation than in any way accurate. The nobleman was sure that Gratian had much better maps than his enemies. A small advantage, certainly, and Maximus had many men among them who knew the whole area very well. But the eternal suspicious and despicably cautious deserter didn't like the fact that if his enemy had an advantage for which he couldn't compensate.

His teeth clenched, and he drew his attention to the general who, with the description of the whole situation, continued where he had stopped before the interruption. Maximus had an excellent memory. He didn't need any repetition.

"We are north of Nemetacum and will occupy the city without problems," the general said. "The local military leaders have already agreed with to us in advance. From Nemetacum, we march toward Bagacum, as we want to join other border troops there. After that, we should go directly to Treveri, which is only a few days' march away, even if we proceed slowly. I suggest that the troops should not be too exhausted. Our Alan allies have sent mounted scouts in all directions; they will warn us as soon as Gratian is moving."

"What will he do?" Maximus asked the crucial question. "Malobaudes will try to persuade him to take a cautious approach so that we can win time and allies."

In addition, weapons and ammunition, von Klasewitz added in his mind, as the cannon manufactory in Britain worked day and night on further guns, as well as on the production of black powder and cannon balls. They had to compensate not only for possible losses, but, if everything worked out, wanted to establish a second artillery company. Maximus had given precise orders for this. Two transport galleys were always ready to take the finished cannons across the English Channel. Every single gun could prove to be decisive in this war.

"Malobaudes won't be lucky," Andragathius said, shaking his head. "Gratian will be looking for a quick decision. He has the German soldiers on his side and is convinced that he is superior to us."

"He could be right," Maximus said. One had to give it to the Comes that he wasn't inclined to the same chronic self-exaggeration under which von Klasewitz suffered – a knowledge that gave the German mental pain, and helped Maximus to plan realistic.

"We'll find out soon enough," the General said. "Gratian, as I see it, will seek an engagement under the command of Rheinberg, as fast as he can. This is an advantage, because the time-wanderer has no idea how to properly lead a big Roman army. He is a naval officer, and he lacks every experience."

"He has Arbogast and Richomer by his side, possibly Theodosius and other experienced soldiers," Maximus reminded him. "And we may all agree that despite this man's disgraceful influence, he is not the one to deliberately ignore the advice of his comrades."

"Then there would be the Emperor himself," the General added. "He will nominally lead the army in order to instill loyalty into the remaining undecided units in his reach. There is nothing else left for him to do."

"This is the smartest thing he can do," Maximus said. "It's also the greatest risk. For when Malobaudes kills him, the command structure of this army will collapse, and those units which have only opted recently for his side will come to us."

"Then there remains Rheinberg."

"Yes, that is indeed true. But he only enjoys his high office because he has the confidence of Gratian. The distrust in regard to his sudden career is great in those circles of the military administration who are otherwise loyal to the Emperor. Rheinberg's legitimization is based on Gratian. Once Gratian is dead, this support is gone. He won't be able to hold office just by himself. That is why we expect him to flee to his ship to Ravenna in such a case. Gratian's army will then be finally dissolved. We can march freely."

"But the East," Andragathius recalled.

"The East is weak. I know the story of what happened in the time-wanderer's past. At that time, I didn't start my endeavor until years later. The East had time to recover from the invasion of the Goths. Theodosius could use the East to fight and finally defeat me. But he does not have this power any more – he or whoever will try. Aside from the remains left of Valens's army, there are some freshly raised units, many of which put into the service before Rheinberg has abolished forced recruitment."

Maximus paused. "By the way, one of the reforms of the time-wanderer I intend to keep."

Andragathius didn't interrupt him. His face didn't reflect what he thought of this second praise for his opponent. He had known Maximus for many years and knew how to judge him.

"Then everything is said. We will certainly repeat this discussion one or the other time. I would like this exchange to be repeated after each further step so that we can discuss whether something has changed in our assessment. We mustn't assume that our plans are perfect or remain invariable."

The General wanted to reply, but was abruptly interrupted. Breathlessly, a messenger rushed into the tent. Maximus had given orders that if there were important news, he should be notified at any time of day or night.

The man was dust-covered and obviously an Alanian rider. One could see that he had a hard ride behind him. He bowed to the Comes, but Maximus waved his hand.

"Report."

"Lord, Gratian's legions. They departed from Treveri. They march directly toward our location."

Maximus looked at the messenger for a moment, then nodded.

"As expected. He takes the direct path and wants the quick decision. So we have to work with the troops we've got so far. How far away are the legions of Gratian?"

The messenger looked uncertain. "If they march hard, they'll be here in a week. But I don't know if Gratian will spare his men."

"He will, he will," Maximus muttered, glancing at the map. Andragathius dismissed the messenger with a gesture.

"We'll stick to our plan. We go to Bagacum. Gratian's scouts will find us there, of course, and the Emperor will command his army to that same location. This is where the decisive battle will take place."

Maximus pointed to the marked village with his forefinger.

"Bagacum, gentlemen, decides the fate of the Roman Empire – and therefore ours as well."

Von Klasewitz stared at the point in front of Maximus' finger and felt the rising nervousness, although the decisive battle was still many days away.

The Comes was right, of course. But what was more important than Rome and the insurgents was his own destiny. And Maximus had just said it.

Von Klasewitz breathed a sigh of tension.

It was time for him to inspect his cannons again.

33

"He'll be waiting for us at Bagacum."

Rheinberg was dust-covered. It was a dry summer day, but not too hot. The way ahead of them was filthy, and the marching legionaries swirled dust. Rheinberg had stopped his horse beside Gratian's beast. The Emperor, General Malobaudes, and Captain von Geeren, were resting at the side of the march, watching the seemingly endless stream of legionaries heading northwest like a worm.

Bagacum, Rheinberg could see from the map was in his time, the French city of Bavay. A very ancient city, originally the capital city of the Nervians, which under Roman rule had developed into an important junction in the province of Gallia Belgica, where many long-distance roads met. Rheinberg didn't know anything else about the settlement. The city itself was not the most important. She could fall into the hands of Maximus. The fortifications were not large enough to defend an army like that of the insurgent, with their strong cavalry elements. Besides, the Comes didn't want to hide. He, like Gratian and his master militium, had the intention of achieving a victory as fast and decisively as possible.

"We'll pitch camp ten miles from Bagacum," Gratian said, pointing to a place on the map. Malobaudes leaned over to look attentively. "There we have the well-cultivated fields around the city. A large, flat surface with few scenic features."

"That's not good," von Geeren said. "My men don't operate well in the open, where they are very vulnerable. I need a free field of fire but also good coverage. A forest, perhaps. Or a hill from which we can shoot. Solid buildings, which we can take as a base, especially for the installation of the MG-positions."

Rheinberg nodded. The MGs would play a decisive role in this battle. Their placement was of central importance.

"Our map is not good enough to say anything about those issues. There will surely be some forest or a hill. We must, therefore, send out scouts as quickly as possible, in order to find such a position."

"I'll take care of it," von Geeren said, guiding his horse aside, and rode away. A small section of specially trained Roman scouts had been attached to the German infantry. Von Geerens's people had told the Romans how the most advanced modern weapons of the time-wanderers could be deployed, so they knew what they were looking for. It was the only task of these scouts to identify positions that were well suited for the MG-positions. Rheinberg knew this task in good hands.

"Equally important to us," he continued, "is the question where Maximus and von Klasewitz will position *their* guns."

They didn't know how many pieces the mutineer had been able to produce under orders of Maximus. It couldn't be many, but Rheinberg preferred to be pessimistic and decided on a significant number. For cannons, the same was true as for the machine guns, and to an even greater extent: Their position on the battlefield decided their effectiveness. In addition, they could be moved less quickly than the MGs and were therefore inflexible. Rheinberg was sure that the deserter had paid attention to this problem, and that the cannons were mobile enough to be relocated, although with some effort. The dry weather benefited their enemies: Transporting MGs into mud and dirt was still relatively easy, heavy cannons on wheeled vehicles would be unequally more problematic. A decent shower could also damage the powder. Rheinberg wished for plenty of rain. But any look into the bright blue sky, where no cloud could be seen, made this prospect very unrealistic.

"He will use his artillery like in the Napoleonic Wars," Rheinberg muttered.

Gratian looked at him questioningly. Rheinberg tried to remember the lessons in military history during his officer's training. Since he had taken a completely different career, these aspects had only been touched on. Von Klasewitz definitely knew his stuff better than he did.

"It also depends on how far the pieces can fire and with what cadence," Rheinberg continued. This was understood by his comrades.

"That cannot be much," Malobaudes said depreciatingly. "I mean, how much time did he have? And what resources were available in Britain? This can at best be inferior cannons, right? Probably not even a dozen, half of whom will explode during the battle!"

"That can be, but I wouldn't underestimate von Klasewitz," Rheinberg replied. "He has certainly subjected his cannons to extensive tests. He will not go to war with poor quality weapons. To this end, too much depends on him personally in regard to the outcome of this battle."

Malobaudes waved his hand. "You are too pessimistic, General. It may be that the traitor understands his craft. And Maximus has allowed him leeway, fine. But all this on the economic basis of a single province and in secrecy! Not much could have been achieved. We have to adjust ourselves to some loud noise and with luck one or the other cannonball will hit something and provide for some confusion. But we Romans are accustomed to onagers and catapults, and the effect may not be much greater."

"That's right," Rheinberg admitted. He wiped his forehead and took a sip of water. Although he was now quite capable with a horse, he found the movement on horseback still very tiring. He could also have used the Opel truck of the infantry, but that one stoof motionless as an object of observation in one of the training workshops of Johann Dahms – not least because the fuel supplies threatened to end.

Malobaudes stretched in his saddle. "Give me a determined cavalry unit, and we'll eradicate these cannons at once. We ride down the gunners, and then these great inventions are no more than a bunch of useless metal."

"Von Klasewitz will have been careful to protect the pieces against exactly this type of attack," Rheinberg said.

Malobaudes snorted contemptuously.

"That may be. But a quick advance – and you won't need a legion. I think we're too afraid."

Rheinberg didn't know whether the old general was right or not. The cannons of the nobleman were an unknown quantity, and his own tendency to assess the risk as high had something to do with his relationship to von Klasewitz, whose sneakiness he had experienced many times. Possibly the assessment of Malobaudes, who knew exactly what modern weapons could accomplish, wasn't wrong at all. Certainly, the mutineer didn't provide the usurper with modern field howitzers, but at most cannons as they had been developed in the Middle Ages.

Rheinberg said goodbye to the Emperor and rode along the long lines of the legionaries. The men were focused on the march, and he was greeted only occasionally.

He greeted back and tried to spread a feeling of confidence he didn't feel – and the worst was that he didn't even know why he couldn't master at least some optimism.

He hated it when dark premonitions plagued him.

34

"The situation is developing."

Sedacius showed mental unrest, marched up and down in front of his officers. Secundus and Levantus gave Volkert a glance which the latter ignominiously ignored.

They were on their way to Ravenna and had made camp. Volkert had been surprised when he heard that Sedacius wanted to meet with some officers, though he had already reached Ravenna with the bulk of the troops. The small group of the recovered legionaries had been equally astonished when one morning Sedacius, with the centurions Levantus and Secundus, had appeared in order to hold a meeting with Volkert. Volkert himself had been unpleasantly surprised. In his eyes, he now occupied a position which didn't correspond to his own sense of his importance.

The Tribune seemed to see that differently.

"Gratian marches toward Maximus. The battle will soon take place," Sedacius had informed him. "Now that the two are engaged, it is time to take the next step in our plan."

Volkert was not sure whether it really was "their" plan, as the goal was to make the Tribune an emperor. But he'd rather not contradict him.

"I used my contacts," Sedacius continued. "At the moment, I cannot negotiate properly with those officers of Gratian who are with him, so I concentrate on those who command the Eastern Army, as well as those who organize the second line of defense at Ravenna. I have found an open ear with some of the men, especially those who regard Maximus as a religious zealot, whose usurpation would be a great danger for the inner peace of the realm."

Magnus Maximus, everyone knew, was a convinced, even ardent, defender of Trinitarian teaching. He would resolutely proceed against

Arians, other Christian sects, and against the old state religion. This would inevitably lead to further unrest, possibly a permanent division of the Empire, as the East was largely Arian.

"I've thrown my dice," Sedacius said, pausing for a moment in his movement. "I have assured everyone that I won't touch the edict of tolerance, and that I am setting up a council for the purpose of the settlement of any Church divisions, with the aim to have a good agreement between the various factions."

A task, as Volkert knew, in which Constantine the Great already had failed. But he kept it to himself. For Sedacius, it was important that he had been able to give the moderates the assurance that they would receive their support.

"The central question will be how Richomer will position itself. IIe is a faithful follower of Gratian. If Gratian fails, it is very unlikely that he will immediately join Maximus. He must look for an alternative."

"What about Theodosius?" Volkert exclaimed. All eyes were directed at him. This was unpleasant.

But the Tribune nodded approvingly. "That is the second problem. Theodosius is in Ravenna. He knows that in that other time he became an emperor of the whole realm. He has joined Gratian, but that doesn't mean he won't seize an opportunity that is offered to him. The problem is that many know how the other Theodosius regulated the church question. There is a strong faction in the Senate who won't accept him as emperor. And he has no wide support in the army."

"Who will get the support of the time-wanderers? You?" Volkert asked.

Again, the Tribune nodded approvingly. "The third problem. I haven't been able to get in contact with someone at a higher place. The comrades who have escorted us to the east are loyal to Gratian. I'm not involved in the defense of the city itself, which is organized by the prefect Renna. But I need this access, urgently. That is why I'm here."

He now fixed his gaze on Volkert, in whom a dark, unpleasant premonition arose.

"Centurion Thomasius, you have had a good understanding with our German comrades, and you are a very reliable and eloquent man. I need someone who can be persuasive and who is wise, not a barbarian in conversation, who can only swing the sword. In you I see the diplomat as well as the soldier. I need someone who might get in touch the time-wanderers, very carefully and discreetly. That man is you!"

Volkert knew he was turning pale. Probably his comrades thought that this was too much of an honor for him, or that he had been formally overwhelmed by this proof of trust. In any case, the grin of Secundus and Levantus couldn't be interpreted otherwise. But they didn't know what was going on. How could he convince Sedacius to change this order without refusing it?

A glance into the face of the Tribune showed him that this was certainly impossible.

How could he carry out his task without being exposed? Volkert sighed deeply. Sedacius patted him cheerfully on his shoulder, then he continued his exposition, the content of which the young German only perceived as a mist of thoughts.

In his head, thoughts whirled around. He faced a situation for which there was no solution. A great misfortune dawned over him.

And then, almost as an afterthought, almost embarrassingly late, he suddenly realized that Julia lived in Ravenna.

Thomas Volkert recognized that his life threatened to become very complicated.

35

There was excitement in the city. It was not openly visible but felt subliminally by everyone. Godegisel knew this atmosphere. When he had concealed himself in the Greek metropolis shortly before the attack of his people on Thessaloniki, he had noticed a similar mood. At that time, it had been stronger, almost tangible. At that time, tens of thousands of Goths had stood directly in front of the city. Now, the threat to Ravenna was more distant, somewhat diffuse, and the hopes of all who wished Gratian good luck rested on the outcome of the battle that was currently being prepared in the far north.

Renna, who, as a military prefect, ensured that the northern Italian city became the center of a second defensive line if Gratian was to fail, tried his best to spread confidence and composure. The fact that he had only a few soldiers at his disposal, and that the contingents that came from other parts of the Empire were often very small, and that of many of those he didn't know if they would arrive in time – all this couldn't be concealed.

And so the feeling of disaster was in the air. This was true not only for Ravenna itself, but also for the settlement of the time-wanderers. The increased safety precautions introduced by Magister Dahms were visible everywhere. Soldiers patrolled in the streets, and visitors were checked with meticulousness. From the chimneys of the iron ship, steam was constantly visible, as the machines were held in readiness. Two days ago, priests had gathered to a silent demonstration to show that they were happy about the prospect that the time-wanderers would get into trouble with their witchcraft. Rumors made the round that Ravenna would be spared from all calamity if only the time-wanderers were to be delivered to justice. All this posed, until now, no danger as long as the prospect was that

Gratian would prevail in the battle against Maximus. If the outcome of the battle was negative, however, the agitators would certainly ensure that this kind of rumors became most handy plans of action, especially if the usurper's troops were to approach Ravenna.

Something Godegisel expected silently. He was the one who knew Maximilian best among the people he met, and he knew that an important aim of the war was to get to the resources, but also to the knowledge of the time-wanderers.

What role a young Goth played in all this, he didn't know exactly. Until then, he was a kind of informal adviser, but he didn't fulfill a real function. He had the feeling that Dahms wasn't quite sure what to do with him, and he should probably ask him to return to his homeland, the parts of the East now populated by the Goths.

Godegisel didn't ask.

He knew that things were happening here that would determine the future of the Empire. How could he, who had accompanied the Roman Emperor Valens on his escape, now simply retreat and look unimpeded from afar how things developed? He had to be here, in the immediate vicinity, as much as he was allowed to. And since no one sent him away, he simply remained.

That morning he repaid a debt.

Actually, it wouldn't have been necessary, but it was possible that the young nobleman, who had left the homeland escaping from the Huns, wasn't the same person who was now walking along the dusty road to make up for a loss which probably no one would perceive as such. Godegisel, officially alimented by the financial resources of the time-wanderers, wore a simple but new garment, had been allowed to enjoy new sandals and wore a long knife at his waist. There were some coins in his pouch. He was allowed to rest in the canteen of the time-wanderers and slept in one of the community accommodations for factory workers – sharing a room with a foreman who usually had a night shift and therefore slept during the day.

In his arm, Godegisel carried a bundle with his former work clothes, carefully cleaned and folded. When he entered the workshop, which he had once visited a few weeks ago, he felt a certain relief. It was not difficult for him to find the man, who had placed him here after his arrival, had paid him a small sum, and had handed him suitable clothes. The Goth had then run away with all this and had presented himself to Dahms without ever fulfilling the employment contract for which he had been paid in advance.

The elderly man, whose muscular figure crouched behind a wide table, looked up as Godegisel entered a room that apparently was at the same time a place of administration and lodging for the foremen. The giant couldn't remember his name, but probably remembered the face. His eyes narrowed and he stood up. He didn't act aggressively, but also not pleased and opened his mouth.

Godegisel was faster. He put the clean bundle on the table so the foreman could see it well. Then, in a meaningful gesture, he fetched his pouch and counted the sum which he had received as advance and added something to it.

Then he made a bow.

"I apologize. I deceived you. I was a stranger in the city and had to talk with the time-wanderers. In my condition, after a long journey and little food or care, I would never have been allowed in their presence. I needed your advance and your help to get access and to deliver an important message. Then many things happened and I had completely forgotten that I still have a debt to settle. I should have come here much earlier."

He pointed to the table. "The clothes are impeccable, I've only worn them for a few days. They are clean. I am paying back the whole of the advance, with a small surcharge for the annoyance I have caused you. Once again, it wasn't any evil intention that drove me to this deception, but a necessity. This explains my actions, but I don't apologize."

The older man looked at the bundle and collected the coins. Then he focused his gaze on the Goth, who was now waiting, not submissive, but also not too rash.

"I didn't expect that," the answer came slowly. "You were not the only one to take the money and not to work. But you are the first to bring it back and explain why. I have not suffered much damage. Not even now. I accept your apology. I suppose you're no longer interested in work?"

Godegisel nodded. "I'll be in the service of the time-wanderers until further notice."

The foreman made a sweeping gesture. "We all are. Without the strange Germans, there would be no workshops, no manufacturers, no work. We are all connected to them and their mercy with our lives."

"Is that something bad?"

The old man grinned. "A good question. There are some priests who find this very questionable. I see that my people do a lot of work here, and that there are almost every day new procedures and techniques that I have to address with diligent consideration so that I can produce more effectively. I don't complain. In fact, it is usually those who mourn the old ways and the old times who whine the loudest. But I am convinced that one must not live in the past. Now is now."

"Not everyone thinks so."

"But many in this city. Most even. When the insurgents come, we will take weapons in our hands and defend the time-wanderers if this is demanded of us."

Godegisel concealed his surprise. He hadn't expected the deep loyalty that came from the man's words. And he felt the sudden urge to contradict him, even at the risk of losing the newly acquired sympathy of his counterpart.

"The time-wanderers certainly have their merits, but they have brought unrest to the Empire," he said almost against his will. "The revolt of Maximus wouldn't have started if the visitors hadn't begun to influence Roman politics."

The old man grinned. "Rome doesn't work, my friend. There always would have been a reason to put an usurper on the throne. What I've heard of the past of the time-wanderers just confirms this. The question is not whether we can prevent insurrection and turmoil, but rather what will emerge from it: a new, more stable order in which men like me can live their day-to-day life without being constantly under arbitrariness and violence – or further chaos, decay and uncertainty?"

"Safety is a great asset, but it is overrated."

210

"You're a Goth, aren't you? You should know how to appreciate safety."

"It is an illusion when measured objectively. Ultimately, you have to feel safe before you can get safety. If one is continually anxious, the Emperor can still reign for so long and still make wise decisions, but one will never find the peace one desires."

The foreman looked at Godegisel suspiciously. "A philosopher, yes?"

The Goth shrugged. "I've experienced a lot. One becomes thoughtful."

"You are looking for a place to plant roots."

"Everything I have found in this respect has either been burnt or pulled out of the ground. And some was my own fault. Even the time-wanderers won't be able to provide safety for me if I seek it in the wrong place."

The foreman made a helpless gesture. "I can only do what I can do. When the enemy comes, I defend what I think is best for me. What will you do in the service of the time-wanderers? Will you run away or stay and fight?"

"I don't run away from it, but I will not stand in the way of a storm for which I am too weak. And I believe this also applies to the strange Germans themselves. I think they have a very strong survival instinct. They will flee when it is necessary in order to have the chance to return."

The foreman looked thoughtful. "It can be. And it isn't foolish."

Godegisel nodded. "Here are your things. I thank you for your understanding and wish you all the best, no matter how hard the storm will blow."

So he turned away and left.

Outside, on the busy street, he stopped for a moment and took a deep breath. He didn't know what had happened to him, something had caused him have such a discussion with a stranger. It was probably a need for him to be clear about his own position. Now he felt better, knowing that his fate was linked to that of the time-wanderers. Whatever future lay before him, it seemed clear that God had assigned him a role which he might not yet fully understand, but whose task had not yet been fulfilled.

That there was a woman in Gaul, who probably wasn't thinking of him anymore, was all that remained to pity.

36

"Now?"

This simple question comprised everything. Rheinberg didn't press on von Geeren, who stood motionless beside him. It was early morning, the sun was just rising, delicately cool for a summer day. The dew lay on the grass, and one felt a great peace – if one were not, like Hauptmann von Geeren, engaged in observing the battle-formation of a hostile army through binoculars.

Maximus had acted decisively: He didn't waste time with talking. No ambassadors appeared with threats or suggestions, no evading, no delays. When it was clear that the imperial army had approached sufficiently close, the men of the usurper had likewise broken camp on this early morning and offered Gratian battle. It was obvious that Maximus wanted a decision. Rheinberg was right, just as he was at the same time feeling uncanny. This protracted procedure was evidence of self-esteem, although Maximus, with von Klasewitz at his side, had someone who could well explain what the German infantry would be able to do on the battlefield.

It was confidence or conscious ignorance. Or a bluff.

The situation made it clear to Rheinberg that he was not born to be a field commander. Yes, even as captain of a ship, he deemed it necessary to play back and forth conjectures and certainties about the enemy's intentions, calculated and analyzed, in order to either take risks or avoid them, often on the basis of insufficient information. But it was quite a different matter to command a ship than a vast army. And at sea there was wind, waves, maybe fog, but that was it. Here he was presented with a battlefield, which was relatively flat, on which there were farms, small groups of trees, one or the other hill, ditches, streams, higher and lower grass, bushes – it was ...

... it was simply making him a bit dizzy.

Rheinberg was still able to learn a lot from Arbogast and Malo-baudes. The two Generals had quickly begun to do what Rheinberg was unable to do: They read the grounds, they were thinking about the most effective battle formation, trying to get a picture of the strengths and weaknesses of the various units. Rheinberg was a silent listener. Even Gratian had more to contribute to this discussion than he himself. Since his appointment as Magister Militium, the young German officer hadn't felt so helpless.

There were some things about which he and von Geeren were the experts. And that was exactly what they dealt with at this moment.

The infantry officer lowered the glasses. "As we have guessed, Jan. Bronze cannons."

Rheinberg nodded. In such a short time, von Klasewitz could only go the simplest way of cannon production – especially on the basis of a weaker industrial base. Iron was less suitable than bronze, if it wasn't transformed into steel, since the latter material was more elastic and didn't crack so quickly. For this, the bronze gun was inferior in range and penetration power.

"How many?"

"Lots. I haven't seen all of them, I believe, but there are more than a dozen. More than 20, perhaps."

"Our friend was busy."

"He understands his craft, that we have to acknowledge."

"Drawn barrel?"

"I don't think so."

"Limited range and accuracy then."

"They're big calibers, and when they shoot, accuracy isn't the problem. Then they just have to keep up the fire into our general direction."

Rheinberg nodded. It was the same principle as the MGs they had on their side. There was no shortage of targets, and if one didn't kill one then surely the other. "How are the cannons protected?"

"Apparently, there is a larger squad of legionaries who are acting as guards," von Geeren explained.

"Can we kill the gunners from afar?"

"Yes, but they built entrenchments, and, as expected, erected heavy iron plates beside the guns. Von Klasewitz, of course. It is not that we can simply mow them down. They are prepared for that eventuality."

Rheinberg nodded. It wouldn't be good too focus on the cannons too much, as at the same time he needed firepower to fight Maximus' main host of soldiers.

"There's something else," von Geeren said. He handed Rheinberg the binoculars. "Look at the legionaries at the front on the right flank, seen from us. They are closest to us. Look at the belts and what they hold in their hands."

Rheinberg lifted the glass to his eye and looked through it. He had quickly found the soldiers and focused the optics. Then he was stiff for a moment, as if stirred by a very bad surprise. A few moments later he dropped the instrument. He was pale. "Hand grenades," he murmured.

"In fact." Von Geeren took the binoculars from him and stowed it in the reinforced leather sheath hanging around his neck. "Klasewitz really is hardworking. A very simple construction. Half of it may not be exploding."

"One half is enough for me," Rheinberg replied silently. He fixed his eyes on the positions of the infantry. They were also protected against attacks from the background by additional troops. They would be able to focus entirely on one target.

"I must talk to Arbogast and the Emperor," the captain finally said. "You have everything under control here."

"I'm just waiting for the signal."

Rheinberg nodded. He swung himself on his horse. His own bodyguard was already waiting for him, and accompanied him back behind the front of Gratian's army, where the Emperor resided with his staff. When he joined them, his face was already showing that he did bring any good news. He tried to explain to the Roman officers the mode of operation of a hand grenade. Since they understood many of the basic principles of modern weapons, it was not long before the faces of Gratian, Arbogast and Malobaudes darkened with worries. Most unfortunately, Dahms' efforts in constructing a similar weapon had not resulted in a comparable mass-production.

"We have to deal with it," Malobaudes finally said. "The battle line is ready. I will inform the centurions personally about this change. They should prepare their men as far as they can." He rose at once, and hurried out of the field.

"We can still win this battle," Gratian said, looking after the general. "Consider a new tactic."

"No, it will not do much good," Arbogast said. The burly general stroked his beard. "It's bad for morale, and we don't have any effective counter-defense. How did soldiers fight against this weapon in your time, Rheinberg?"

"By killing those who threw them before they could throw them. Once they fly, you find cover and pray that you are not hit or that the grenade is a dud. There isn't much else left to do."

Arbogast sighed. "I expected that. So there is nothing else for our men as well."

Rheinberg rose and nodded to Gratian. "I will inform the field hospital that not only the cannons of the enemy can lead to a certain type of injury, but also the hand grenades. The nurses and paramedics must know."

He looked around and raised his shoulders. "And then we should simply attack as planned."

The glances he got reflected his own determination. There was no more waiting.

37

"This is our problem!"

Von Klasewitz' pointing finger didn't tremble even when he directed it toward the positions the scouts had drawn into the large map. They were marked with the symbol Maximus had chosen for the legionaries of the time-wanderers, the so-called infantry. The nobleman knew that with this discussion he helped to seal the death of his own countrymen, the German comrades who had disappeared with him in time. But he had long since gone beyond the stage of contemplating unnecessarily about moral questions that didn't help him in this situation at all.

Maximus nodded. "And how do we solve it?"

Andragathius, the general under the command of Maximus, laid a hand flat on the map. "Normally, I would suggest that with a large cavalry unit the positions of the time-wanderers would be overrun in a wide, circumventing attack. There would surely be great losses, but the most important aim is to make the threat of the ... how did you call them, Tribune von Klasewitz?"

"Machine guns," the man helped.

"Machine guns ... yes, this threat must be eliminated."

"Why don't we use that tactic, then?" von Klasewitz wanted to know. He was a bit irritated, for he had been consulted when it came to the positioning of the guns, and Maximus and Andragathius had discussed without him the field of fire, but the exact tactics of the battle, they kept hidden. This was a reference to the fact that the two Romans had not yet understood what role artillery played in a battle, and that these weapons had to operate in tight coordination with all other units to be as effective as possible. It seemed to him that above all Andragathius regarded the cannons mainly as a noisy effect, which would pave the ground for the actual battle but would ultimately not be able to make a really important contribution.

"We don't do it because the rear flank of these positions is covered by selected defensive units. The cavalry would be noticed in time, and the time-wanderers would have plenty of time to adjust to this threat. That would not only cause a high loss, but a bloodbath with a very doubtful outcome."

"The alternative?"

"If your cannons had a wider range, we'd be able to solve the problem," Maximus muttered thoughtfully. Von Klasewitz' first reaction was to take this as an accusation, but a glance into the face of the Comes taught him something better. The man didn't want to blame anyone here, but he had recognized an important function of the artillery better than the German had thought possible. Of course, cannons were also used to destroy enemy artillery as far as it was within reach. Unfortunately, Maximus was correct in his statement that the machine guns were able to shoot further than the ultimately crude bronze pieces of the insurgents – a reason why he had paid particular attention to the protection of the cannons.

"What does the alternative look like?" he insisted.

"We must go against the position of the wanderers, but not on detours, instead from all sides at once. We will still pay a high price, but we have a tactical advantage with the hand grenades. Getting rid of this infantry is our first priority. We must move so fast that they cannot react in time, both with foot soldiers and cavalry."

"Leave the horsemen," Klasewitz advised. "They are too easy a target. We stick with foot soldiers. If they behave as we have practiced, we can minimize losses."

"But it takes longer," the General complained.

Von Klasewitz looked at Andragathius. "This may be the case. But through this approach we test a meaningful tactic and show the men that the marvels of the time-wanderers have their limits. It will continue to be important in the future. If we win the battle, the war is not yet decided, no matter what you dream of." Apart from his activity as an artillery officer, von Klasewitz had also prepared other training units with NCOs, especially for the correct use of the primitive hand grenades as well as the changes in approach. So far, Roman legionaries had huddled behind their shields in the battle for cover, especially when a hail of arrows rained down on them. That wouldn't help much against the bullets from the German machine guns. Instead, von Klasewitz, much to the initial amusement of the instructed Romans, had shown what was to be done once the weapons of the time-wanderers spoke: fall flat on the belly, press yourself as hard as possible to the ground and then, as soon as the spray of bullets seemed to be moving away from one's own position, glide ahead on the belly, in the direction of the enemy, all in order to represent as small a target as possible in the shrubbery or higher grass. He had demonstrated it to them with full physical effort, but they had only realized the necessity when he had begun firing with his rifle over their heads. Then their willingness to learn had quickly increased.

"If the instructions I have given will be well-implemented, the men should know what to do when they are fired upon. I cannot tell a cavalryman to get off the horse and lie down, especially because he probably will not have a horse left to ride. No, let's leave the cavalry out of the game. They won't help us here. A determined advance of the legionaries, reaching the range for throwing hand grenades, and from several sides at the same time – that is our tactical approach."

Von Klasewitz had spoken calmly. His comments had been of cold precision. Andragathius and Maximus couldn't resist the impression that the man knew what he was talking about. Finally, it was the Comes who nodded and said, "That convinces me. Andragathius, we rearrange the legions accordingly. Run a force around the enemy's positions so they can attack in time. Use the cavalry to attack the enemy scouts or, better yet, kill them. But no riders in the direct attack against the positions of the time-wanderers. We use most of the auxiliary troops at the other end of the battlefield."

"Very well," von Klasewitz commented. "The enemies have made an important tactical decision that is of advantage for us: Their infantry is more or less concentrated in one place. Their advantage is that they can cause big damage from there and have a clear field of fire. Also, one is more difficult to overwhelm, as we will find out soon enough. The serious disadvantage is the lack of flexibility. The range of the MGs is considerable, yes, and the rifles also cover the whole battlefield. Nevertheless, the more distant parts of our legions will suffer much less from the attack of the enemy. There, I will also concentrate the fire of our cannons. We have to keep one flank moving and slowly work on the position of the time-wanderers; with the other, we must take an offensive approach toward Gratian's troops."

The German sketched the scenario on the map. He had made this argument often, but he didn't tire to repeat it again. Of course, he pursued another goal: His cannons had to convincingly prove their effectiveness and their relevance in battle. His continued grace in the eyes of Maximus depended on their performance. Therefore, he wanted to use his artillery as much as possible to gain prestige and influence. His goal had to be to be recognized alongside Andragathius at least as an equal military leader.

The meeting didn't last much longer. The basic lines of the advance were clear, and the formation of the legions was almost completed. Finally, von Klasewitz said goodbye, stepped out of the tent into the muddy morning, and marched at once to his artillery unit. He tried to radiate confidence and self-assurance, albeit in his own more arrogant version. He was hiding his real feelings as much as he could. A battle, that he had learned during his training, was absolutely unpredictable once it had begun and developed its own momentum. This was all the more true here where hitherto unusual and untrained elements were included in the equation. This was usually the recipe for helpless confusion and coordination problems. It was also the opportunity to establish a new tactical doctrine and to demonstrate its value.

Chances and risks, he felt, had to be considered.

Now it was necessary to put his own weight as much as possible into the balance. And von Klasewitz was determined to do exactly that.

38

"Now is the time, my friends!"

The encouragement wouldn't have been necessary. Captain von Geeren had rarely witnessed his soldiers as concentrated as now. Everybody knew the importance of the day, and they all knew the risks involved. Von Geeren nodded to the centurion, who was lying next to him in the dirt and also armed with binoculars. Lucius Verilius was the commander of the unit that was to protect the infantrymen from the flanks and the back in order to avoid surprise attacks. He was very young, younger than the German, and he had been given this task above all because he was particularly good at getting along with the new weapons of the time-wanderers. The fact that he used the binoculars with the same self-assurance as the German was only an indication of this fact. That he was the first Roman officer to have received a pistol from the Germans' stock and carried it visibly on his belt, and even achieved good results in shooting exercises, was another. Verilius belonged to a new generation of Roman soldiers who recognized the advantages and potentials of the weapon technology from the future and were prepared to rethink old methods and certainties.

They came along really well. This helped to ensure that the language skills of the two men were not a one-way street. With the same soldier, with whom the centurion had learned to master the pistol, he had been part of language classes. What he had learned was bumpy and full of mistakes, but he was ready to speak without fear of errors and accepted corrections with stoic calmness.

Not far from here the war-music of the legions, which had begun with their final preparations for battle, was heard. Von Geeren somewhat missed the drums he was accustomed to. Roman battle music had much more to do with flutes and trumpets, which were often very loud, but ultimately rather disturbing, at least in his ears. He would take the opportunity to speak about drums in due course, but he realized that it was ultimately too late for it now. Once artillery and guns had been brought to their full extent, no one would be able to hear any musicians play, and they would be, as in his own future, confined to festive occasions.

The two gigantic armies, which had finally positioned themselves, looked like oversized sports teams. Although von Geeren and Rheinberg had pointed out over and over again that it was much more sensible to take positions as quickly as possible, in the vicinity of promising cover, the Romans had not been deterred from this rather pompous and now increasingly obsolete mode of battle preparation. Rheinberg had at some point mentioned to von Geeren that his complaints were of no use. They would have to have the bitter experience on their own to understand that classical battle formations became more or less obsolete.

The problem, both officers had also recognized, was that the Goths were the first who had become victims of the German arms. Barbarians. Wild and uncivilized. Now Romans, but ultimately only second-class citizens. Roman legionaries had not yet been confronted with the firestorm of cannons and guns, at least not as targets. It was hard to describe it in mere words. Centurion Verilius was one of the few officers who had absorbed the lessons. His men had had to learn certain things, for instance, to throw themselves into the dirt without any hesitation, no matter where they were.

This was yet to be communicated effectively to the masses of legionaries.

The survivors of this battle, von Geeren thought bitterly, would better understand later. But at that time it would be too late for their dead comrades.

A cavalryman came up, snapped the horse by the reins so that it came to a standstill almost next to von Geeren. The man jumped from the back of his animal; it was one of Rheinberg's messengers.

"The Magister Militium sends his regards," the man said, somewhat breathlessly.

"I hear you."

"The order for the attack will be given at 8:30 a.m., if Maximus should not take the first step."

"Thank you! We are ready."

The man nodded, threw himself back on his horse, and stormed away. Von Geeren looked at the clock. Another innovation for Roman Battlefield tactics: At the *Saarbrücken*, Rheinberg had collected all working watches, whether worn on the arm or on a chain. There had been a decent number. Some of them had been distributed to important officers of the Romans, who had shown themselves very pleased about the exactness of this measurement of time. Since then, tactical commands have been given with times that were unmistakable. It facilitated the co-ordination immensely, although the advantage immediately decreased rapidly with the start of a battle. The biggest problem remained to be battlefield communication, which depended on spotters, signalmen and acoustic signals. Dahms had proposed to introduce widely visible and wisely coded flag signals, with a mast on a hill, so that the enemy couldn't interpret the signals or at least only with difficulty. Unfortunately, the necessary preparations weren't finished before this battle. So the flutists and trumpeters were still essential, and their signal sequences well known to Maximus. No chance for any surprise here.

Von Geeren waved his lieutenants. They just nodded. They all knew. The officer saw how the gunman in his vicinity was checking the seat of the patron's belt one last time, and then formally placed himself behind the powerful weapon, keeping an eye on the targets. Other infantrymen, in dug-out trenches, were protected against the occasional arrow or other thrown missiles. Von Geeren had ordered, where possible, to target officers of the enemy. They were clearly recognizable by their uniforms and, above all, the helmets. The more they got, the more difficult it would be for the enemy to coordinate his attack properly.

But von Geeren did not want to overestimate the effect. Once the battle was well underway, it became quite a challenge to move big units, and some had a tendency to dissolve in the tangle of battle. Good leaders certainly played an important role, but not the same as at the beginning of the slaughter.

Nevertheless, every little advantage was helpful.

And then, as if it had not been announced well before, von Geeren was startled when he heard the trumpet signal. He should have looked at his watch, he admonished himself.

"Targets!" he shouted, and the other officers related the order. It was quite unnecessary – the men had been doing nothing else for half an hour –, but it announced that the next order would follow soon.

In Maximus' army, movement was visible. The men of Gratian, on the other hand remained at their given place, and for a good reason: They didn't want to get into the fire line of the infantry. Geeren raised the binoculars and frowned. A whole wing of the opposing army had changed its direction of march. Thousands of soldiers were on the move, directly toward ... him.

"Fire!" he yelled, louder than necessary.

The infantrymen obeyed. A deafening noise scattered over the battlefield as the guns and MGs sent their deadly bullets on their way. Von Geeren's eyes were glued to the eyepiece. He saw legionaries fall, essentially mown down, pictures that reminded him of Thessaloniki. But then he saw how much more fell to the ground than could possibly have been hit, and he felt both fear and respect.

The legionaries, like a man, fell into cover, lay flat on the grass.

And then, almost as if a gigantic carpet had set in motion, they crawled to the position of the Germans with an obstinate slowness.

Yes, the infantrymen still found their targets. MGs plowed through the ranks of the attackers. Cries of the victims echoed across the field. The attackers made a great, painful, cruel progress.

But the losses were not half as great as if the legionaries would've continued to march upright instead of crouching down. Von Klasewitz had instructed the men of Maximus well. They would suffer, but what von Geeren had secretly feared would become reality: They would approach the positions of the Germans, bleeding and full of injuries, but in a certain and inevitable wave, and then, at some time, crude grenades would fly and blades would flash in the summer sun.

"Verilius!" von Geeren demanded.

224

But the Centurion was not at his side. Von Geeren lowered the glass, looked around, and his eyes widened as he realized that the Centurion did what was his job – to protect the Germans from an attack from behind.

"Secure flanks!" von Geeren shouted, pointing to the direction from which another, massive wall of opposing legionaries slowly approached them, kept in check by Verilius's men, who evidently had the disadvantage in numbers. "Messenger!"

A man appeared next to him. Von Geeren scribbled something on a piece of parchment, handed it to the cavalryman, who immediately disappeared with it.

A loud, crashing sound made the German huddle down.

Von Geeren looked in awe.

An avaricious legionary of Maximus' troop had thrown his hand grenade, which had not even come close to the positions of the Germans.

But it had exploded. Loud and audible. Frightening.

Von Geeren dropped into the nearest MG-hole and fixed the binoculars back to his eyes.

He hoped the rest of the battle would be more pleasurable. Then the cannons of the traitor opened fire.

Now at last, Captain von Geeren had the certain feeling that they were in very deep shit.

39

"Stop it! Hands off!"

Von Klasewitz rushed forward, pulled the gunner backwards. The torch fell to the ground, and the nobleman trampled the fire out. The frightened legionary staggered back and didn't know what was happening to him. A bullet whirred around their ears, and von Klasewitz tore the man into the cover behind the entrenchments. Dirt flew up, where the bullets of the German infantrymen swept the ground. Then they had looked for new targets, and it became quiet, even if only for a very brief moment. The two cannons to the left and right of the German were firing with a deafening bang.

The gunner stared at von Klasewitz, still confused. The nobleman extended his finger, pointed to the hairline that had formed on the cannon after the last volley. The eyes of the Roman broadened, then he nodded eagerly. He understood that another shot and the gun might have exploded in his face.

Von Klasewitz cursed as he half-straightened up to hurry to the still operational pieces. This was already the third gun that had fired five shots at the most, before it fell silent forever. The continuous use, the fastest possible shot – all this had required more from the cannons than all exercises before.

Von Klasewitz again threw himself behind the entrenchment, looked frantically to the left and right and backwards. The guards had already had to ward off an attack by Gratian's troops on the artillery under heavy losses. Von Klasewitz had asked Maximus for reinforcements, and he had received them. The image of the bodies of the enemy's legionaries, which had been torn into pieced by the first volley of his cannonade, had evidently impressed the Comes. He wanted to keep the cannons. They should continue to fire.

Von Klasewitz felt the heat of the cannon next to him, casting a sorrowful glance at the bronze construction. He would have liked to order a break to allow the pieces to cool off. At the same time, this was also a great danger: the cooling bronze could deform imperceptibly in the process. This could possibly lead to further damage once the bombardment would resume.

If the battle lasted much longer, von Klasewitz would lose his complete unit. The higher the stress, the faster the remaining guns would fail. He rushed from position to position to control how his cannons were stressed. If they failed, that was one thing. If they exploded unexpectedly among them, it was a completely different one.

Von Klasewitz kept his ears shut. His experiment with candle wax as earplugs hadn't worked so well. The cannon fired. The powdered odor penetrated his nose, but he immediately, almost instinctively, scrutinized the weapon for any damage. He maintained his rapid pace of inspection.

Von Klasewitz crawled to the edge of the entrenchment and stared at the battlefield. The massacre was in full swing. The German targeting had demanded numerous sacrifices among the invading troops. But the soldiers of the Comes had now come near enough, often flat on the ground, that they cast their hand-grenades, and a few squadrons began to throw themselves at the positions of the infantry. Von Klasewitz suspected that the men had planted their bayonets, and that they were supported by Roman guards. It was a very unpleasant, cruel melee, and the traitor was glad to be far away. He was an artillery officer. He killed from distance. There was nothing in this fight that concerned him.

Shouting. The metallic sound of impinging blades.

The nobleman stood up. He saw that the legionaries, who were stationed as guards for the cannons, were suddenly active again. Up to now, Gratian's troops had not attempted to attack the artillery items for a second time.

Another scream. Von Klasewitz nipped the gun out of his holster. He had a total of 16 rounds, the only cartridges he still had left. His gun, he had left behind; he preferred the pistol, and it was quite sufficient for any melee.

A troop of Gratian's legionaries had slumped and crouched near from behind, apparently unimpressed by the cannonade. The men had been in safety since the beginning of the battle.

A scream and a soldier threw up his arms, sank to the ground, a few yards away from the entrenchment. He had been hit by a bullet, right into the chest.

But as he had turned the back of the battle, von Klasewitz discerned that some of the German infantry were among the attackers.

Von Klasewitz felt hot and cold. Even a handful of the infantrymen would dispatch the legionaries, if they proceeded decisively.

Now the traitor heard their shots; they came from the nearby undergrowth, close to a group of trees, in which the marksmen were hiding. Three other legionaries collapsed. Fear grew among the guards. Then a shouting of angry voices, as more of Gratian's men became visible from behind the trees and hurried to the cannons with drawn blades.

"Cease fire!" Klasewitz shouted at his men. "Defend yourself!"

The cannons turned silent, the men whirled around, took spears and swords, and prepared to defend their weapons.

The nobleman aimed at one of the attackers.

He had a steady hand. Pulled the trigger once. A whipping bang. A legionary falling to the ground. Safe and calm, with an outstretched arm, von Klasewitz aimed at the next target. Pulled the trigger. The gun jerked up. An enemy legionary grabbed his chest and collapsed. A new target. The bullets whipped through the air, and the rifles, apparently only a few, were seeking their victims. Von Klasewitz, however, they seemed to magically miss.

The man was completely focused, sought his victims, aimed, shot, got them every single time, aimed again. Men gathered around him, defending him against attackers who had come near enough. They were many. Too many. The traitor shot, and he never failed, but for each fallen, two new ones seemed to grow out of the ground. And the group of his own defenders shrank more and more. Then trumpets sounded, and the ground trembled.

Von Klasewitz looked around, recognized horsemen, who rode wildly toward the cannons. Hundreds. Alanians. The allies. The nobleman felt a sudden relief.

Maximus had to know about their situation.

It clicked.

Von Klasewitz stared at his empty pistol. He fingered for the second magazine until he remembered that he had just shot it. He lowered the tired arm, stuck the pistol away.

He raised the shortsword, which he also carried on the belt, but then he realized the attack had subsided.

And then it was completely over.

It took a while for a Roman officer to approach him. Von Klasewitz didn't know the man, but he belonged to Maximilian's liaison with the Alanians. He looked at the cannons and nodded his satisfaction.

"We have driven the enemy away, Tribune!" he announced. "Your thunder-pipes are undamaged."

Von Klasewitz looked around and saw that the man was right.

Nothing had happened to the cannons.

But that didn't matter. For when the traitor saw about the ranks of his men, it was also clear that the cavalry had really come at the very last moment. The artillerists had already had to defend themselves against the enemy, and it had been a bloody struggle. Everywhere, the scattered bodies of the dead and wounded were visible. Many of them were once his men.

The nobleman shook his head.

"You must resume fire," the Roman officer said. Von Klasewitz made a weak hand movement toward his men.

"I still have enough trained soldiers for two cannons," he replied exhausted. "Report this to Maximus. Only two cannons. The rest of the men are dead or too badly wounded."

The officer looked around as if he hadn't noticed the consequences of the enemy's attack. He fell silent, then nodded and stepped off.

Von Klasewitz turned around, looking at the battlefield, on which the fight still raged, evidently with unbroken intensity.

For him, however, the battle was over.

40

The hand grenade flew high. The legionary who had thrown it fell, struck down by three or four bullets, stumbling to the ground and was probably already dead when he hit the dirt. But his grenade flew directly toward von Geeren, in a beautiful curve. The officer looked at it as if in slow motion. A good number of Maximus' grenades had proved to be crude and unreliable. They had something like an impact fuse, which didn't work in more than half of the cases. The front line was littered with non-ignited grenades. They could be thrown back and some enterprising soldiers did, and sometimes they would even detonate at the second try. But the German infantry had their own hand grenades, not many, but much more reliable. When the enemy legionaries had approached them, the prepared order had been given, the salvoes had ebbed for a moment, and instead, each man had hurled two German hand grenades onto the advancing, crouching opponents. Where the cover helped them not to be hit by the rifles, the attackers had no protection against the grenades. When a whole front line of bodies was torn by the explosions, and the succeeding legionaries reached the dead and wounded comrades, bleeding from partial wounds, the enthusiasm of the attackers had visibly diminished. Von Geeren had even discovered first legionaries who had cautiously made their way back.

But not all of them. And this grenade flew at him with terrifying certainty. Von Geeren didn't know where to throw himself. An explosion would catch him anyway.

A hard fist tore him down, a shadow fell on him. Centurion Verilius dragged him behind the large, square shield, forged from iron. Normally, the Roman army had no use for such strong shields; they were too expensive and too heavy. But when it became clear that the enemy had grenades, Rheinberg had plundered the Emperor's honor guard, and left the great shields to Verilius and his men. They offered some protection against an explosion, especially against the flying splinters. However, a certain distance was necessary. In the immediate vicinity of the detonation, the shield would also be in danger of contributing to the generation of shrapnel.

Von Geeren heard the warnings of his men. He reminded himself to shout as well. He opened his mouth, but then he heard the dull sound of the grenade reaching the ground, and all his muscles tightened in instinctive expectation of the explosion.

Nothing happened.

He peered past the edge of the shield, saw the grenade lying on the ground a few meters in front of him. The impact fuse had failed, but the weapon was a permanent danger. An unintentional touch could already trigger the detonation.

Two large sandbags fell on the dud, expertly thrown out of the cover by two German soldiers. Sandbags, which had been used as defense against arrows. However, the attacks of the enemy archers were not half as dangerous as these duds. When the two heavy and voluminous sacks hit the grenade, von Geeren once again expected the detonation. But nothing happened. Three more sandbags were quickly piled up. If the grenade was now going to explode, it wouldn't do much harm.

Von Geeren had little time to relish his feeling of relief. When he wanted to turn to Verilius to express his gratitude, he was already pushed aside. Out of nowhere, an enemy soldier had appeared out of the ground in front of them. Either he had approached with greatest care, or had been so muddled in the chaos that he had escaped general attention. He was a muscular, strong man, who jumped forward with determination, the sword forward like an extension of his own body, and at once appointing the German officer as his victim.

Verilius raised his blade, took a step forward, pulled with his left von Geeren behind himself. The blow of the attacker was powerful but hit the wrong target, bounced hard against the Centurion's shield. Verilius threw the cover away at once, as it hindered him in the fight. Fearless, almost with contempt, the Centurion awaited the next move of his opponent.

It didn't come. Geeren had taken advantage of the distraction, raised his pistol, and pulled the trigger. The impact threw the legionary back, he stumbled, the arm with the sword suddenly lowered. He gave von Geeren a last look, half disappointed, half confused, then he fell to the ground and died.

The young German looked at the corpse for a moment. Then he raised his eyes, looking for more attackers. But it remained quiet. Was the enemy's onslaught broken? The officer moved behind the entrenchment, looked at the battlefield. The traitor's cannons were hardly firing. But the legions of the usurper pressed forward. The part of the formation, which was closest to the infantry, was grouped together. Warning calls arose. Again, the flank of the German position was attacked. Verilius raised his arm in greeting, then he had already disappeared to hurry to his men, who were now under pressure.

Von Geeren wiped sweat from his forehead. A glance at the clock informed him that only an hour had passed since the beginning of the battle, and yet he felt exhausted. He took a sip of water from his bottle. The attack of the legionary had been very purposeful, directly against him.

This couldn't be a coincidence. The officer had been easily identifiable. Von Klasewitz had passed on the information about the appearance of officers so that the legionaries could identify someone like him with no doubt. The only one who had abandoned his uniform was Rheinberg, since he felt compelled to look like the Magister Militium was supposed to. He wore the mixture of "armor and skirt," as the Germans secretly called it, which was similar to that of other Roman officers. Von Geeren was quite glad not to have to wear it. He didn't assume that he had particularly beautiful legs.

"They're attacking again," one of his men shouted. The Captain didn't have to use the binoculars. The legionaries were well to be recognized, though they had repeatedly thrown themselves down on the ground, crouching like a flood toward the German position. Other divisions remained standing and began rapid storm attacks to direct the fire of the guns. Von Geeren bit his teeth when he took note of this kind of heroism, which bordered on complete self-sacrifice.

The problem was that this tactic could work. The first targeted shots of the infantrymen met.

"Save ammunition!" von Geeren shouted. "Aim carefully! No waste!"

Even the MG shooters fired with only short bursts of fire. This was their biggest problem: After the skirmishes and fighting so far, they slowly and surely ran out of supplies. Dahms couldn't compensate for losses through his workshops in the foreseeable future. It wouldn't be long before they were left with only the bayonets, which had already been attached to the mouths of the rifles. For von Geeren it was clear that he would at this moment command full retreat. In close combat with the blade, his men, despite all the exercises, were far inferior to an experienced legionary. It would be a quick and very one-sided slaughter.

A machine gun barked. A row of rushing legionaries ran against a wall and fell to the ground.

Quick and one-sided like this.

The Captain looked toward the place where he knew Rheinberg and the other generals. No new flags, no trumpet signals, no messages – no new orders. Rheinberg had other problems.

Von Geeren wasn't happy about it. He suddenly missed Jonas Becker. The burden of responsibility pressed heavily on his shoulders.

Shots fell. Victims screamed. The Captain saw another hand grenade fly, landing too short, detonating without damage. Nevertheless, von Geeren had his face in the mud again.

He was trembling.

He was actually quite terrified.

41

"We are not simply doing well, we have the advantage!"

Rheinberg nodded with delight. The Emperor had described the situation to the point. Malobaudes grunted affirmatively. He seemed to share the judgment of his Lord.

Just now, Gratian had given the order to use the favor of the moment. The battle had already lasted almost two hours. The extensive elimination of the enemy's artillery had above all a very positive psychological effect on the Emperor's troops. The fact that the German infantry didn't have the same effect as hoped for was due to the fact that Maximus threw many men against their positions, and although he had not yet overcome them, he nevertheless tied the firepower of the Germans. The lack of ammunition was also noticeable. Rheinberg sensed that this was the last great battle in which he could massively involve the infantry. And he had to talk to Dahms. No matter what projects the engineer also pursued, he had to ensure ammunition supplies.

Gratian had ordered to throw the reserve, including some his own hand-picked bodyguard, into the battle. There was a certain irony in the fact that a good part of the Guard consisted of Alanian riders, who now fought against their countrymen. In another time, in the past, these riders had betrayed Gratian to fight with Maximus. But now everyone wanted to be on the side of the winner, so at least Rheinberg's impression was.

The fresh troops, boosted by the prospect of an imminent triumph and the promise of considerable loot, put Maximus's army under great pressure. The usurper's legionaries were brave and extremely disciplined. But it was clear that the momentum was now Gratian's side. If they didn't readjust now, the Comes' front lines would soon break. And with that, this nightmare of an uprising was ended once and for all.

Malobaudes bent over the great representation of the battlefield. Different pieces of wood symbolized the units of both sides, their position constantly updated by scouts, who had tirelessly rushed from one side of the battlefield to the other. The old general looked thoughtful.

"Maximus doesn't have too many options," he said.

"He can end the battle and seek his salvation," Arbogast, who also belonged to their council of war, presumed.

"Maximus isn't stupid. He will not throw away his men in a senseless gesture," Gratian said. "On the contrary, I expect him to send an emissary to begin negotiations."

Malobaudes looked up. "What will Maximus get from us?"

Gratian features hardened. "Nothing for him and his officers, General. He is a traitor, an usurper. I was gracious with him, though I knew what he had done in Rheinberg's time. But he had to hit even faster than planned. There is no mercy and no excuse for him. I want to give him the chance to judge himself, with his sword, honorably. The same option should be given to his generals and all other high-ranking conspirators. I want to readily spare them the shame of an execution. But I will not be able to assure my position if I'll be too forgiving."

Gratian's expression grew softer, tired, as he continued. "The soldiers and the allies, however, should enjoy my willingness to show some grace. They are professional troops, I cannot just let them go. They'll receive the offer of pardon and may remain in the service of the Empire. I will transfer those legions far into the East, and exchange the officers. Fresh troops are to be relocated to Britain. The men have executed the commands of their superiors, and they have been promised great honors."

Gratian sighed. "I know I haven't done enough in the past few years, especially in some remote provinces like Britain. There is still a lot to catch up. I won't make those legionaries suffer for my own mistakes."

Malobaudes seemed to think about what he had said.

"But Maximus' attempt has a much deeper reason than that, Augustus," he said. He nodded his head in Rheinberg's direction. "Whether we like it or not, it has both a political and a religious component. Ambrosius is involved, as we now know. Is the Bishop to die?"

Gratian shook his head. "No. I will force him to a more private life. It would be fatal, however, to make him a martyr. And of course you're right, General, if you say that the cause for this uprising is to be found deeper. Nevertheless, I believe that both the economic and political reforms introduced, as well as the approach of tolerance in religious matters, are indispensable. It may destabilize the situation in the short term, but the long-term benefits will be enormous."

Malobaudes looked at Gratian. There was a sudden determination in his features. "Very well, sir," he muttered. "If this is your will ..."

The sword leaped into his hand, so quickly had he pulled it. Malobaudes uttered a loud cry. It was no battle cry, it was a signal, Rheinberg was sure. He rushed forward, but the General's blade, which was a few steps closer to Gratian, was already swinging from behind into the chest of the young Emperor.

Gratian made a helpless, almost gentle defensive move.

But any strength had already left his body. He looked at Malobaudes with the bewildered astonishment targeted toward a person who had enjoyed trust and then turned out to be a traitor.

Gratian sank to the ground, glancing at the tip of the sword that protruded from his chest. A quick stab, right on target, powerful, by an experienced fighter, but the heart had probably just been missed. Not by much. Blood leaped from the wound, the heart artery was intersected.

Gratian, Emperor of Rome, died without another word.

Then the tarpaulins of the tent were cut up, and soldiers, recognizable as men of Gratian's own cavalry, became visible. The betrayal went deep, Rheinberg realized. He had his pistol in his hand, aimed at the murderer, but he was already surrounded by his allies, who now pulled their swords.

Legionaries from the bodyguard, who had remained at the tent, stormed in, saw the bleeding body of the dead emperor lying on the ground, saw the hated barbarians. Shouting arose. Blades were drawn.

Somebody dragged Rheinberg by the arm. It was Arbogast, the old general, and like a child, Rheinberg stood aside.

"You must go," Arbogast said. "You are next!"

Rheinberg's arm went up, a shot cracked, then a second. Two enemy warriors fell to the ground screaming. More legionaries pushed forward.

Arbogast pulled Rheinberg's arm again. "Go. Here is nothing to gain for you!"

How true, the young German thought. He heard the calls from outside the tent: "The Augustus is dead! Gratian is murdered!"

Rheinberg stumbled back. He shot again, as if mechanically, fighting warriors, one, another one, one more, while he retreated, led by Arbogast. The General chopped up the tarp, peered through, waited a moment for Rheinberg to kill another attacker up close, heard the empty magazine's click, a sound he could well understand, and dragged Rheinberg into the open.

The German acted like in trance. He heard trumpets bleed to mark the retreat. Rheinberg reared up. "I have to lead the army," he hissed to Arbogast. "The battle ..."

"The battle is lost," the old man returned. "The death of the Emperor will break the soldiers. This day belongs to Maximus now. But the war is not over yet. We'll regroup at Ravenna!"

Rheinberg didn't know whether he should rely on that so easily. "The infantry ..."

"Have their orders for this, right?" Arbogast asked. "If Tribune von Geeren is clever, he will already let his men fall back. Verilius will take care of it. Maximus' legionaries will let go of their attacks when they realize that they have won the battle. The bloodbath ensuing if they would attack the escaping infantry would be too great. The Comes cannot give that order now, and he knows that too. The battle is won, that is enough for him."

"But ..."

Arbogast cursed. Impatience was clearly visible in his face. "No more. We need to regroup. We must appoint a successor to Gratian.

And as soon as possible. The Senate is in Treveri. He must declare Theodosius emperor."

Rheinberg was dizzy. Where does all of this lead to? He had been so anxious to change the course of time, he had been so confident as to be able to avert the greatest catastrophes ... but fate had proved to be persevering, not wanting to be avoided by him. It had pushed Maximus into insurrection, had killed Gratian, and now would make Theodosius emperor?

It was all pointless?

Rheinberg shook his head, let Arbogast lead him, whose iron will and energy were now enough for two.

There was turmoil in the camp. Everywhere soldiers ran around. Rheinberg saw that the General was right with his speculation. The army dissolved. Officers had probably managed the situation so far that it became an orderly retreat. With a little luck, the part of the army that didn't go over to the victorious Maximus, would be able to retreat to Ravenna.

"Here, on horseback," Arbogast said.

"I cannot leave now," Rheinberg said, breaking from the old General's grip. "That would make me a coward. I am the Magister Militium."

"Maximus' people will be hunting you."

"That's the way it is."

Rheinberg exchanged the magazine in his gun, loaded it, and put it in the belt. "We're collecting the troops that still want to follow us," he decided. "We'll move back to Treveri. You there!"

Rheinberg called for a man who had passed by. It was one of the soldiers from the messengers unit. "Sir? The troops ..."

"I know. Ride back to Treveri. The court is to set off for Ravenna immediately. They should send a message to Richomer, so he knows what happened. Get on your way!"

"Yes!"

Rheinberg stopped Arbogast, strutting toward the camp.

A moment later, the General was with him, the blade shining in his hand.

The tent was now almost empty. The traitors had helped Malobaudes to escape. Legionaries stood helplessly around the body of the Emperor, apparently under the command of a decurion, who also didn't know what was to be done. When Rheinberg and Arbogast entered, all faces turned toward them.

"Cover the body!" Rheinberg ordered. "Take him to one of the carts. Then escort him directly to Ravenna. Wrap him in a cloth. We have no time for a major effort in preserving the corpse. Hurry up. We shall later bury him as it befits. He mustn't fall into the hands of Maximus!"

Grateful to receive clear instructions, the legionaries immediately set to work. Other men appeared. Arbogast began to issue orders to retreat.

Then von Geeren rushed in. He was unharmed, as Rheinberg was pleased to see.

"The men of Maximus are approaching the camp! We must get away!"

"How is your unit?" Rheinberg asked.

"I've lost 17 men. We've been carrying weapons and ammunition. When we left, the attacks subsided."

"Your men are ready for the march?"

"Any time."

"We're still waiting. The legionaries who want to leave with us need cover."

"Maximus doesn't seem to want to enact a massacre among the fugitives," von Geeren contradicted.

"No, he's hoping for deserters. But once it is clear which units don't want to follow him, he will pick up the pressure. He should be encouraged to think twice about any attempt."

Von Geeren nodded and turned away. He didn't need more specific orders. They had prepared for this probability in their planning. The escape route was known. The Captain would position his men along the military road and ward off attacks by Maximus' legionaries, most likely cavalry. Rifle bullets and horses were unequal opponents. It was to be hoped that the Comes, who had hitherto proven to be a very sensible opponent, would also see this.

Some minutes passed, during which Rheinberg and Arbogast

gave orders and gathered an overview of the situation. Gratian's corpse had now been removed. They actually managed to conduct an orderly retreat.

Finally, the reports became more and more urgent indicating that Maximus' army approached. Rheinberg saw that he couldn't do much more. The first of his own units were already marching along the military road toward Trier. All the officers were informed.

"It's about time for us to go, too," Rheinberg decided, nodding to the General. They didn't dismantle the tent but ensured that every information contained on the map and important documents was either burned or taken along.

Then Rheinberg and Arbogast sat on the back of their horses and accompanied the stream of the refugees. They also received the reports of messengers, officers and clerks. A picture of the defeat was slowly emerging.

"We lost a good 8,000 men in the battle," Rheinberg summed up after receiving the last reports. "And as it seems, more than 10,000 legionaries, but above all auxiliary units, have deserted to Maximus' side. No one of the very high officers – apart from Malobaudes – but many from the middle hierarchy, especially those who are at the same time tribal princes or nobles. Maximus seems to have developed good communication to these people."

Arbogast didn't flinch at Rheinberg's somewhat clumsy way to express himself in Latin. He had learned to correctly interpret the strange allusions of the time-wanderer from context.

"If Richomer did his job well, then we have the foundation for a second line of defense to work with," Arbogast concluded. "It all depends on what Maximus will do next."

"He will go to Treveri and hope that the Senate will confirm him there, directly after Gratian's death, as the new emperor. Even if the Senate wouldn't succumb to his wishes, he will surely be appointed by his troops, and by so many provincial politicians and leaders of the military administration as he can scrape together in order to assert the legitimacy of his claim."

Arbogast nodded. "We must appoint our own successor as quickly as possible. It must be someone who is capable of acting decisively and is able to bundle the different forces of the Empire. Someone with legitimacy. I remain with Theodosius as the appropriate candidate."

Rheinberg said nothing. Perhaps the idea wasn't so stupid in the end. Perhaps the present Theodosius wouldn't commit many of the errors of his alter ego in Rheinberg's past, now that he knew what had happened there. Perhaps one would be able to work with the Spanish nobleman, to focus on his qualities. Theodosius was no enemy of Gratian. He wouldn't approve of the murder by a traitor. Maximus would find in him an opponent who was just as exasperated as the Theodosius of Rheinberg's time.

He took a deep breath and watched the long column of disciplined and exhausted legionaries. The struggle wasn't lost yet.

It had only become much, much more difficult.

42

It was a beautiful child.

Everything had happened as the two midwives had said.

"The first child," they had told Julia, "needs the longest. From the second, it is faster, then the body knows what all of this is about. But the first will strain your patience, noble Julia."

After the first eight hours of labor, Julia had felt anything but noble. At the end of the second eight hours, when the new human had finally appeared, she could no longer express her own feelings. She had been at the very end of her strength and had done nothing but what the midwives advised her, with one objective in mind, that this merciless torture might finally come to an end.

When the shrieking bundle had been laid upon her arm, she had been completely exhausted, but the feeling of happiness left the torment forgotten, at least for the moment. A midwife had happily assured her that the baby was complete and healthy. It was true that the old practice of placing maligned children immediately after birth in front of the city walls had been officially banned for some time, but above all, elderly women were still – often unspoken – of the opinion that it was for the best to immediately surrender such children to death.

The question didn't arise here. To check the completeness, it was also necessary to determine the gender of the child. The real problem began here: Julia had repeatedly told Martinus Caius, the alleged father, her conviction that she would give him a heir, a son. The warm bundle in her arm, however, was a beautiful and active daughter.

Now, a few days after her birth, with Julia a little bit recovered, the young mother's husband had also been able to take a look at "his" offspring. When it was revealed to him that it was a girl, a most unfavorable expression had been visible on his face.

For Julia, it was ultimately no matter what Caius thought about her daughter, which was not his. She knew that Thomas never expressed an immediate and single-minded interest in a son. She also knew that daughters built a special relationship with their fathers, if the latter were only sufficiently interested. After all, she had been able to successfully manipulate the feelings of such a bond with her own father for ten years. So she didn't worry much about Thomas.

Martinus Caius, also under pressure from his own parents, wouldn't wait very long to take action to secure the desired offspring for his own family. That wouldn't have mattered to Julia, if these actions wouldn't involve her. But they did, unfortunately.

Until now, she had been able to reject such advances. It helped that her mother, Lucia, who watched over her granddaughter like a guard, and the two nursemaids jumped to her side, and made – in the absence of the Caius – blasphemous commentaries on his "amusing manners." The common female bulwark against all too early desires of a frustrated husband held the – so far – rather clumsy attempts to overcome them at bay. But the more days turned into weeks, the weaker the line of defense. Julia had changed her tactics. Suddenly, sufficient and even generous supplies of wine and German liquor had appeared in the house, and eager, almost imposing slaves almost forced the alcoholic beverages on her husband. Caius, without any aversion, yielded to drunkenness. This usually led to the fact that he had had to break off any attempt at an approach because he simply lacked the strength.

But that too wouldn't work forever.

So it was almost a gift from the Lord, when the news of the battle in Belgica came to Ravenna, and General Richomer placed the whole province under direct imperial administration to organize the defense.

This lead to a number of consequences. Martinus Caius' father decided that the young mother and her daughter, who had received the name Lucilla, had to leave Ravenna. Since the family of Caius had extensive possessions throughout the Empire, they decided to evacuate the women and the children of the family to the east, which had been very quiet for almost a year. A large *latifundium* on an island in Greece was considered her new place of residence. There were also many servants at her disposal. They wouldn't miss anything.

The good thing about this arrangement was the exclusion of all adult male members of the household. On the contrary, the patriarch of the family said that all men had to work for the defense of the town and the possessions of their relatives. Private militias were organized by the city's well-to-do families to guard special buildings and warehouses. Last but not least, the fear of a possible attack were increased by the prospect of plundering or arson. It wouldn't be the first time a competitor would use a military situation to settle old bills. And Caius the Elder had buried a lot of corpses in his cellar. That his son was now recruited to participate in an effort to ensure that these bodies remained hidden, was very favorable for Julia. For months, she was sure, Martinus wouldn't be able to touch her.

And with a bit of luck, he would be fighting for Ravenna's defense. And die in the effort.

Deep in her heart, Julia bore the gracelessness and hardness of Rome, which had led to growth of the Empire and its continued existence. Asked, she would not even want to deny it. She was not the only one with this attitude. Her own mother, Lucia, was proof enough for the thesis that behind every Roman leader there could be a more ruthless Roman wife.

Apart from this fortunate coincidence, the impending attack of Maximus, however, filled her with concern. Especially since she absolutely didn't know where Thomas Volkert was in this confusion. Was he still in the East in search of the Huns? Had he, like so many other troops, been summoned to Ravenna to risk a new battle against the usurper? Nor did the occasional letter from her slave Claudia's brother in Noricum tell much. At last she had heard some of the troops sent to the East had returned. But was Thomas among them? It was this kind of uncertainty that filled her with great inner unrest. That made her very irritable, together with the lack of sleep due to her daughter's needs. Everyone kept himself as far away from her as they could. Even Mother Lucia seemed to have developed more respect. Of course, she could have given Lucilla away, like many rich women, to a nurse-maid, a slave girl who had just given birth to a baby and was able to breast-feed both. On the one hand, Julia had developed a different attitude to slavery with time, surely under the impression of very clear words from Thomas. And on the other hand, Lucilla was her living, breathing connection with the man who was her "real" husband. So she didn't want to cut that connection with Thomas even for a moment. When, together with a few other female family members, she entered the transport galley en route to Greece along the coast, she was very, very tired.

Lucilla, it seemed, liked the fresh sea air.

When the galley departed, Julia took a last look at Ravenna.

She wondered what the city would look like once she returned.

And then she wondered if she'd ever come back here at all.

43

Late in the evening Rheinberg arrived in his villa, sweaty, tired and very depressed. He let Felix and the other slaves of the house take his armor without comment. He stank terribly, but the slaves didn't flinch. They had all heard the bad news, and all of them sat on packed cases and boxes. The major-domo had correctly assumed that the whole household of the Magister Militium had to be moved to Ravenna, and the preparations for the journey had commenced immediately as soon as the first messenger had arrived with the news of the battle's outcome.

Tomorrow morning they would leave at once. Parts of the administration were already on their way to Ravenna. Relatives of those who wanted to fight Maximus moved as well. All those who basically didn't care who'd be emperor or who had hopes for new benefits and posts from the new man remained. There were no criminal courts and no official decrees. If at Ravenna the advance of Maximus could be brought to an end, it was inevitable that the Empire would have two parallel administrations, at least for some time. The situation in the East was still unclear. How would the military hierarchy decide? This depended not least on the negotiating skills of the new emperor, who was to follow in Gratian's shoes. The name of Theodosius had spread like a wildfire. Everything seemed to gear into his direction. Theodosius himself, it was said, had already arrived at Ravenna.

But what most disturbed Rheinberg was the fact that he had heard rumors that there were more aspirants to the mantle of office than expected. It was, of course, not surprising in such a situation that some adventurers smelled an opportunity. Nothing could be done, but Rheinberg's agents reported at least one serious candidate, who had secretly convinced powerful senators and had sympathies in the East. The young German had noticed these reports with increasing frustration. He felt overwhelmed. The political machinations, the ruthlessness with which one was struggling for positions and power, all this was foreign to Rheinberg, and he didn't have the necessary experience to deal with it appropriately. He felt, deep in himself, not as a politician, not even a mediocre one, and that was very painfully obvious now.

Not only that. Everything was painful. Especially his butt.

Toasted, full of thoughts swirling around in his head, Rheinberg was almost irresistibly led into the bathing area of the villa. This house had only the best facilities. A large bathroom with three different basins, of different temperatures, a massage area, and a sauna were of course included. Rheinberg was undressed and finally sank with a pleasant groan in the hot water of the small basin right next to the massage table. The heat encompassed him and almost immediately released the cramps in his muscles. His body ached with every movement, and almost more than the endless rides, it was the inner tension that had spread to his muscles. Rheinberg closed his eyes and wished that he would be able to remove his giddy thoughts as easily as the pain in his limbs. But as much as he endeavored, his spirit remained active, even hectic, and the image of the fallen Gratian, the bitter feeling of treason, the retreat of the imperial troops, all returned with stubborn regularity. For a moment, Rheinberg thought about simply drinking away the tension with a considerable amount of wine. But he knew he had to make decisions tomorrow morning, and a hangover wouldn't help him very much with that.

And so his body rested without his mind relaxing. He noticed that this inner unrest also spread to his limbs, that he was moving in the water, although he wanted to remain calm. He opened his eyes, gazed at the steam rising from the hot water. Through the refraction of the liquid he saw the blurred image of his hands, with the roughened skin, slightly reddish due to the warmth, sullen and not too vigorous. He could still feel the pistol's handle squeezing into his palm, drawing a pattern on his skin, and pulling the trigger, again and again, until the magazine was empty. The picture of the dying soldiers in front of his eyes, stifled by his striking shots, bloody and fading, intermingled again and again with that of Gratian, cut down by a sword. How secure the Emperor had felt after he knew that the future, which had once led to his early end, now no longer existed – only exchanged, as Rheinberg bitterly thought, by a much earlier demise. Hubris, that was what he had to accuse himself of. The assumption that with a handful of men, a ship, and sparse knowledge of the past, he could change the course of the world in the face of all emnity, even like a messiah, and could do everything so that all would be so much better.

What foolishness.

The bitter thoughts engulfed Rheinberg again, and he felt the sudden need to cry. He knew that his depression had much to do with the leaden fatigue that gripped him, but even this rationalization didn't help. It was not that he would wake up tomorrow morning and the world would look quite different. The problems marched toward him a very literal sense. The fact that he could retreat to the *Saarbrücken* at any time, and escape with the cruiser from the confusion, held only a temporary consolation. He wouldn't be able to look into the mirror again if he didn't try to save what could be saved. And yet, in spite of all the comrades and friends who would support him, he had been very much disturbed by Jonas Becker's death. He knew how someone like Gratian must have felt, young, inexperienced, surrounded by people of whom he never knew very well whether he could trust them or not, equipped with power of which he was more a tool than anything else. Yes, Rheinberg came to the conclusion that it was probably this feeling of being driven, which was particularly nagging at him, the painful realization of being a toy in someone's game, which he had for a while considered to master.

Bitter. Very bitter.

There was a rippling sound beside him. Rheinberg looked up. Tanned skin, a slender leg sinking into the water, followed by a female body. The young man recognized the shape, moistened by steam, of a beautiful woman, slim, with full breasts, a wide, inviting hip. He saw her face and recognized Aurelia. For some reason, he wasn't surprised.

248

The former slave, who had been his guest at dinner ever since their renewed encounter in the archives of the palace, slid beside him on the hot stone bench. He felt her hip touching his, soft and compliant, and her hand, as if by chance, on his thigh. She didn't say a word, and he didn't talk as well.

For a few minutes they just sat there. Rheinberg didn't move. Whether from fatigue or shyness, he couldn't tell. He looked at Aurelia, a little cautiously from the side, wondering what he should say, and saw in her face something like determination, as if an important decision had been made, which had to be put into action. Rheinberg's gaze then fell on the thin leather sheath, which lay between the breasts, down the slender, long neck of the woman. From there the grip of a thin blade protruded, a knife often used in assassinations. Whatever heat Rheinberg had felt, now it was suddenly very cold. He stared at the blade. Aurelia followed his gaze. Then she talked.

"I was promised a lot," she said.

"What exactly?" Rheinberg asked hoarsely. He didn't know if he should look at the breasts or the knife. It was a combination that allowed somehow the heat return to him.

"Freedom. A livelihood. Some land. Slaves."

"For what?"

"To use this blade to kill you."

Rheinberg stared into the water, shocked and rattled to the bone, feeling very weak and sad.

Aurelia, there was no doubt, was part of the network of betrayal and intrigue that had been woven around Gratian and himself. She had been a gift to Renna. Did the military prefect, who together with Richomer organized his second line of defense, also belong to the conspirators?

And why did she tell him all this?

"You've had your chance. I didn't hear you enter the bathroom. You decided against it," he said quietly.

Aurelia reached behind her neck, loosened the ribbon on which the blade hung, rolled it around the leather case and handed it to Rheinberg. He automatically reached for it, weighed the light blade in his hand, then placed it casually on the edge of the basin.

"I've been thinking about it. I reconsidered," she said.

"Why? It was a clear assignment. I was an easy target."

Aurelia nodded. "Too easy."

"I don't understand."

"You've already given me most of what I've been promised. Freedom. Some gold."

"That was all?"

"I've found a good position, difficult enough for a freed slave. I could never have had this opportunity before."

Rheinberg frowned. "I've released you. You weren't so happy at first."

"Oh, I was perhaps a bit uncomfortable. And it would have been much easier to kill you if I had remained your slave. It was important to me at the time."

"What's important to you now?" Rheinberg wondered that he could ask this question so calmly. He was struck by a wild confusion of feelings that pushed the political and military situation into the background. Such an wild storm of emotions, all at once, could be overwhelming. He felt the sudden need for a sip of Köhler's brandy.

"That I do the right thing," Aurelia said. She played with the index finger, curling the short hair on Rheinberg's thigh. But she didn't look at him, just at the steam of the bath.

"You have decided not to kill me."

"Yes."

"Why?"

Aurelia hesitated. "That might sound silly now, my lord."

"Do not call me that. You have already freed yourself from addressing me that way."

The former slave girl smiled. "There were many reasons to kill you. Some have lost any meaning. Others are no longer so important. I cannot at the same time be grateful to you for giving me my freedom and then kill you. I'm not a doll in the hands of those who want you ill. Also, I like you."

Rheinberg sighed. Should he be satisfied with this explanation?

250

"You have trouble believing."

Rheinberg nodded. He was very tired.

Aurelia's hand wandered slightly. Her search found what she was looking for, and to his own astonishment, Rheinberg noted that he was not as exhausted as he thought.

Without thinking about it, he leaned over to Aurelia. His lips found hers in a gentle, almost hesitant kiss, followed by a second, not so hesitant anymore.

His mother, remembered Rheinberg at the most unfavorable time, when the palm of his left hand closed around Aurelia's breast, a damp, cozy feeling of soft warmth, had always warned him about such girls.

He kissed Aurelia again, intensely, long-lasting, almost breathlessly.

Who gave anything to the warnings of a woman who wasn't even born yet?

Jan Rheinberg sank into the heat that surrounded him in so many ways.

He decided not to have any further doubts for the moment.

44

The military headquarters in Ravenna was full of vigorous activity. A seemingly undisciplined mixture of officers ran around the premises, orders were given, messages forwarded. The chaos was actually well-structured. In the middle stood four men to whom all the different threads seemed to flow. General Richomer, Military Prefect Renna, the Spaniard Theodosius, and Johann Dahms, who was present as the official representative of the *Saarbrücken*. On a table beside them, a mountain of messages lay; numerous scouts kept them up to date with the latest news.

"When Rheinberg arrives with the remnants of Gratian's army in two days," Richomer said, "there is not much time left to unite them with our troops. We will keep them separate, and only use them in a unified movement if we cannot do otherwise."

"Maximus will appear a few days later, if he keeps his marching speed," Renna said thoughtfully. "There really is no time."

"And it doesn't look good," Dahms said finally.

They all looked at him. In the discussion of the last half-hour, the engineer had increasingly perceived that the Roman officers were trying to hide some unpleasant truths or didn't want to make a point. For this he had no sympathy.

"We are doing very well, and your leadership is exceptional," Dahms said in one of his rare approaches to diplomatic expression. "But the situation is as follows. First, the remains of Gratian's army are exhausted and demoralized after their defeat. The losses are considerable, there are still deserters, discipline is therefore questionable. I guess we can count on maybe 15,000 men. Secondly, the relief troops assembled here in Ravenna are miserable. There are a few recruits, a few reinforcements from the East, we are talking about 10,000 men, and I don't want to speculate how well and

252

disciplined they can fight. Third is the mood in the population. Nowadays the Church, under the careful guidance of the Bishop of Milan, is very effective in fomenting the unrest among the population and against the time-wanderers. They put the blame for the entire fiasco on us. The people are restless, are rightly afraid of a siege of the city or a house-to-house fight. The spies and agitators of the insurgents are hardly kept in check. Right now, after Gratian's death, Maximus is brought into play as the guarantor of stability and, above all, of religious righteousness. The Trinitarians call him their man, and that is not a coincidence. Moderate voices are silent or aren't heard. What happens, gentlemen, if Maximus attacks Ravenna and at the same time a popular uprising is organized? Do you expect us to direct the guns of the *Saarbrücken* to the city and inflict a massacre among the citizens? This is a very different situation from Thessaloniki! And finally, fourthly, if the reports don't deceive me, Maximus has more than compensated for the losses he suffered in Belgica by means of defectors and new auxiliary troops. We are talking about an army close to 40,000 men, well-motivated, a victory on their scorecard, and convinced of the legitimacy of their own actions. Is Gratian's death not correctly to be interpreted by the Trinitarians as the finger of God, who indicates to everyone who he prefers and whose contemptuous, fickle, overbearing attitude toward heretics he condemns? Four points only, gentlemen, and I could continue the list: The ammunition supplies of our infantrymen, for example, are almost exhausted. We must use the guns of the cruiser during an attack. However, the prospective battlefield lies much further away from the ship than at Thessaloniki, which makes misses inevitable. I repeat: If we, the time-wanderers, cut away the civilian population of Ravenna, then our future in the Roman Empire is doomed. We're not going to do that."

Dahms paused, a little exhausted. It had been a long speech for a man who was more likely to hold back with verbal utterances. Thoughtful silence of the three addressed Romans was the immediate reaction.

Renna sighed softly. "The issue of agitation among the population is well described. And it is not limited to the civilians. I see how the priests approach my men. If I get them, they say that they will only bless the soldiers, so that the Lord will protect them in the coming battles. What should I say? At least I cannot forbid the Christians among my men to speak with priests. This would tend to increase disquiet and mistrust, and at the same time be detrimental. There are also Arian churchmen. I'm not sure what we can do to solve this problem."

"What you say, Magister Dahms," Richomer added, "is that our plan to make Ravenna the second line of defense is already doomed."

"Those are hard words," the addressee replied. "I don't doubt there are many among us who will fight bravely and honorably against Maximus. But yes, I think that the matter is gradually slipping out of our hands, and we are in a most unpleasant situation."

Theodosius, who had hitherto been silent on the discussion, cleared his throat. "Gentlemen, I have seen senators and other officers for supper last evening," he said in a low voice. "There it was discussed that I should be appointed the successor of Gratian, all to be done in front of the legions and the Senate after the arrival of the retreating troops."

None of the men were surprised. Everyone knew that this step had become increasingly unavoidable.

"As soon as I am Emperor, I can make decisions. Dahm's words convinced me. I believe that we cannot hold Ravenna. Instead, we must retreat to the East, to Constantinople. The city is impregnable. From there, with the human potential of the East, we can fight Maximus." The Spaniard looked at Dahms and smiled. "I've learned that I did something similar in another time, your past."

Dahms nodded. "That's true. It took quite a long time, but the conditions were different. I have sympathy for your proposals. But I fear that it is already too late to realize your plan to move the troops assembled here successfully to the East, to use them as a base for the army, with which we can then proceed against Maximus."

"Why?"

Dahms pointed to the map, which hung behind them on the wall.

"Maximus is too close. Even if we march today, the usurper would get wind of it. He would change his direction and cut off our path. For a large field battle, our troops are too few, badly trained, too little experienced, without the important tactical advantage of the German infantry because of the ammunition deficit already mentioned. The likelihood of Maximus killing us without the cover of the *Saarbrücken's* cannons and without the protection of the city walls is relatively large. We simply have not enough lead to run away from him in that direction. We also do not have enough ships to move larger units. The fleet is in Constantinople. We should have made such a decision much earlier. Now it's too late."

"So we're tied up here and have to make the best out of the situation," Richomer summarized. "We should evacuate as many civilians as possible from the city, to the south. If we can only win with the support of the firepower of the *Saarbrücken*, the city will inevitably be damaged."

"Many citizens don't want to leave," Renna interjected. "An evacuation order will add to the general displeasure."

"We're going to force it through," Richomer said, clenching his fists. "We want to save the lives of these people!"

"They'll say the best way to do that is to avoid battle," Renna said gloomily. "To surrender to Maximus would finally solve all problems."

Dahms looked strangely at Renna for a moment. He was silent, however, as the future emperor again took the floor.

"That is absurd," Theodosius said. "This would jeopardize what we have achieved so far. Maximus is not incapable, but he is a fanatic. With him as emperor ..."

It was quite astonishing to hear these words from the mouth of Theodosius, especially remembering the fact that in Dahms's past he had been given the nickname "the Great" for his efforts to establish the trinitarian state church. He didn't differ essentially from the ambitions of the usurping Comes. However, this was no longer the same Theodosius.

"I don't suggest we capitulate," Renna murmured. "But we should take Dahms's words seriously. Rheinberg will not order to attack the city with the cannons. In fact, I rather believe that we will enter the *Saarbrücken* together with Theodosius, Rheinberg and send the senators gathered here to Constantinople. We stay here and try to keep Italy. We continue to the South, playing games with Maximus. Then he cannot afford to concentrate all his attention to the East, and we gain time to establish a new army over there and then take the enemy from two sides. The additional strategic advantage is that we are able to dominate the Mediterranean with the *Saarbrücken* and the steam boats. We can communicate quickly, regardless of weather, and move troops, even if not too many."

Richomer looked approvingly at Renna. "That's an excellent suggestion. We are not looking for the ultimate and final battle here! We dance with Maximus! He is to follow us throughout Italy, always beautifully in a wide circle. And he will wait until you, Theodosius, together with Rheinberg, prepare the East for the counterattack."

The men looked at each other. Sudden confidence, indeed enthusiasm, was visible in their faces. Then they bent over the map.

When Rheinberg arrived, a complete plan would be ready for execution.

45

Ambrosius passed through the entrance hall. Two legionaries stood in the alcove, looking at the Bishop without suspicion. He who had been admitted to the palace many times, somehow belonged here by now. The clergyman was not alone in the hall. In the middle of the sunny courtyard two more men stood, evidently engrossed in conversation. The Bishop went up to them. When they recognized his presence, polite greetings were exchanged. Maximus Magnus knew just as well as General Andragathius that much of their current success was due to the fact that the Bishop was openly supporting their cause.

A little respect couldn't hurt. In the new Rome, under an Emperor Maximus, Ambrosius would be the most important representative of the Church. The Bishop himself exercised a humble, modest attitude. He hid his triumphant feelings of victory and his satisfaction about Gratian's demise quite well. He was surprised that he felt only the slightest regret about the death of the young emperor.

"Augustus," Ambrosius greeted Maximus, whereupon the latter raised his hands.

"Not yet, Bishop, not yet. We arrived in Treveri this morning, and will be heading to Ravenna by tomorrow. I intend to have the proclamation done this evening, if you like to attend."

"I do. I will be there and bless you."

"That would be good."

Ambrosius's public support was important in order to confer legitimacy to the appointment of Maximus as emperor – just as important as the two dozen senators who had been present in Treveri to give the Comes some political blessing. It was indisputable that his troops had already provided him with the purple the day before. But Maximus placed great emphasis on appropriate protocol and the widest possible support. He wanted a strong mandate in the coming confrontation, and that there was still a lot of work to do, everyone was aware of, even after the victory in Belgica.

"So you march at once to Ravenna?" Ambrosius asked.

"That's the way it is planned. I'll let the troops relax for one night; we have many hasty marches behind us. The sooner we are in Italy, the faster we can prevent a serious military opposition forming there. Our spies report that Richomer and Renna, together with Theodosius, have been preparing their defense for some time. I don't want to underestimate these men. It's not over yet."

"What about Malobaudes?"

Maximus hesitated for a moment. "He has done his duty."

"And?"

"I cannot use him as a general right now," the Comes said with a glance at Andragathius, who merely nodded mutely. "Malobaudes is a traitor. He is, of course, on the right side, and has given us good advice – but many of the defectors will not be very pleased, despite the fact that they have abandoned Gratian. I can only give him a more responsible position after memory has faded over time."

"But these men are all traitors," the Bishop said.

"Yes, but most of them came to us only after Gratian's death. In their own eyes, they never betrayed him. This is somewhat different in the case of Malobaudes. I have discussed it with him, and he sees the matter like me."

"Indeed?"

"He's not a fool. He remained in Belgica with some border troops to secure the rear flanks and to show that the normal imperial administration is completely unencumbered in its work. I want to return to normality as soon as possible. We work with very volatile political capital. We need the support of the population. And we need all the righteous rebels desire peace after all has been done. And I will make sure that it will happen that way."

Ambrosius nodded. "A good decision. Tell me if the Church can help. I want to use all my influence to stabilize the situation in your sense."

Maximus bowed. "I will accept any support."

"The question remains how do we continue with the time-wanderer von Klasewitz," Andragathius muttered. "I must admit, despite his unpleasant way of dealing with his men, he has proved himself in battle. His cannons have made an important contribution to our victory. And he is brave as a person, no doubt about that."

"That's right," Maximus asserted. "I intend to strengthen the usage of this new type of weapon. The man should have his own, large artillery unit as soon as we manage the situation in Ravenna. We need to keep an eye on him, but I think he needs us more than we do need him. He strives for revenge and for confirmation, and according to the development of things, we can help him with both."

Maximus looked at Ambrosius. "What does the Church think?"

"I am not the Church," the Bishop replied. "But good that you ask. I'm less concerned with one single time-wanderer – we have him quite well under control, and he is not half as smart as he thinks. I will also look after him, work on his loyalty. He is a man who is strong in his faith and weak in his personality. I will know to use this in our favor. Leave it to me."

"Not quite," Andragathius grumbled. "He's got an official guard assigned by me. Let him know that we have him under observation."

"So be it," Maximus decided. He looked at Ambrosius.

"What else can you tell me?"

"The Church, Augustus. Think of the Bishop of Rome, the Pope. We must strengthen its authority, now and officially. I am striving for no further office, but the Church needs a strong representative, a leader, someone who has the first and the last word in secular and spiritual matters. Meet with him in Rome as soon as you can, Augustus. It is important. Very important." Maximus looked at Ambrosius, nodded slowly. The Bishop was sometimes hard to understand. Was he actually not striving for personal influence, was it sufficient for him to establish and strengthen an official state church? Or was he simply someone who preferred to exercise power from of the background so that he seemed less vulnerable?

"I will take your advice, Bishop," Maximus said. He had to go to Rome anyway, a symbolic deed that had been waiting for him. It would be appropriate to lend legitimacy to his claim.

For a moment, the men were silent, each occupied with his own thoughts.

"So there's only one thing left for today," the Bishop finally said, staring at the ground before his feet.

"What would it be?"

"May I, Augustus?"

Maximus opened his arms in an admissive gesture. Ambrosius turned away and walked through the hall. In front of the door stood one of his priests with a heavy bundle in his hand, and the Bishop took it without words. The man dragged it back into the hall to the place where the two were waiting for him. With astonishment, Maximus and Andragathius observed as a heavy hammer emerged from the sack, a powerful tool which the Bishop could only move with great effort. The guards looked at each other briefly. The hammer didn't appear to be a threat to their masters.

"Would you please take a step to this side?" Ambrosius asked. Maximus and Andragathius did him the favor. The Bishop stared again, recalled his last visit to the place when the craftsmen had been working on the mosaic, his last attempt to dissuade Gratian from the error of his ways. The image on the ground, which not only showed the Emperor but also the carefully represented body of the iron ship, the origin of all blasphemy and witchcraft.

At that time the Bishop had decided something.

He was glad that he was now ready to put this resolution into action.

He lifted the hammer with considerable effort, and then, with a liberating outcry, let it crash onto the mosaic. Stone chips flew through the area. Maximus and his general flinched involuntarily. Ambrosius didn't let go. Again and again, he tore the heavy tool up, and again and again, it hit the carefully embedded stones. With each stroke, the mosaic pieces were splintered, the foundation more broken, the dried mortar dissolving between the colorful pieces.

It didn't take ten minutes, then the contour of the *Saarbrücken* was erased.

"Damnatio memoriae!" Ambrosius gasped, breathing heavily, dropped the hammer carelessly, bowed to Maximus, and left.

46

On this evening in the late summer of 379, two emperors were crowned in the Roman Empire. It was not the first time that emperors and counter-emperors had existed, and many observers of the events didn't even expect that this would be the last time in Rome's history. Both festivities had remarkable parallels – an illustrious crowd of guests, high-ranking personalities, roughly equally distributed. The festivities were both relatively modest, unpretentious, almost bureaucratic, with strong military presence and little involvement of the normal population. Both ceremonies were carried out under noticeable time pressure, with military preparations and work taking place in parallel. There would be no proper festive mood, there were few smiling faces, hardly cheerfulness, but some satisfaction, at least in Treveri. In Ravenna there were glances full of fear, mistrust and doubt, though such feelings were well-hidden behind masks of polite attention and ostentatious observance.

However, an important difference was discernible: While the ceremony in Treveri was predominantly testified by ecclesiastical dignitaries of trinitarianism, representatives of the Arians as well as the traditional Roman religions, like priests of the Mithras cult, which was important for the armed forces, were only present in Ravenna. The fact that the Trinitarians had sent only a subordinate priest, not even the elderly Liberius, Bishop of Ravenna, made a point in regard to the division which added to the separation of the Empire after Maximus's attack. Theodosius, who had given a brief speech after the purple had been presented to him, didn't address this. He saw no point in stirring up religious feelings.

Both the newly appointed emperors acted wearied that evening, living through the ceremony with a certain determination, but without the spark of enthusiasm that could have carried the audience with them. Both emperors chatted with high-ranking guests, accepted congratulations, listened to requests and suggestions, observed how men and women positioned themselves at the newly established courts, how small power struggles and intrigues had already begun on this first evening of their newly won rule. But both of them looked distant and were seen as their gaze turned thoughtfully, staring almost as if they were looking into the future. Both knew the seriousness of the situation, and none of them was willing to question the legitimacy of their own actions. Both men thought of tomorrow. Maximus Magnus, who would start his march toward Ravenna to bring the matter to an end. Theodosius, who, after the arrival of Rheinberg, would take his army and flee before the expected advance of Maximus, with one or two days' advance, near enough to irritate the usurper, far enough away to avoid an immediate battle. Avoidance and temptation. A strange dance would begin, a dance that would comprise thousands of legionaries and hundreds of miles. Theodosius himself, it was decided now, would take command of the troops. Rheinberg was to move with the *Saarbrücken* to Constantinople and organize the troops of the East. The declared goal was to attack Maximus subsequently from two sides.

In both cities, the ceremony ended relatively early. In this case, the festivities were not extended until the early morning hours of the next day. Both rulers had instructed their people to commence important work the next morning right away, and to retire early. It was surprisingly silent in the palaces. Although in itself a good event, the mood, if not depressed, was very serious. Celebrations, something in which both emperors agreed, would be possible at a later time.

Once only one of them remained.

On the next day, both emperors sent embassies to every corner of the Empire, demanding more or less unmistakably the loyalty of their subjects. How, above all, the countless bureaucrats and provincials would react to these letters was of great importance to them both.

And then both of them were left with not much more than prayers for their success.

47

Actually, he should have retired two years ago, Domitius Modestus thought and looked into the mirror. He saw an old man whose office rested on his shoulders like a heavy burden. As a Praetorian Prefect in Constantinople, he had been something like the Prime Minister of Valens, the second most powerful man in the East. With the takeover of the entire government by Gratian, his influence had risen even more, since the Emperor had mostly stayed in the West. Modestus had a only sympathy for the new, tolerant policy of the new Emperor; he was, indeed, one of the officials of Rome, who had subscribed to the Arian faith. Under Julian, whom they called the Apostate, he had been an ardent advocate of the ancient Roman religions. It was only later that he had been converted to Christianity when he realized that the influence of the old religions was dwindling and that the East seemed to be largely in the hands of the Arians.

It had been both politically as well as spiritually opportune.

In addition to his political instincts, his clever handling of finances always had made him indispensable. As chairman of the consistory, he had ensured that Valens's increasing irrationality had not been too damaging to the state's finances. This was also the reason why the financial situation here was currently better than in the West: despite the formal reunification of the Empire under Gratian, relatively separate coffers were continued, even though Gratian's reforms had been faithfully executed in regard to taxation also in the East. This had rather strengthened the financial situation of Constantinople.

Much had happened recently. The death of the Valens, the subsequent rule over the entire Empire by Gratian, the emergence of the time-wanderers – Modestus had noted all this with great serenity. He had done his work, and it had been to manage, reform and rebuild Eastern Rome. A work he had done quietly, efficiently, and above all unspectacularly. And he had stayed in office because young Gratian had assumed that an old man like Modestus wouldn't have any greater ambitions. Rightly so, as the Prefect found.

And so he had some regret about Gratian's death. The successful revolt of Maximus, whose fanatical inclination to the trinitarian confession was widely known, filled him with sorrow. Nor was the appointment of Theodosius as successor to Gratian something which caused great enthusiasm in him.

Yet he had shown the Spaniard his loyalty. He had last heard that the iron cruiser of the time-wanderers, the *Saarbrücken*, was about to leave and travel to Constantinople, with high-ranking officers on board who wanted to organize the planned counterattack on the usurper. As soon as he had received the news through the coastal messenger system, Modestus had made all necessary arrangements. He would do what was his duty. He wouldn't be responsible for any delay.

But now he was supposed to be.

The old Prefect sat in his office, and after he had sent out all his staff he crouched directly at the window, and let the warming sun fall on the parchment, which he held in his already somewhat trembling hands. What was more important now?

The words of Maximus were clear and unambiguous. *Submit yourself to my will, Modestus,* he had written in a very direct manner. *Act according to my wishes.* Modestus would normally have burned this request immediately in the fireplace, being only a little bit annoyed at the foolish presumption of an usurper.

But there were other things happening.

A week ago, his wife Anastasia and his youngest daughter had disappeared without a trace. Their two litters, supported by loyal and well-trained slaves, guarded by a half-dozen legionaries, had never reached the festivity to which they had departed. Modestus had at once initiated a great search, but in spite of all thoroughness there was no trace of the disappeared. Before his mind's eye, the puffy bodies of the women were already floating somewhere in the brackish harbor water, plundered by merciless street robbers.

No, the good news was that they were obviously alive and well.

The second letter, written by his wife's well-known, careful writing, had only briefly reported what had happened, apparently under the strict editorship of those who had abducted her. They all lived, were well-cared for, were uninjured, but trapped in an unknown place.

And they would, as their kidnapper had told her, continue to remain in good health, and even be brought back to the Prefect's villa, if the latter only behaved as Maximus Magnus wanted. And this well-being, Modestus could read, had something to do with the way in which preparations for the *Saarbrücken's* visit to Constantinople went.

Modestus read the two letters again and again. He probably didn't want to believe what was written there. He looked for a way out in those words, but the door remained closed.

He stared out the window, unable to think for a few minutes. Of course, he felt torn between his patriotic duties and the love and care for his family. Then he wondered what was the most important thing for him at his age, the priority in a life whose autumn had already passed and whose winter had already begun for quite some time. How long would the Lord leave him in his place? Another year or two? And what was he going to do? What was of importance? His honor as Prefect and servant of the Empire, or the life of his daughter and his wife, who had been loyal to him for so many decades?

Domitius Modestus stared out the window for a long time. The two letters had long since fallen from his tired hand and lay on the ground as he sighed and lifted them again.

He had made his decision. With that, he felt better.

48

Diderius peered into the cloudy shimmer of the lamp. The Lord was in support of his cause, there was no doubt. It was pitch-dark, and the torches and lamps, as numerous as they were, barely illuminated the streets and alleys of the settlement of the time-wanderers. He knew it very well now, knew about various hidden approaches, had learned where the guards were doing their patrols. He was well prepared, very excellently so, and therefore full of courage.

He had spent another night of love with the naive and not-hard-to-please Flavia. Then, when she had fallen asleep with a smile, he had left his house, the key of the ugly woman in the pocket. Flavia had told him where the fresh supplies had been landed, and he was ready to prepare for the great day when Maximus's troops stood before Ravenna. Then he would have to act. Diderius was a clever man. He placed great emphasis on detailed preparations and reluctantly left anything to chance.

So he did an exercise. He would not pass the poison tonight. But every movement, every step should be perfect. He would soon no longer need Flavia. Her fate didn't trouble him. If all was done, he would leave Ravenna quickly. Everything was prepared for this too.

Diderius was a thorough man.

He entered the dark backyard of the canteen where Flavia was working, and listened. Nothing stirred. A couple of stray cats scuttled past the trash, but no human soul could be seen. The watchmen came here, too, but not more than twice a night, and they didn't spend too long here either. The first tour was already over. Diderius had time.

He felt secure as he moved. He had been very observant about the environment, in the daylight, every time he had picked up a happy and joyful Flavia after her shift.

Diderius was a thorough man.

His right foot stepped on something soft. There was a squeaky sound as the sandal fell into something sticky. Food remnants, no doubt. Diderius didn't want to think about what he had touched. The uncomfortably moist feeling between the sole and the foot excited almost as much nausea in him as the sight of the naked, voluptuous Flavia. So everything fit together. But it didn't matter. Diderius had some spare sandals in the little bag he wore around his shoulder. He was ready.

He was a very thorough man indeed.

He had arrived at the back door, secured with a mighty lock. He took the key he had stolen from Flavia and tried to use it. A perfect fit. Carefully, he turned the heavy key; it clicked and the lock was open. If he wanted, he could open the door now and have access to the kitchen and the storage room.

Soon, he exhorted himself. Not tonight, but soon.

He turned the key again, this time in the other direction. It clicked. The lock was closed. He pulled the key out. Enough for the night.

He turned and breathed deeply. That was perfect. Everything was ready.

Then he saw a light approaching. A small oil lamp only, a weak glimmer.

He narrowed his eyes, tried to recognize something. A mighty figure appeared indistinctly. Heavy, safe steps. No caution, no hesitation.

"Hello Didi!"

Flavia's voice!

Diderius flinched, involuntarily taking a step back.

"But ... but ... dearest ..."

"Ah. Yes. I forgot."

A fast movement. A sharp, brutal pain. He looked down at himself, saw a heavy, big meat knife in his belly, led by a heavy, reddish hand.

"Do not worry, Didi," he heard Flavia's voice. "I'm a professional!"

Then she opened his guts with the strength and efficiency of a butcher. When the man's body sank to the ground, his eyes gazing gloomily into the skies, she let the knife lie beside him. She bent down, tore the purse from his side, and put it to the other belongings she had plundered from her former lover's dwelling.

Of course, a year ago, when she'd taken the place as a kitchen aid, her hope had been to spy on some rich officers to be able to lay hands on their valuables. Or time-wanderers, with their magical equipment. There was a market for this.

But now the ground was too hot for her. Maximus came. War was not good for business. It was time to leave, despite all the painstaking preparations. For now, what she could plunder from Diderius had to suffice. After all, it was enough to provide her with proper supplies for several months.

Flavia laughed and pushed a strand of hair from her full face. Men were fools.

This one had at least tried hard in bed. A nice toy that considered himself a great conspirator.

He had not been thorough enough.

And now she had even done the time-wanderers, yes, the Empire a favor. In her pouch, besides the gold of Didi, she found the package with the poison.

They had always treated her decently, despite her lowly status. It didn't hurt to leave a present before departure. On the other hand …

Who knows, Flavia thought, when she turned away to disappear into the night.

Who knows, perhaps she still had use for this special parcel.

To the bleeding corpse behind her, she gave no more thought.

She had to hold on to herself in order not to whistle happily.

Register of persons

Aurelius Africanus: Roman Trierarch

Ambrosius of Milan: Roman Bishop

Andragathius: Roman General

Aurelia: a slave

Peter Behrens: Infantry NCO

Gebre Berhan: Governor of Adulis

Bertius: Roman legionary

Claudia: slave of Julia

Martinus Caius: Son of a Roman businessman

Johann Dahms: Chief engineer of the *Saarbrücken*

Diderius: a conspirator

Erminius: King of the Quadians

Josef Feldmann: Medic

Flavia: a cook

Godegisel: gothic nobleman

Dietrich Joergensen: First officer of the *Saarbrücken*

Julia: daughter of the Marcus Gaius Michellus

Harald Köhler: NCO of the *Saarbrücken*

Klaus Langenhagen: Officer of the *Saarbrücken*

Levantus Roman: centurion

Magnus Maximus: Governor of Britain

Malobaudes: Roman General

Marcus Gaius Michellus: Roman senator

Mehadeyis: Emperor of Aksum

Dr. Hans Neumann: Physician of the *Saarbrücken*

Ouazebas: designated heir to the throne of Aksum

Petronius: a priest

Pina: friend of Godegisel

Marcus Flovius Renna Roman military prefect:

Jan Rheinberg: Captain and Magister Militium

Richomer : Roman officer

Septimus Secundus: Roman NCO

Markus Tennberg: Ensign on the *Saarbrücken* and deserter

Flavius Theodosius: Emperor of Rome

Thomas Volkert: Roman Decurion

Klaus von Geeren: Infantry officer and company commander

Johann Freiherr von Klasewitz: former First officer of the *Saarbrücken* and deserter

Made in the USA
Middletown, DE
06 July 2018